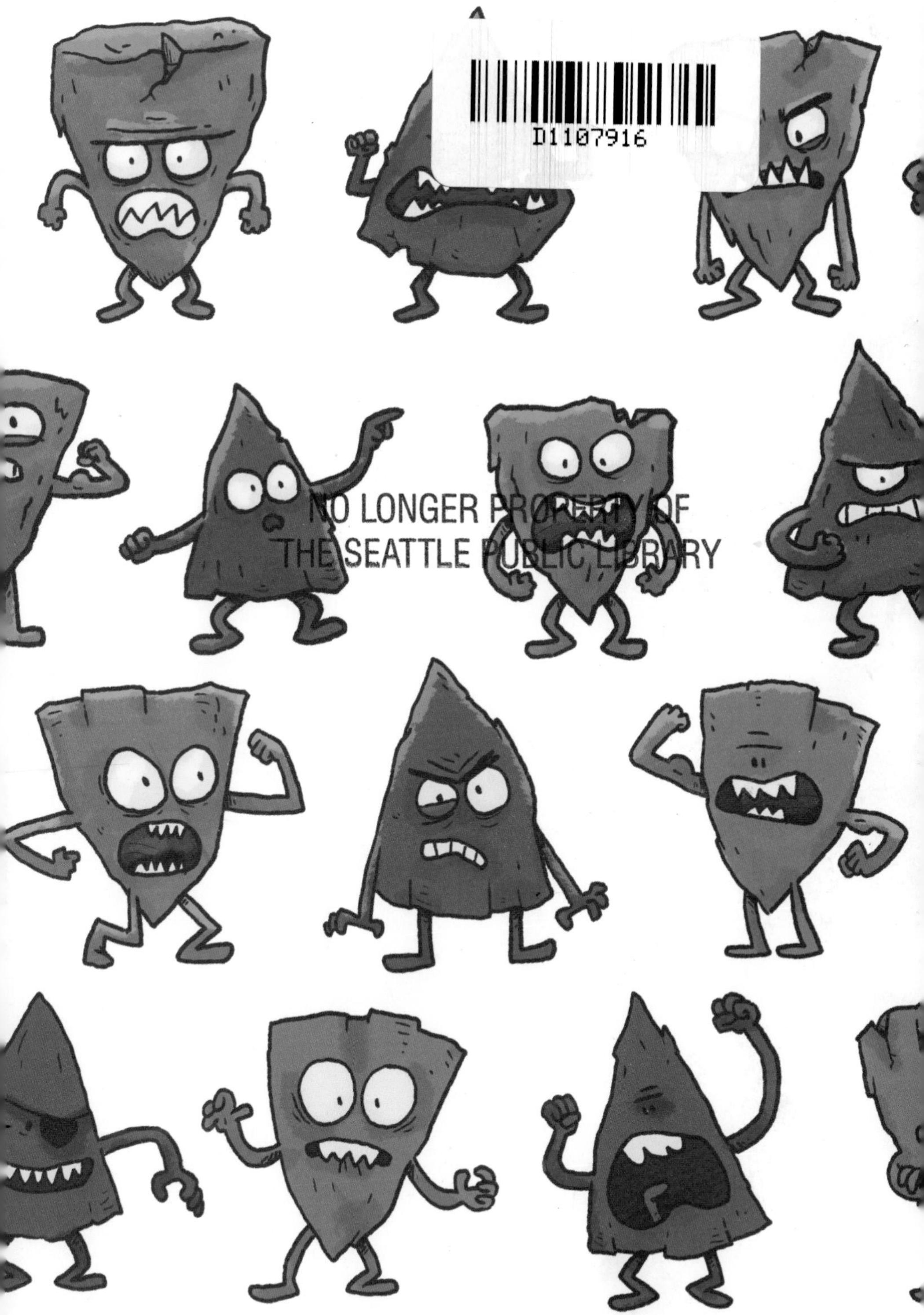

Blue, Barry & Pancakes

ENTER THE UNDERGROUND THROWDOWN

Blue, Barry & Pancakes

ENTER THE UNDERGROUND THROWDOWN

by
Dan & Jason

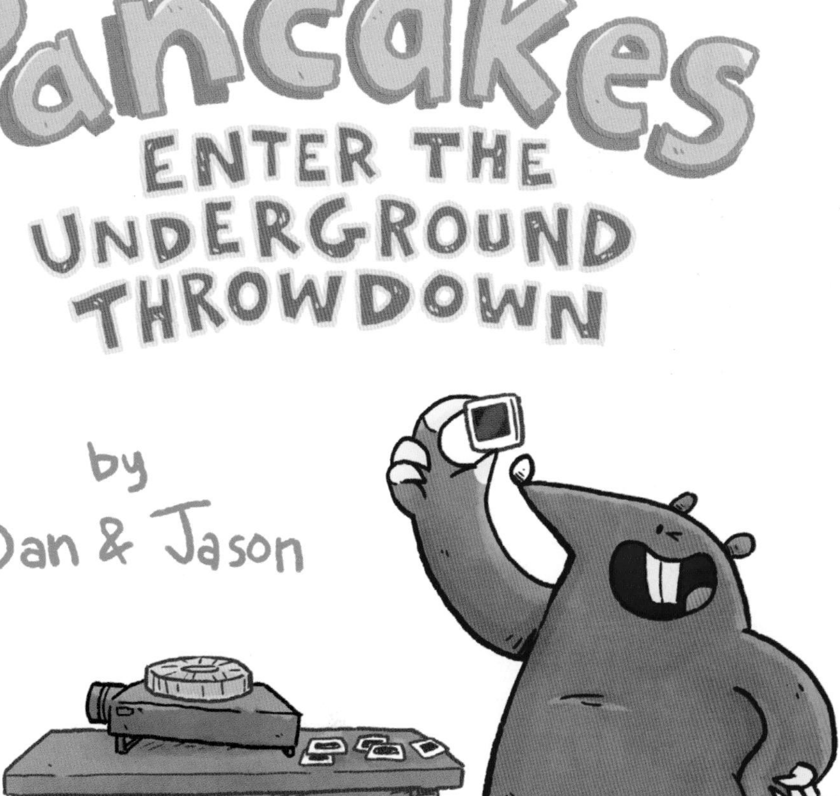

:01
First Second
New York

FOR:

My big brother Abe. Who let me read his X-Men comics in between wrestling matches. —D.A.

Phil and Roger. They took me on many magical adventures, especially the ones beneath the waves! —J.P.

First Second

Published by First Second
First Second is an imprint of Roaring Brook Press,
a division of Holtzbrinck Publishing Holdings Limited Partnership
120 Broadway, New York, NY 10271
firstsecondbooks.com
mackids.com

Library of Congress Cataloging-in-Publication Data is available.

Our books may be purchased in bulk for promotional, educational, or business use. Please contact your local bookseller or the Macmillan Corporate and Premium Sales Department at (800) 221-7945 ext. 5442 or by email at MacmillanSpecialMarkets@macmillan.com.

First edition, 2022
Edited by Calista Brill and Alex Lu
Cover and interior book design by Sunny Lee

This book was drawn mostly on a Wacom Cintiq and iPad Pro. Dan & Jason write, draw, color, and letter together in Photoshop and Procreate. The font is a unique Blue, Barry & Pancakes typeface created specifically for these books.

Printed in June 2022 in China by RR Donnelley Asia Printing Solutions Ltd., Dongguan City, Guangdong Province

ISBN 978-1-250-81696-2
10 9 8 7 6 5 4 3 2 1

Don't miss your next favorite book from First Second! For the latest updates go to firstsecondnewsletter.com and sign up for our enewsletter.

BY ART
WE LIVE

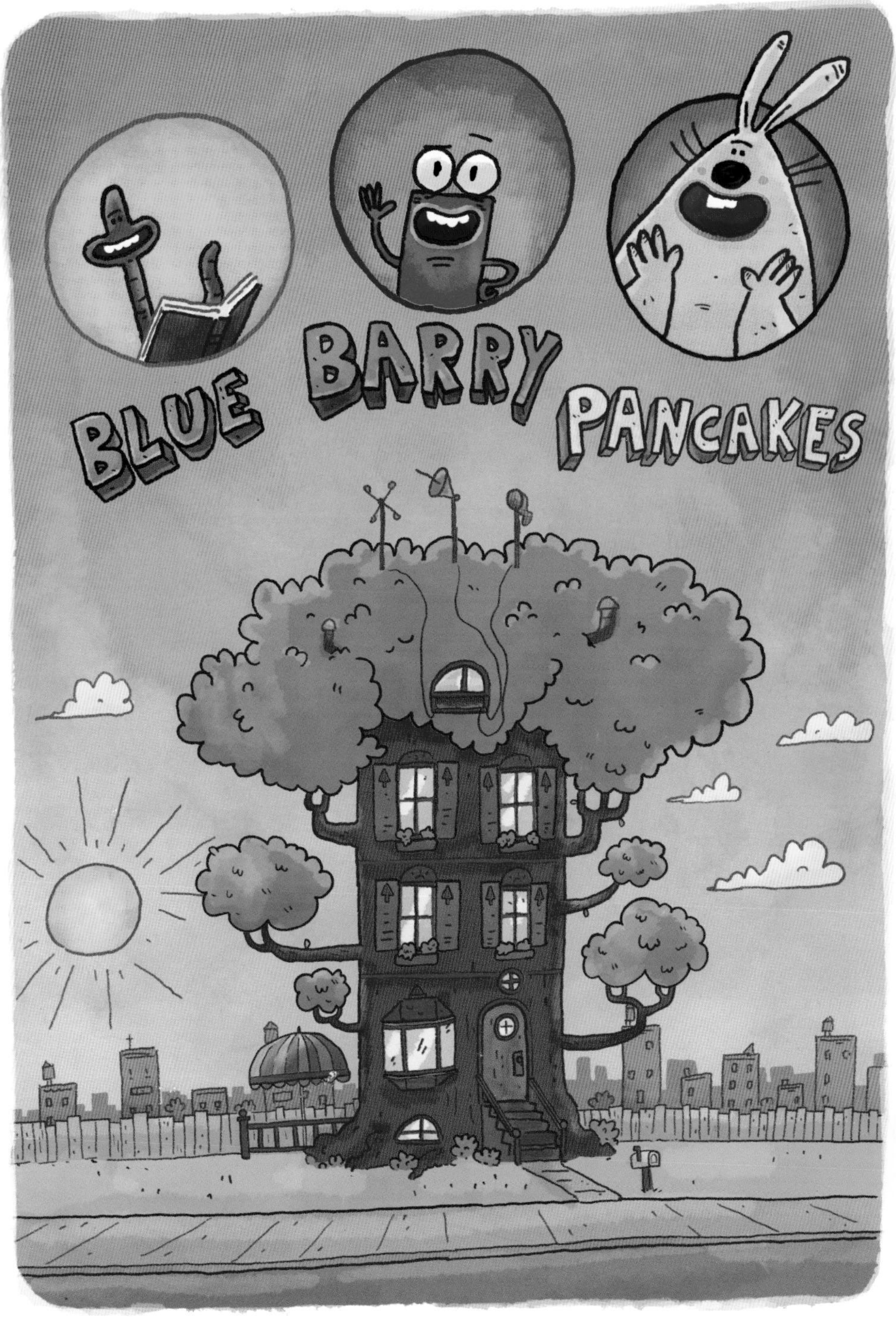
BLUE
BARRY
PANCAKES

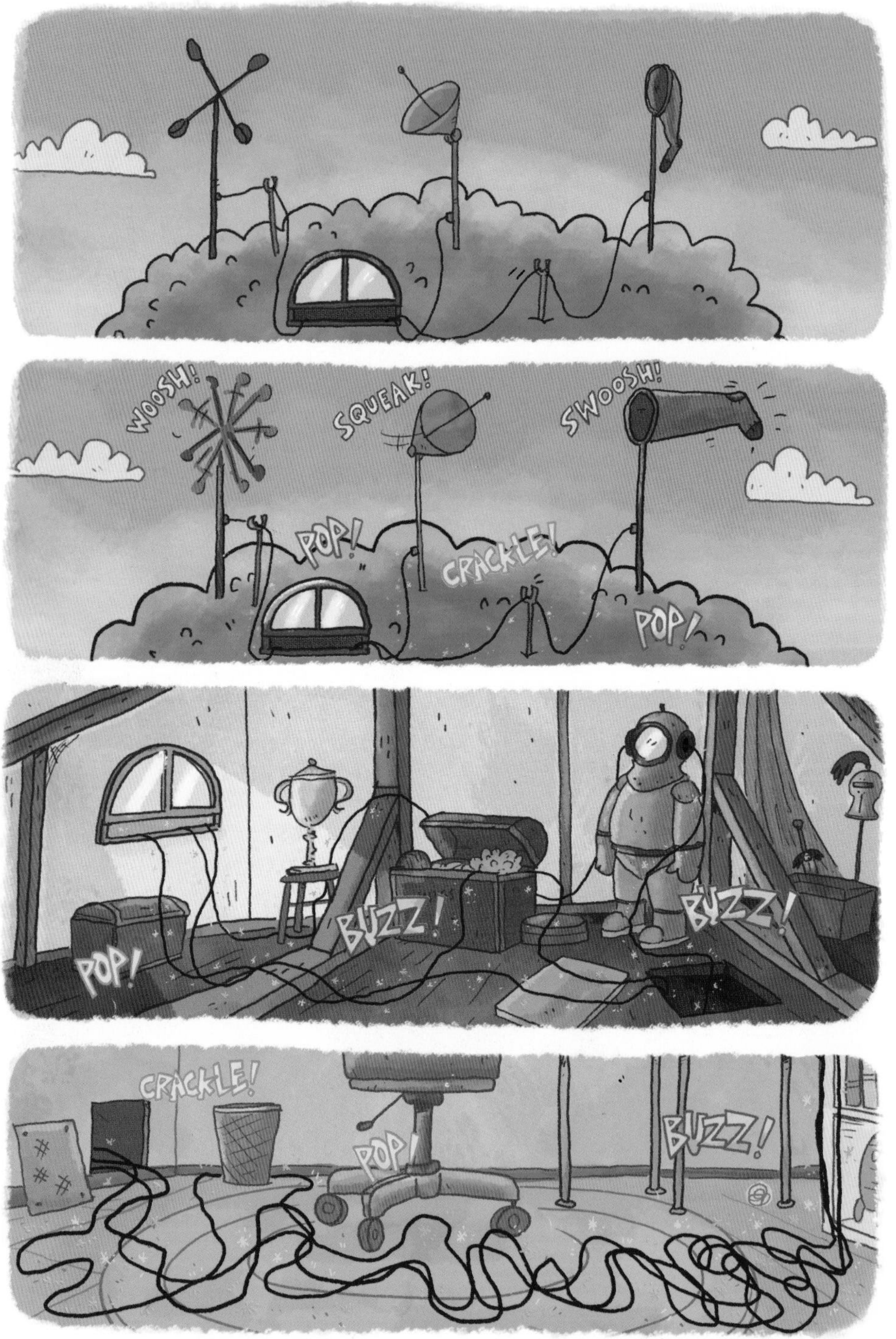
WOOSH!
SQUEAK!
SWOOSH!
POP!
CRACKLE!
POP!
BUZZ!
BUZZ!
POP!
CRACKLE!
POP!
BUZZ!

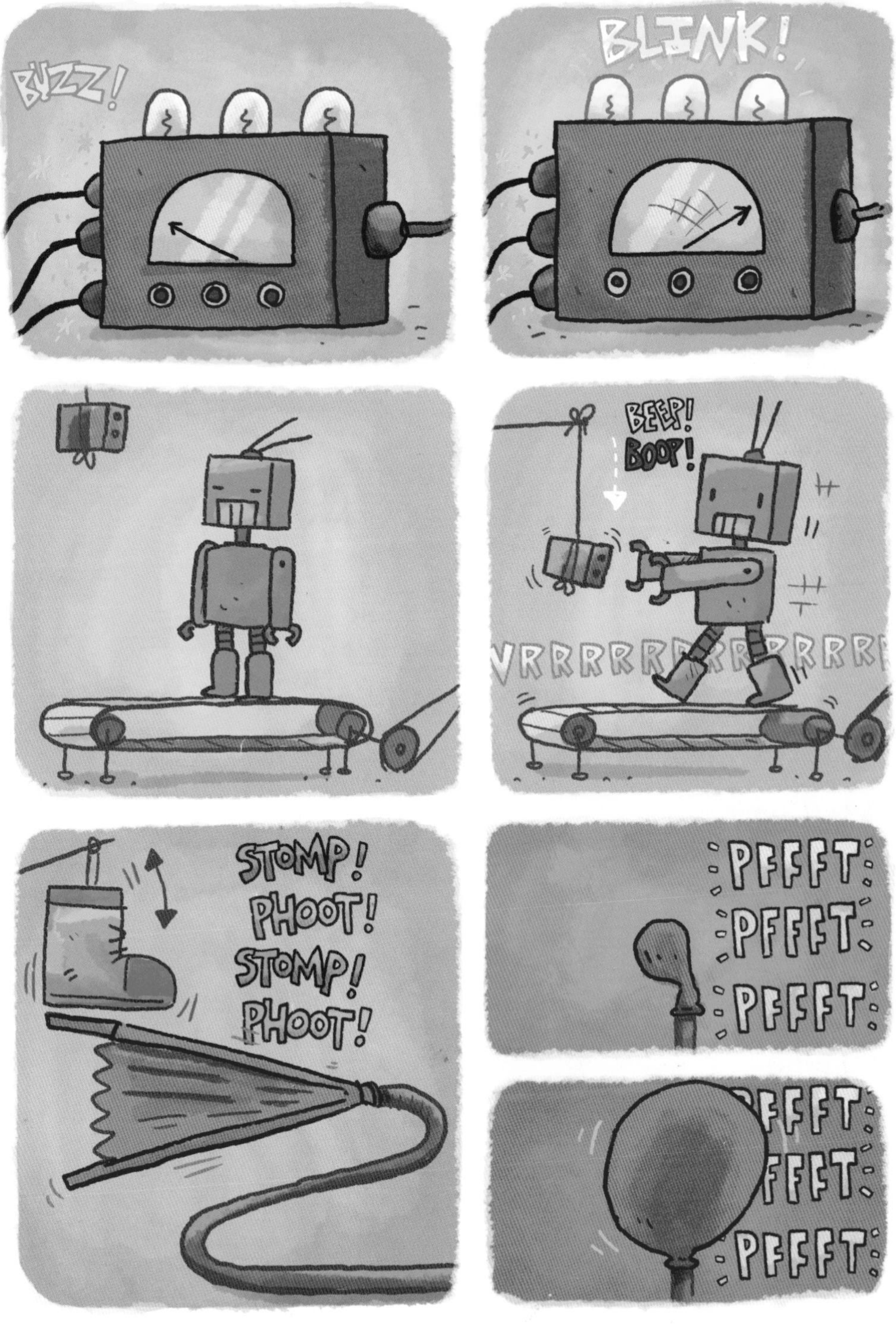
BUZZ!
BLINK!
BEEP!
BOOP!
STOMP!
PHOOT!
STOMP!
PHOOT!
PFFFT
PFFFT
PFFFT
PFFFT

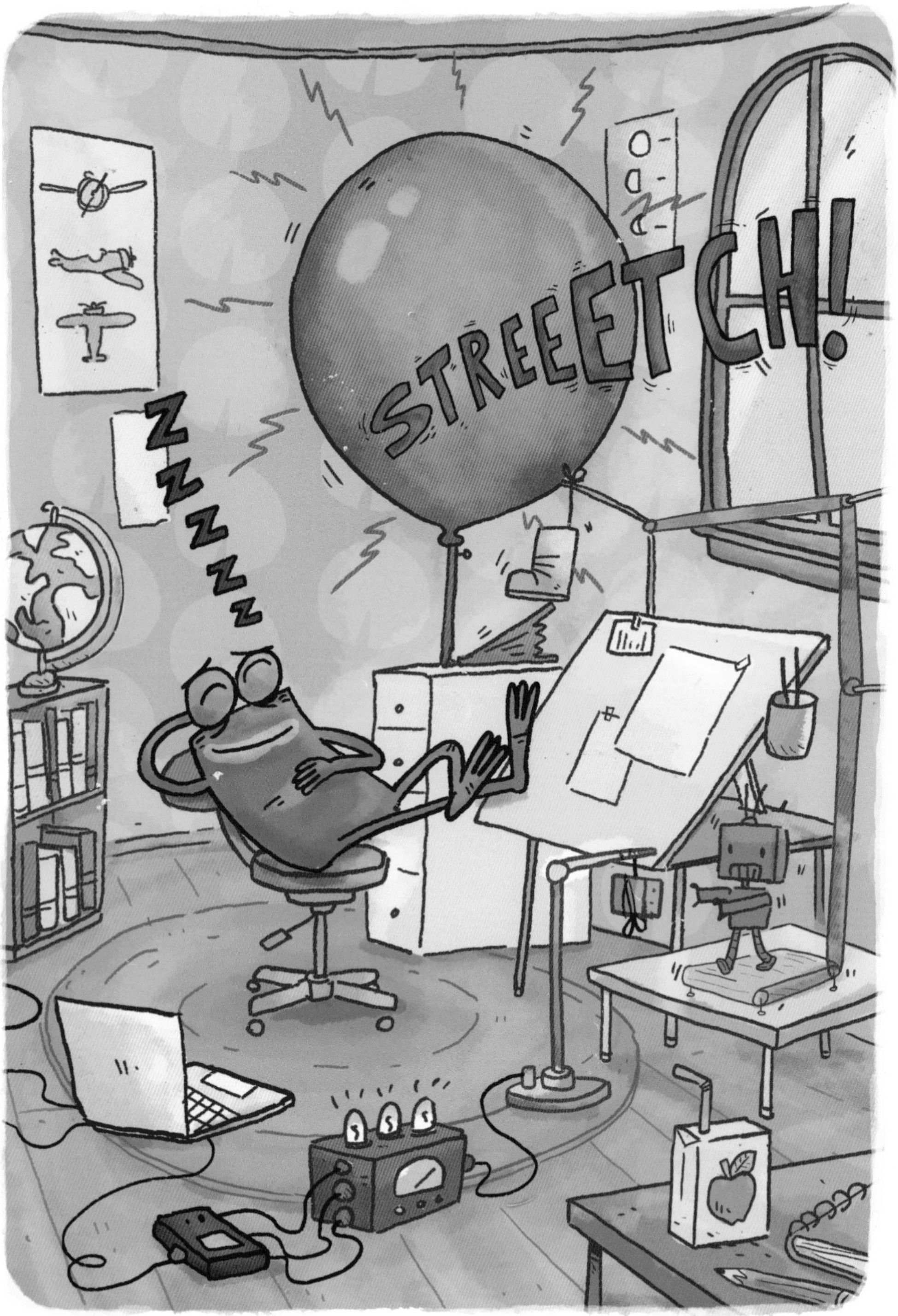
STREEETCH!
ZZZZZZ

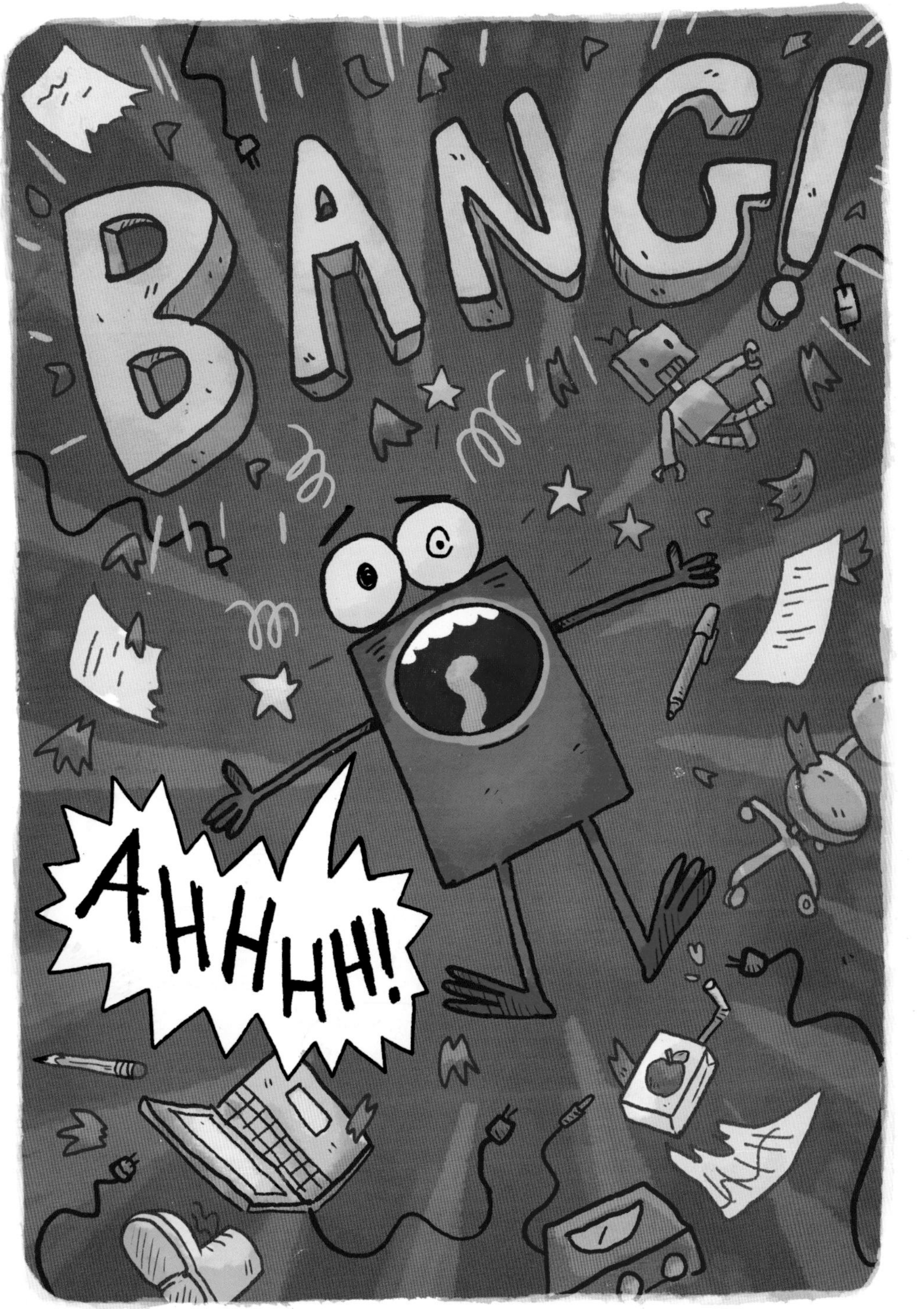
BANG!
AHHHHH!

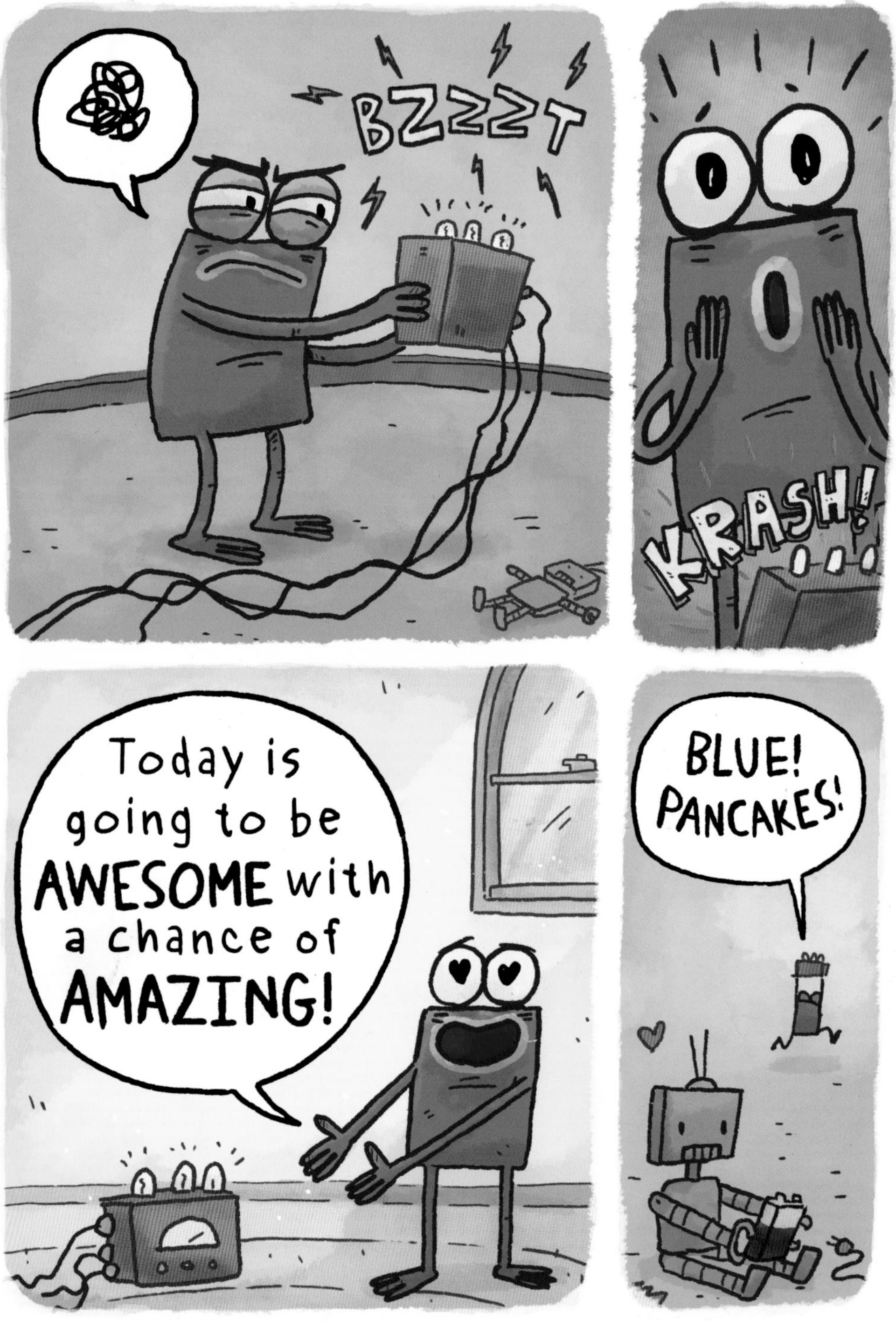
BZZZT
KRASH!
Today is going to be AWESOME with a chance of AMAZING!
BLUE! PANCAKES!

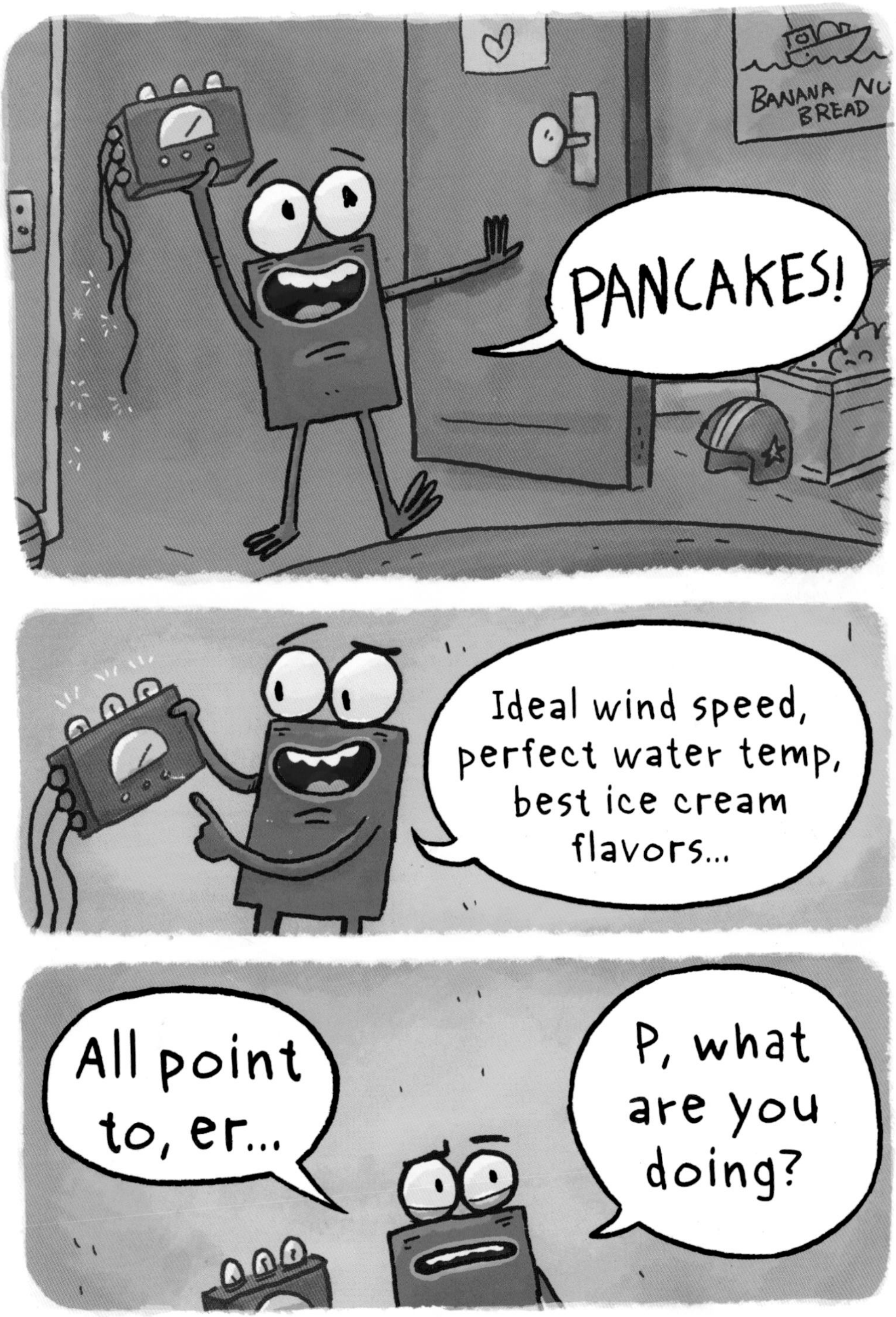
BANANA NU
BREAD
PANCAKES!
Ideal wind speed, perfect water temp, best ice cream flavors...
All point to, er...
P, what are you doing?

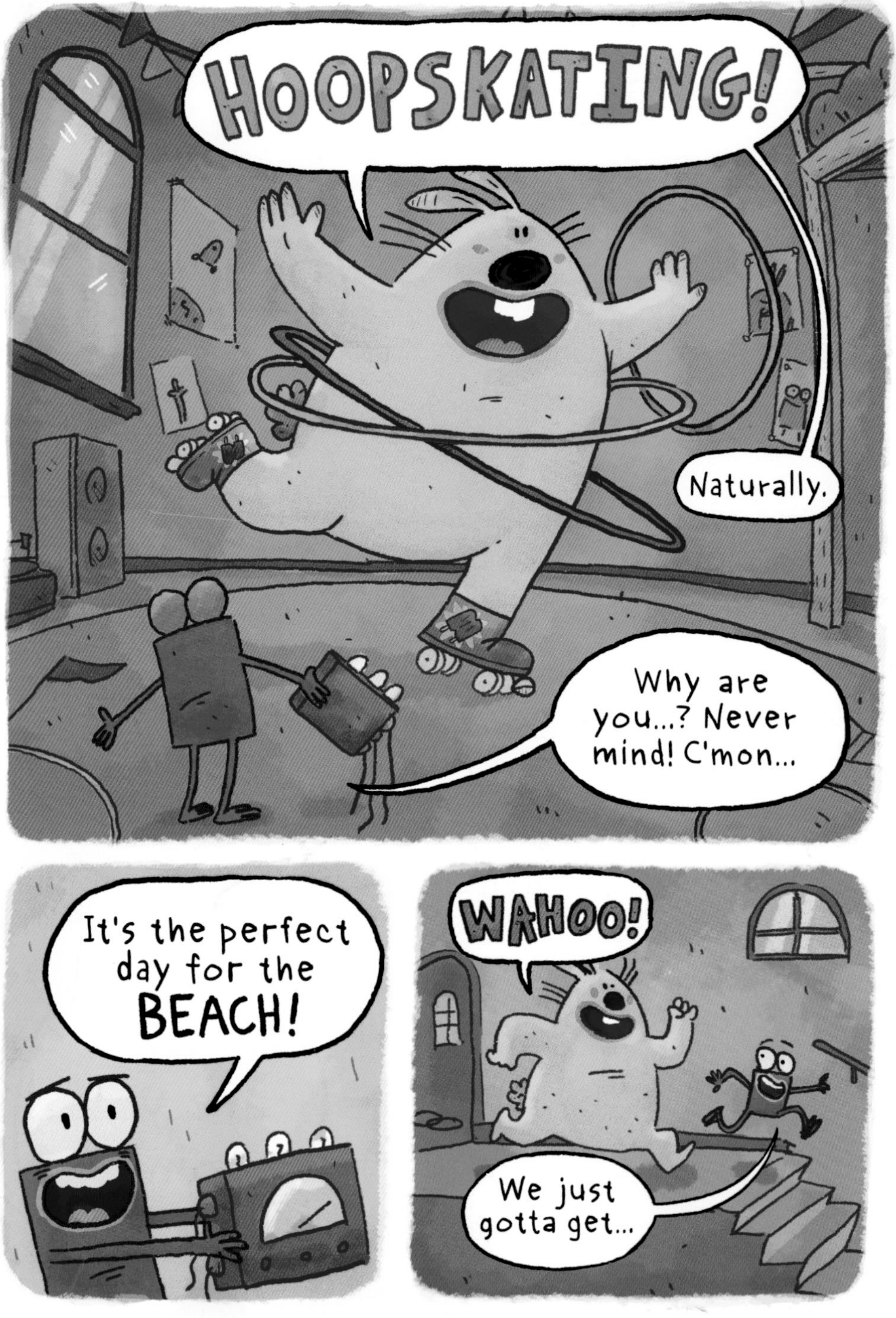
HOOPSKATING!
Naturally.
Why are you...? Never mind! C'mon...
It's the perfect day for the BEACH!
WAHOO!
We just gotta get...

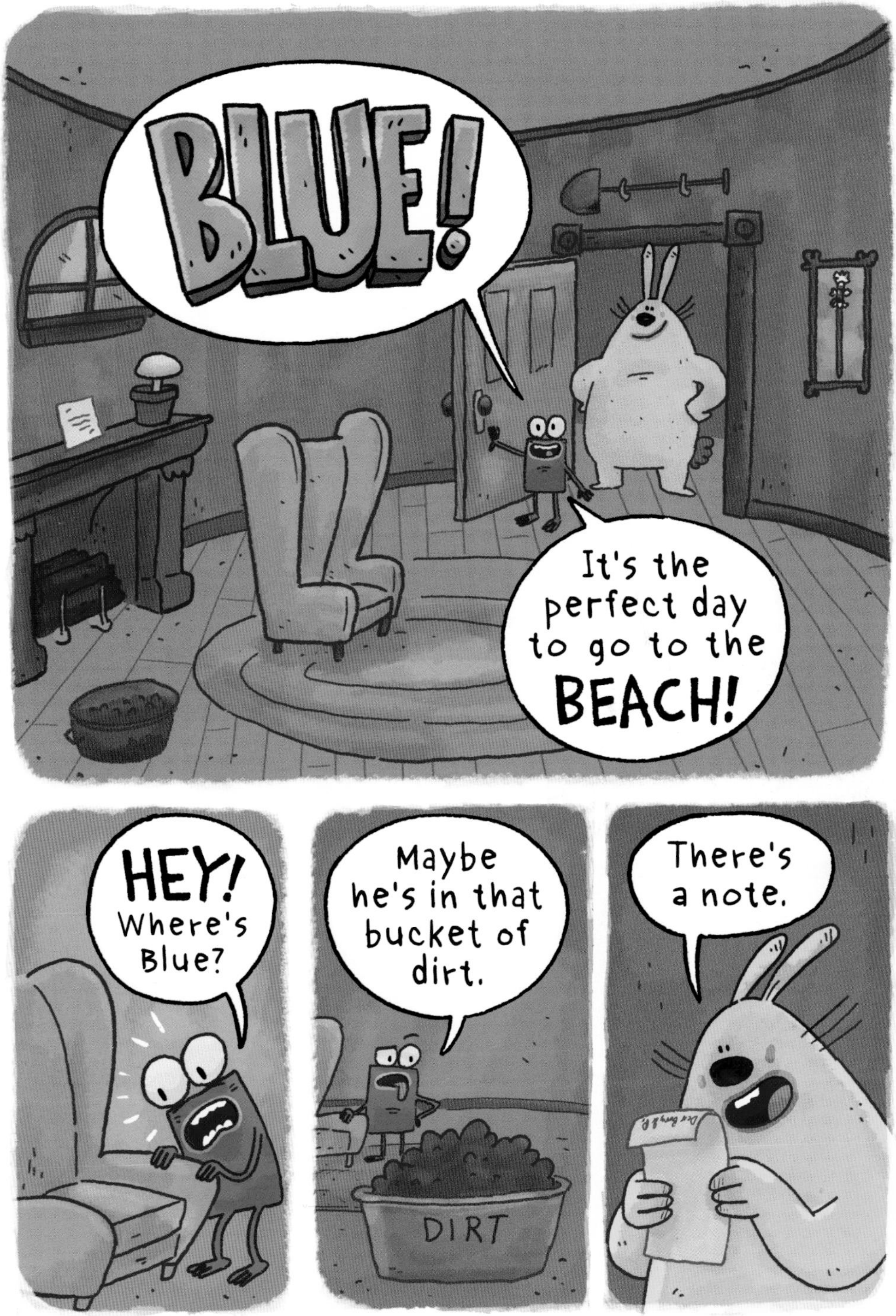
BLUE!
It's the perfect day to go to the BEACH!
HEY! Where's Blue?
Maybe he's in that bucket of dirt.
DIRT
There's a note.

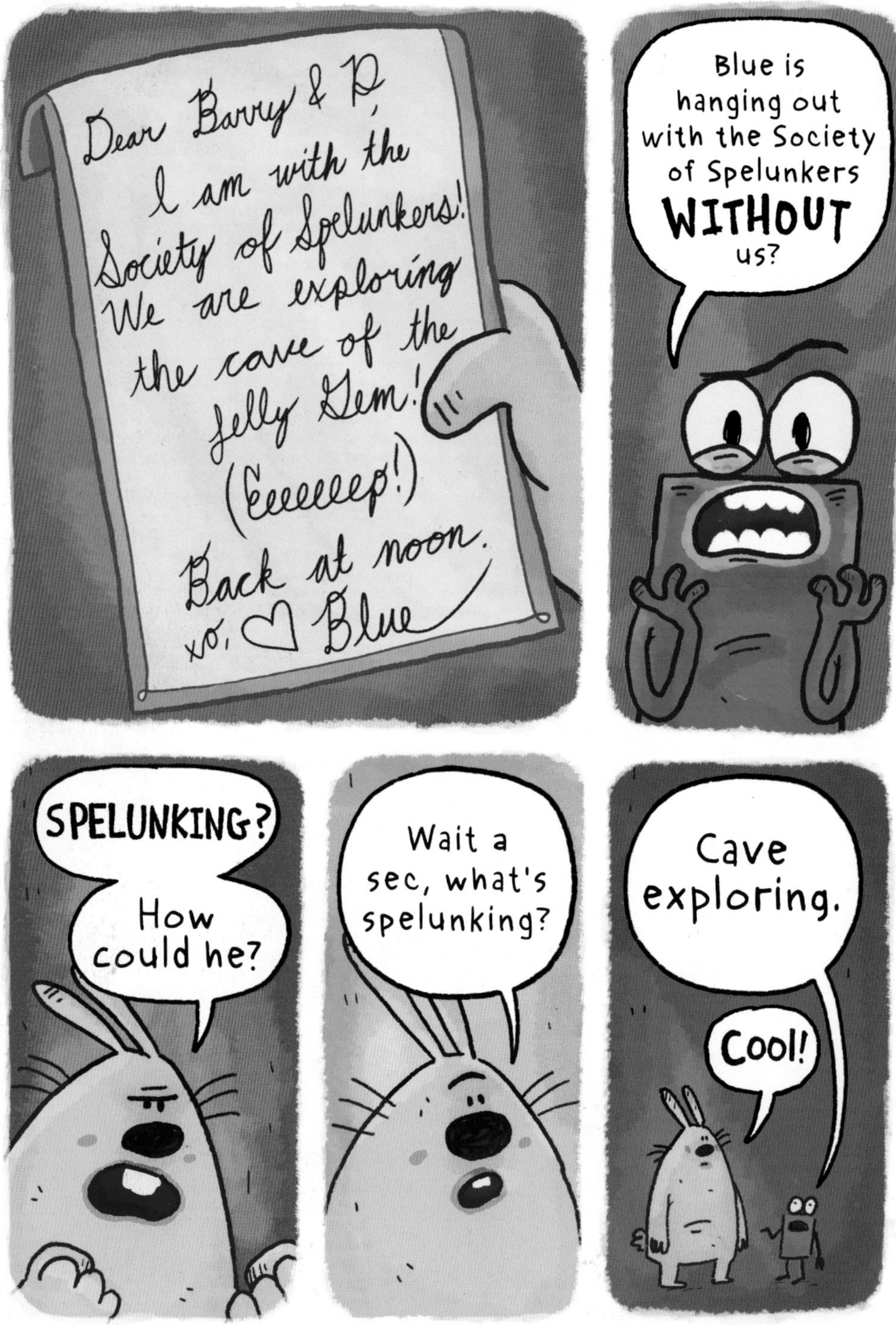
Dear Barry & D,
I am with the Society of Spelunkers! We are exploring the cave of the Jelly Gem!
(Eeeeeeep!)
Back at noon.
xo, ♡ Blue
Blue is hanging out with the Society of Spelunkers WITHOUT us?
SPELUNKING?
How could he?
Wait a sec, what's spelunking?
Cave exploring.
Cool!

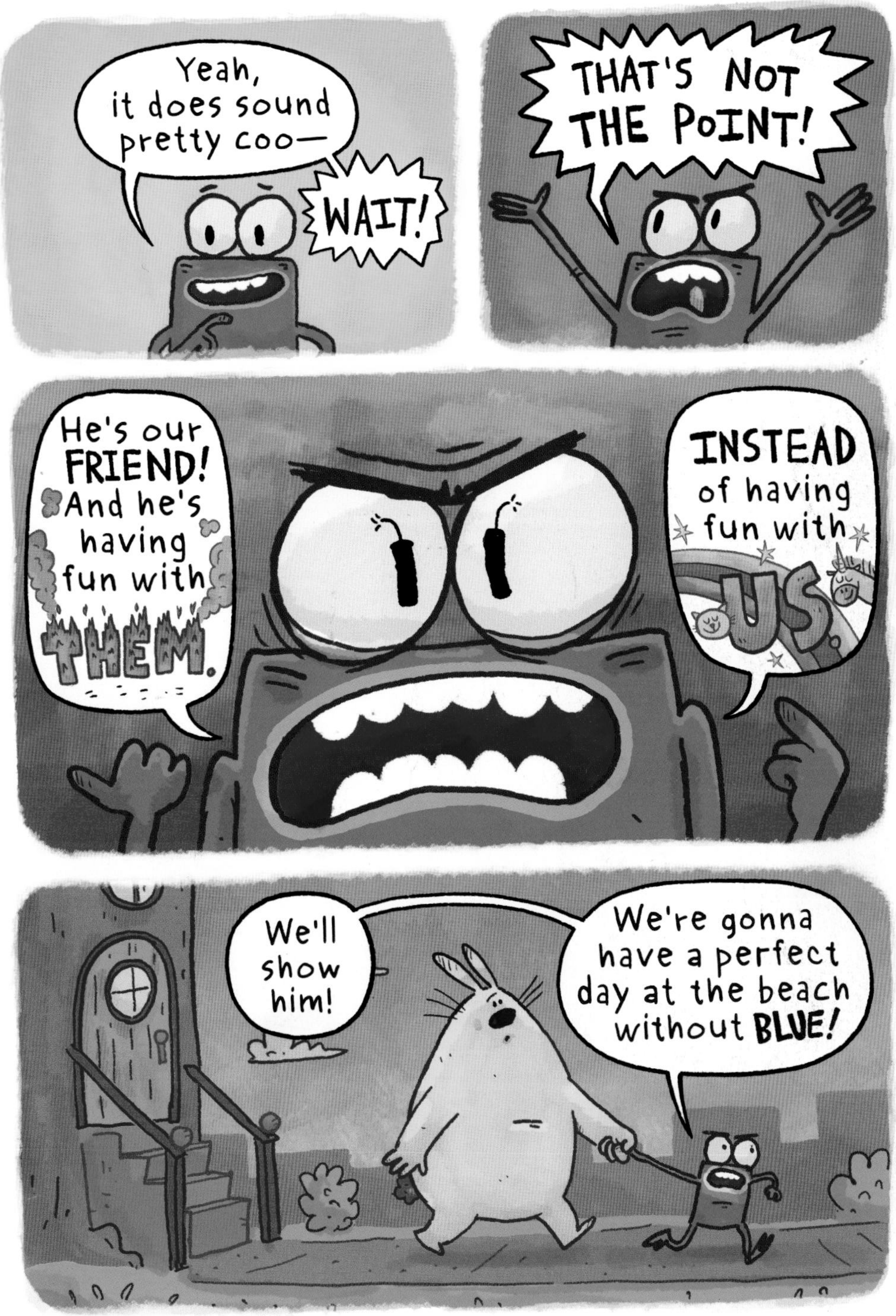
Yeah, it does sound pretty coo—
WAIT!
THAT'S NOT THE POINT!
He's our FRIEND! And he's having fun with THEM.
INSTEAD of having fun with US.
We'll show him!
We're gonna have a perfect day at the beach without BLUE!

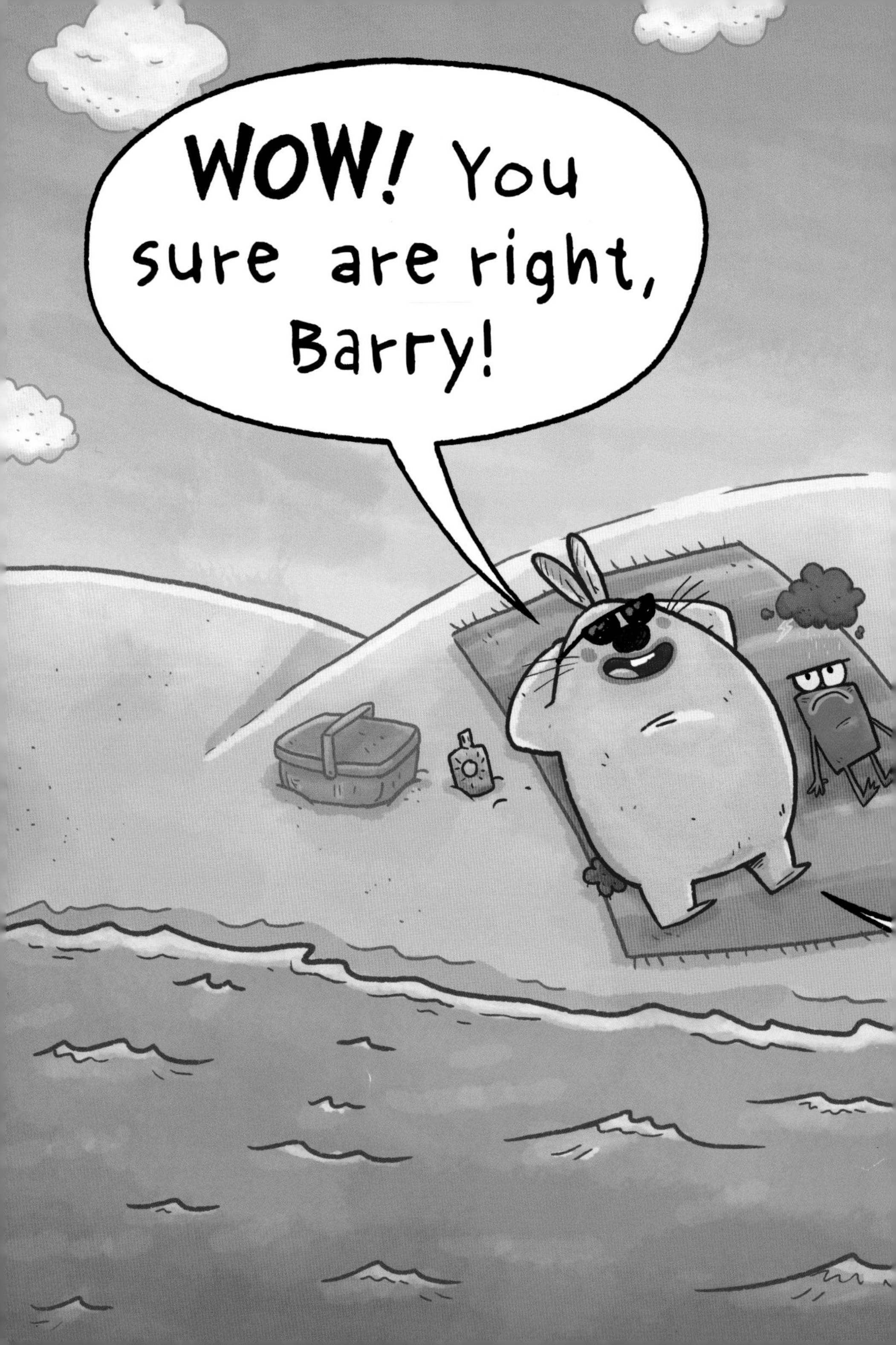
WOW! You sure are right, Barry!

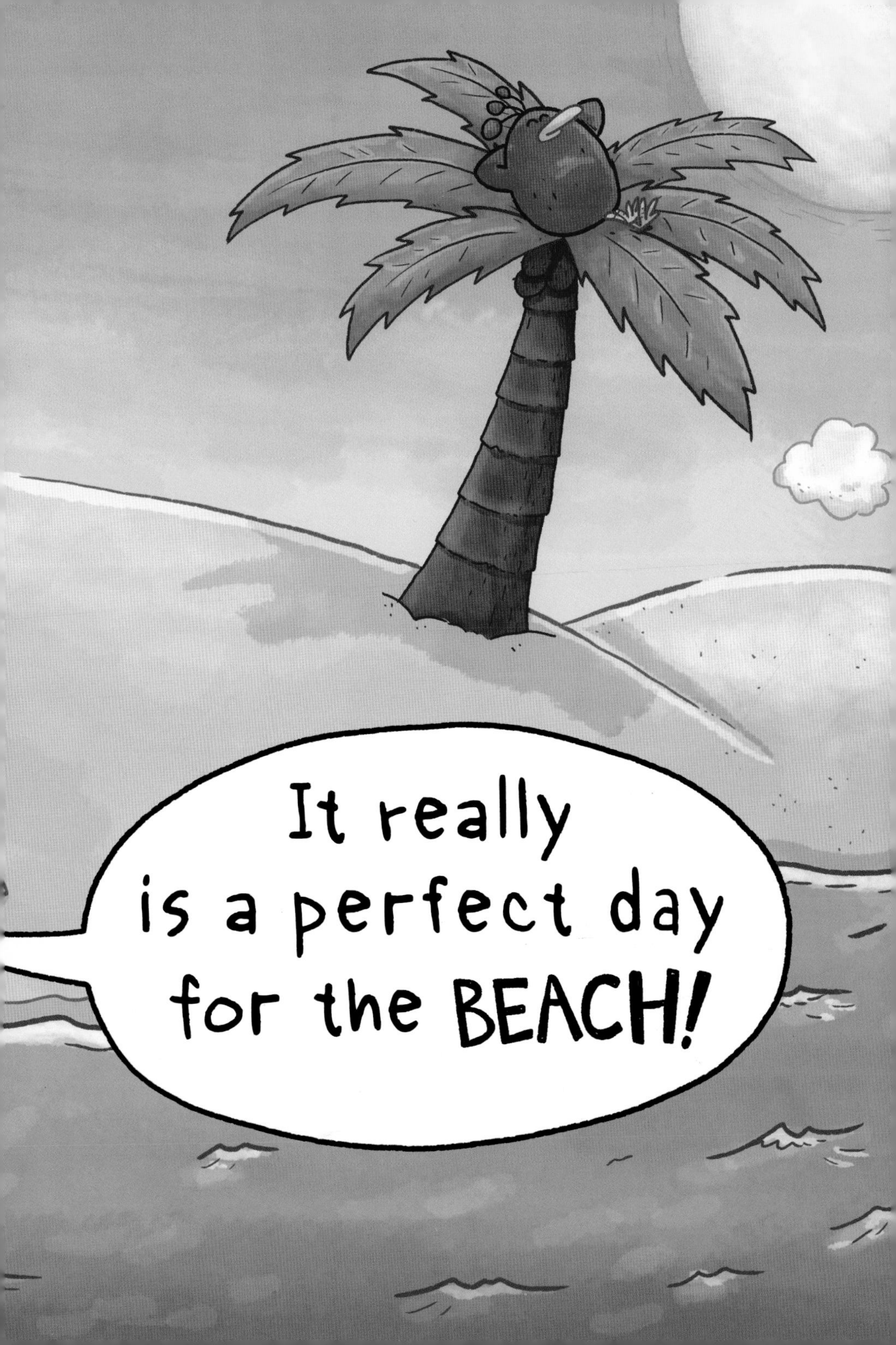
It really is a perfect day for the BEACH!

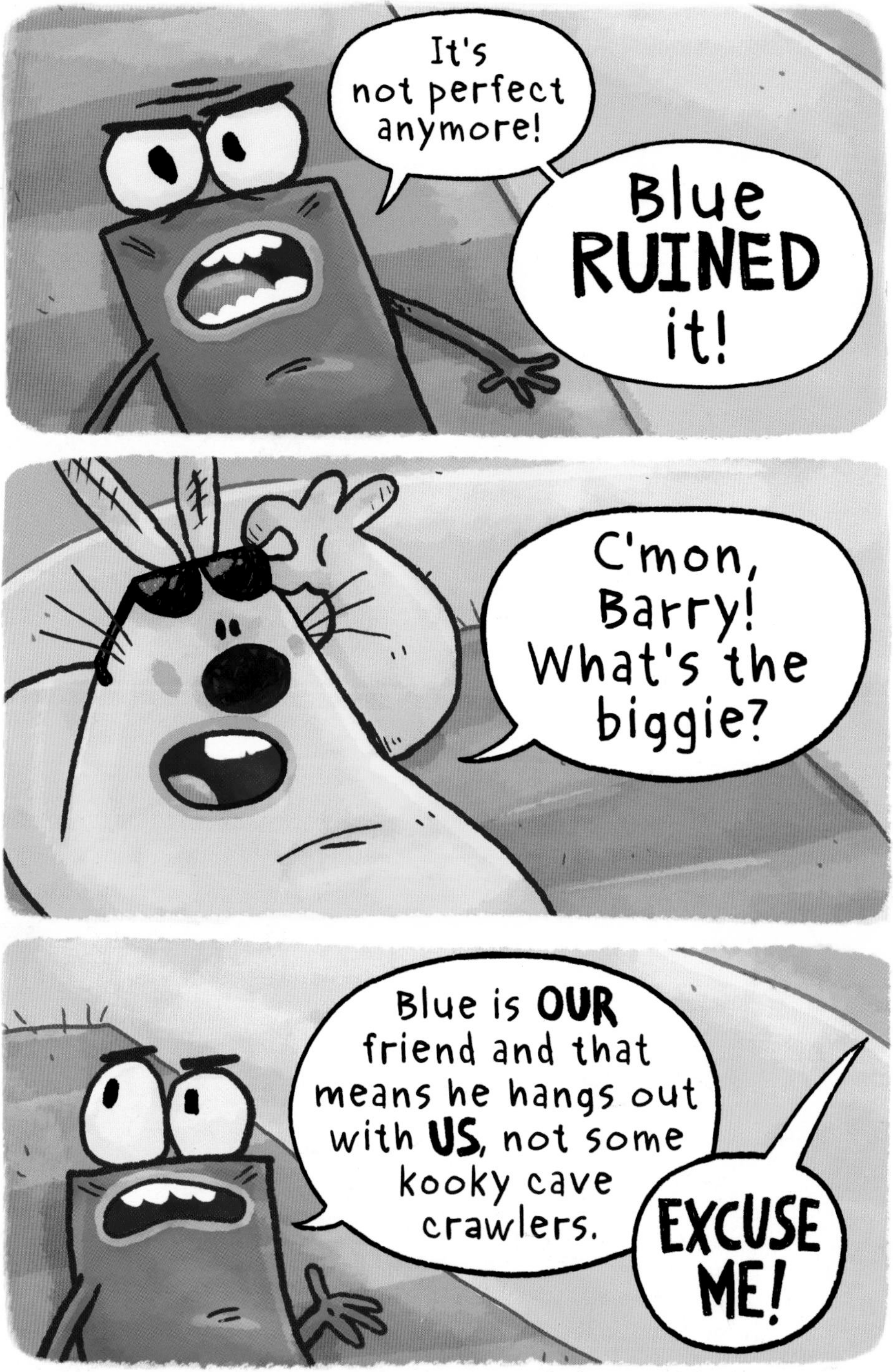
It's not perfect anymore!
Blue **RUINED** it!
C'mon, Barry! What's the biggie?
Blue is **OUR** friend and that means he hangs out with **US**, not some kooky cave crawlers.
EXCUSE ME!

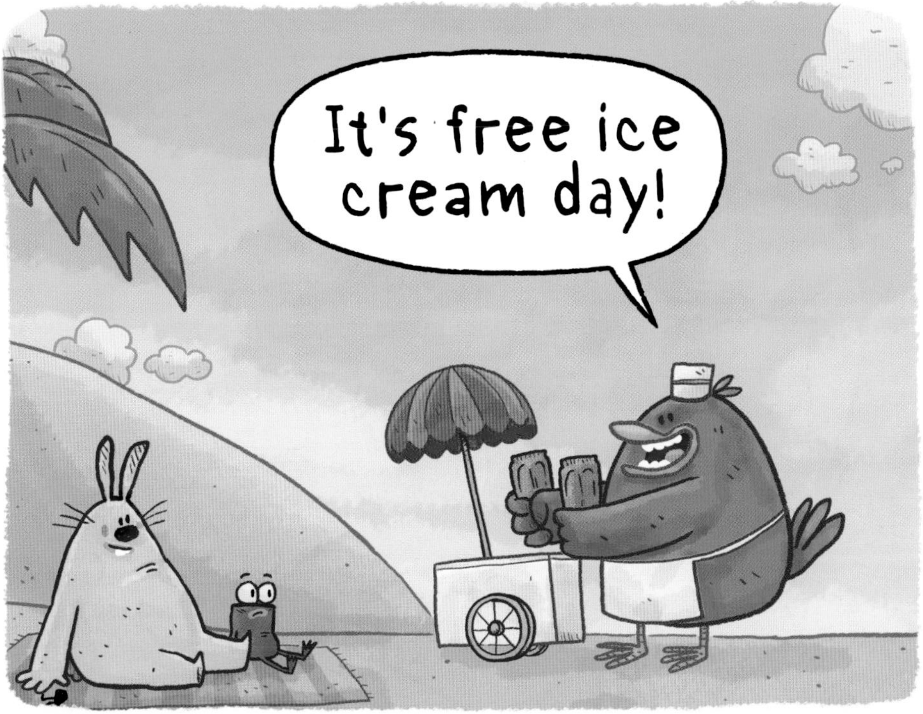
It's free ice cream day!

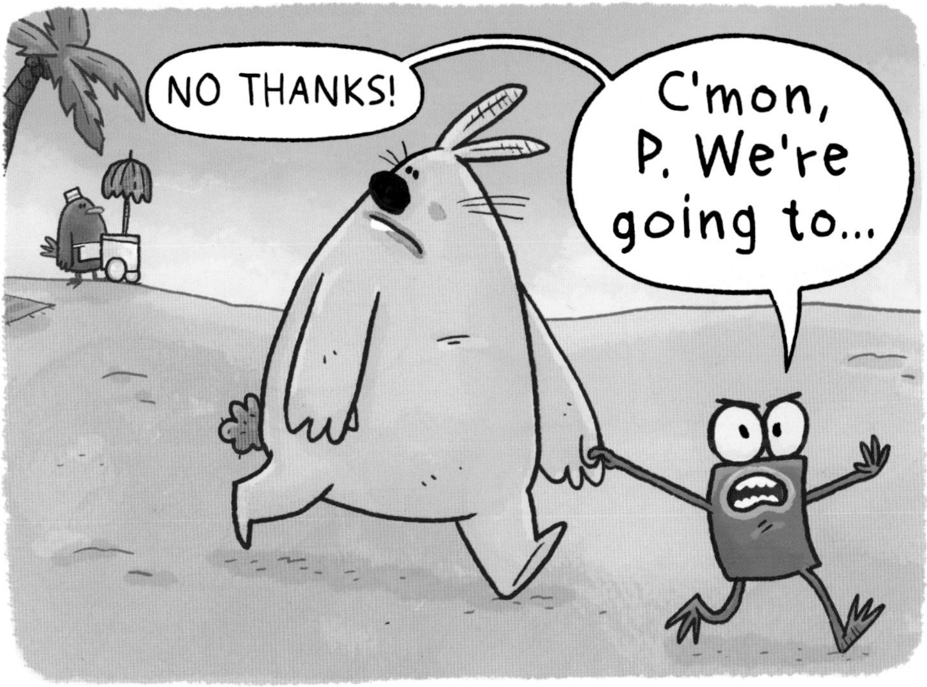
NO THANKS!
C'mon, P. We're going to...

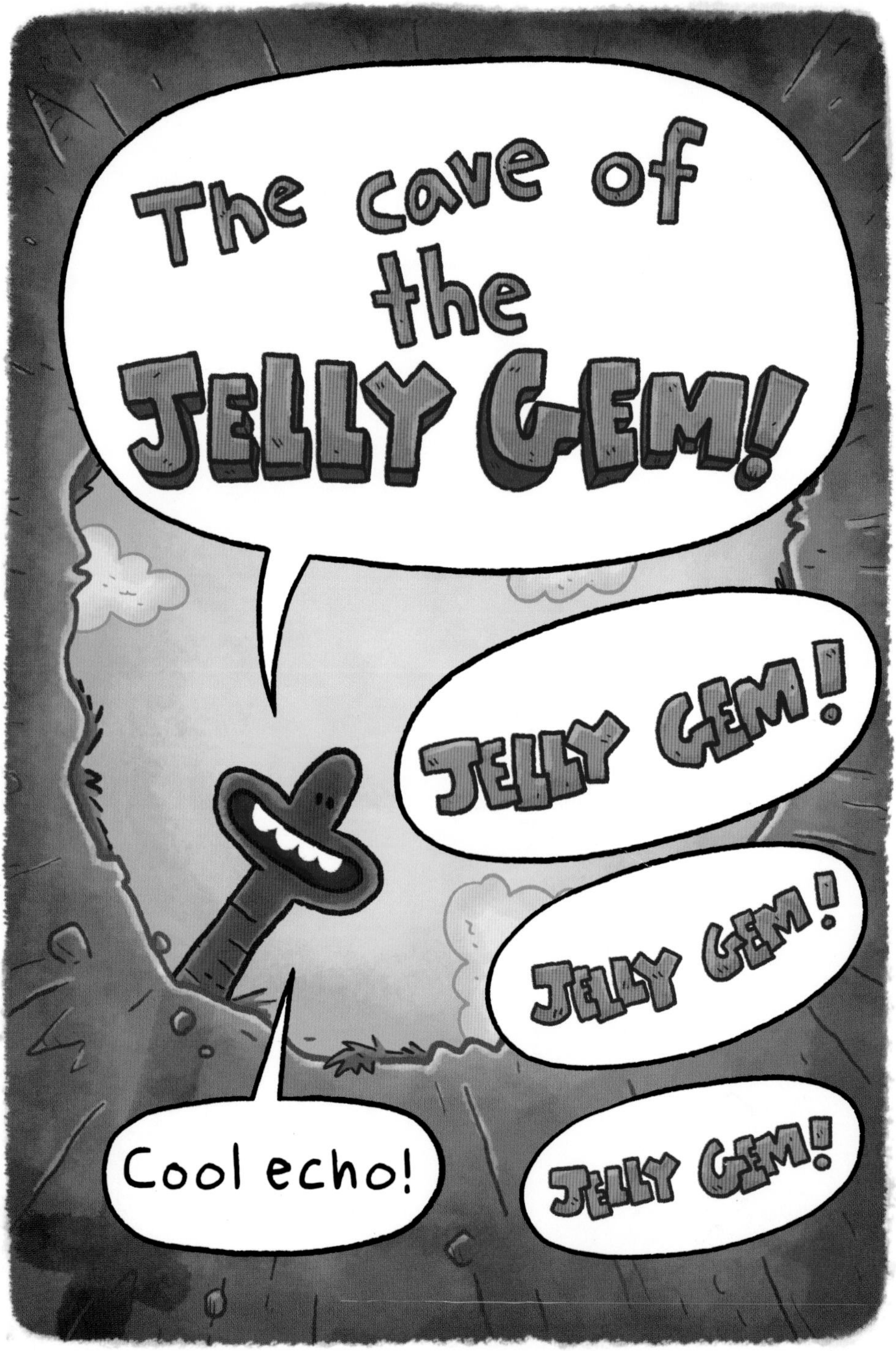
The cave of the JELLY GEM!
JELLY GEM!
JELLY GEM!
Cool echo!
JELLY GEM!

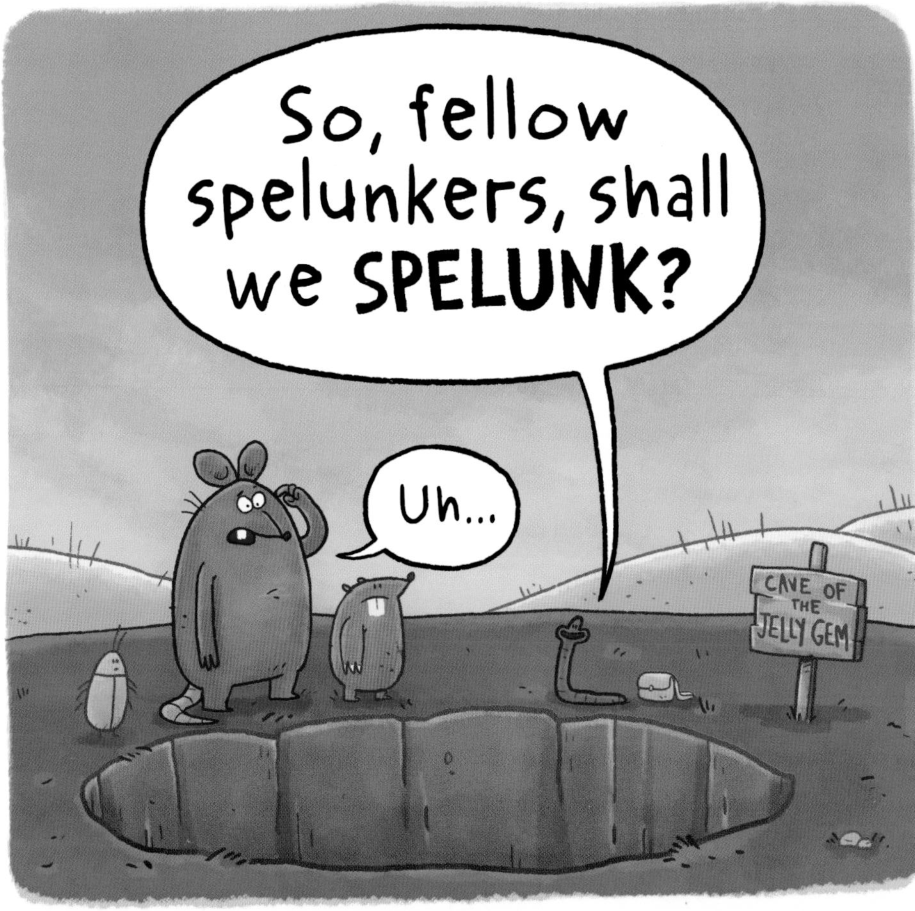
So, fellow spelunkers, shall we **SPELUNK?**
Uh...
CAVE OF THE JELLY GEM

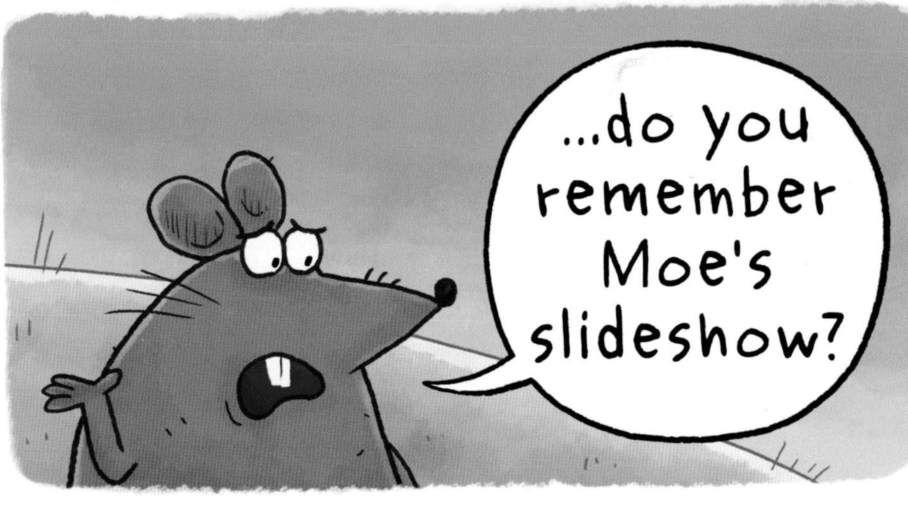
...do you remember Moe's slideshow?

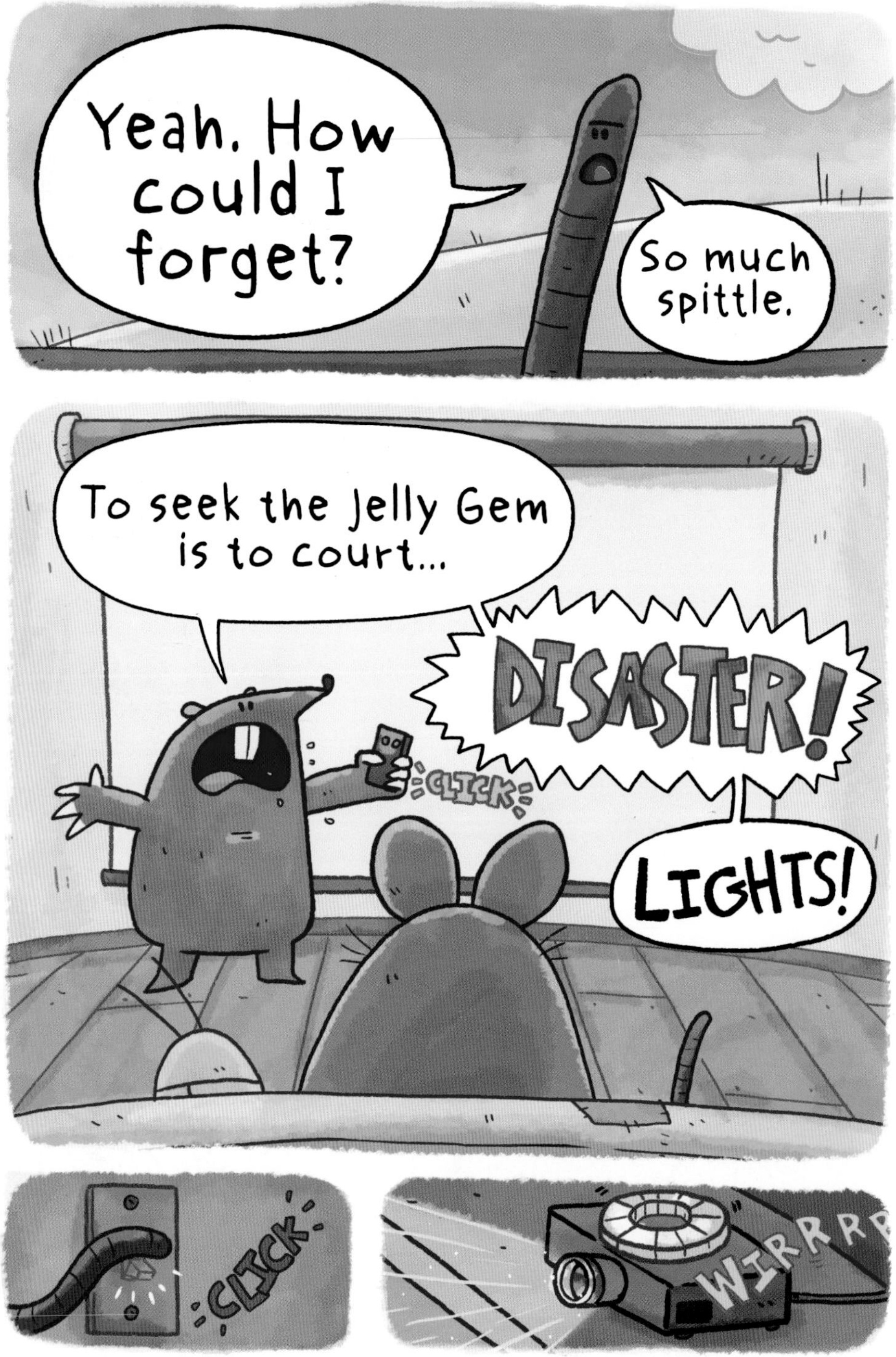
Yeah. How could I forget?
So much spittle.
To seek the Jelly Gem is to court...
DISASTER!
CLICK
LIGHTS!
CLICK
WIRRR

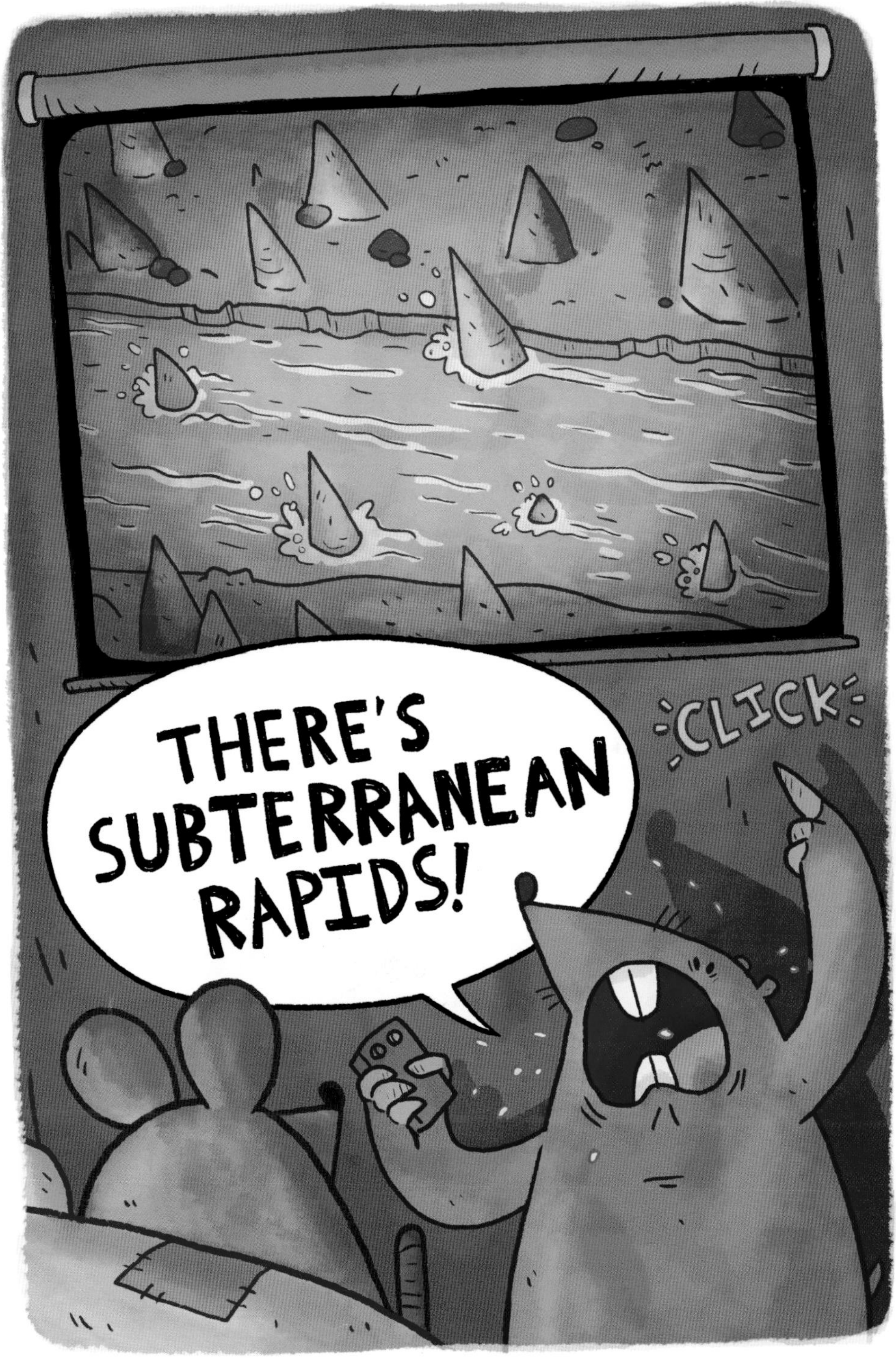
THERE'S SUBTERRANEAN RAPIDS!
CLICK

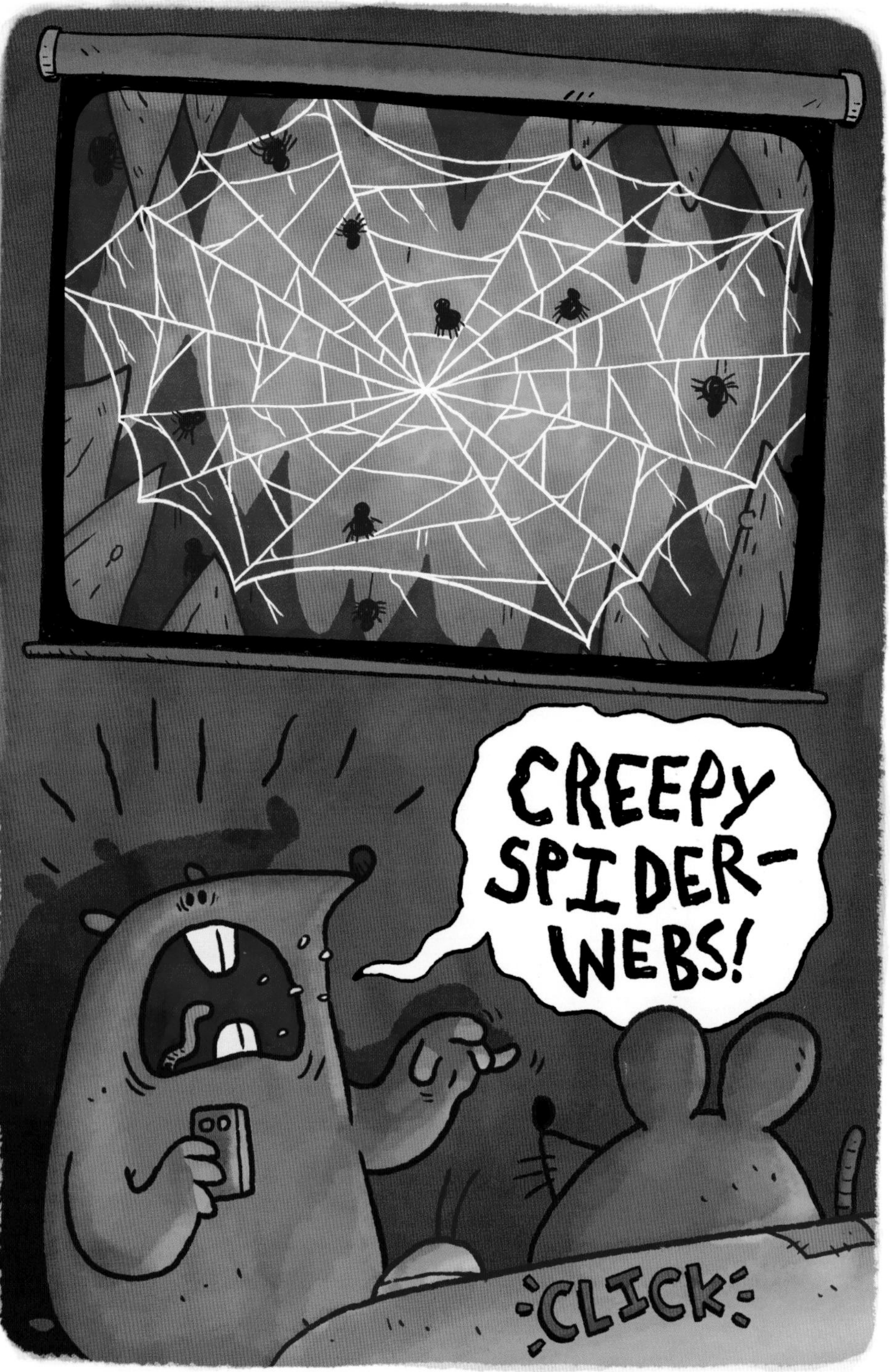
CREEPY SPIDER-WEBS!
CLICK

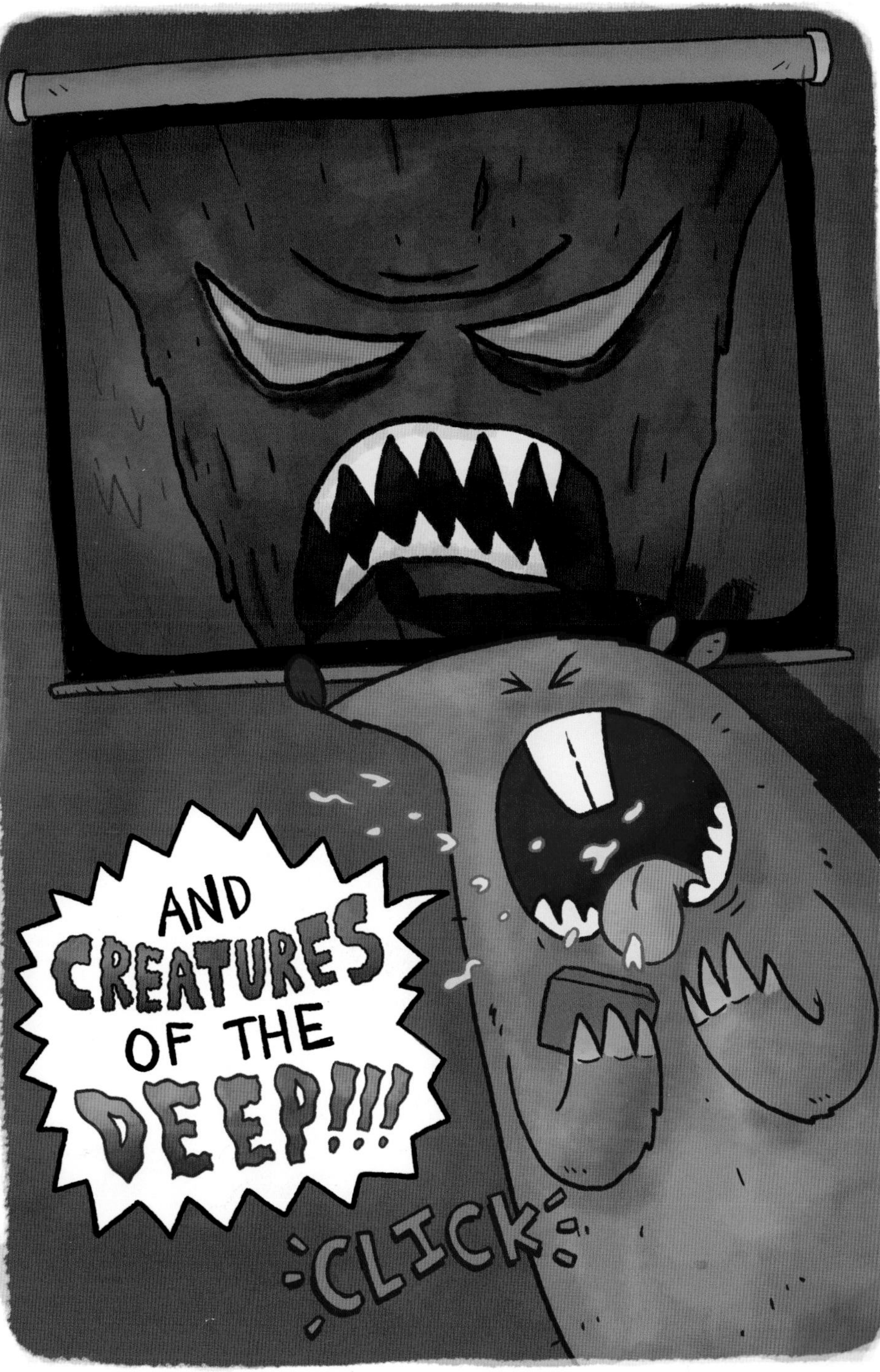
AND CREATURES OF THE DEEP!!!
CLICK

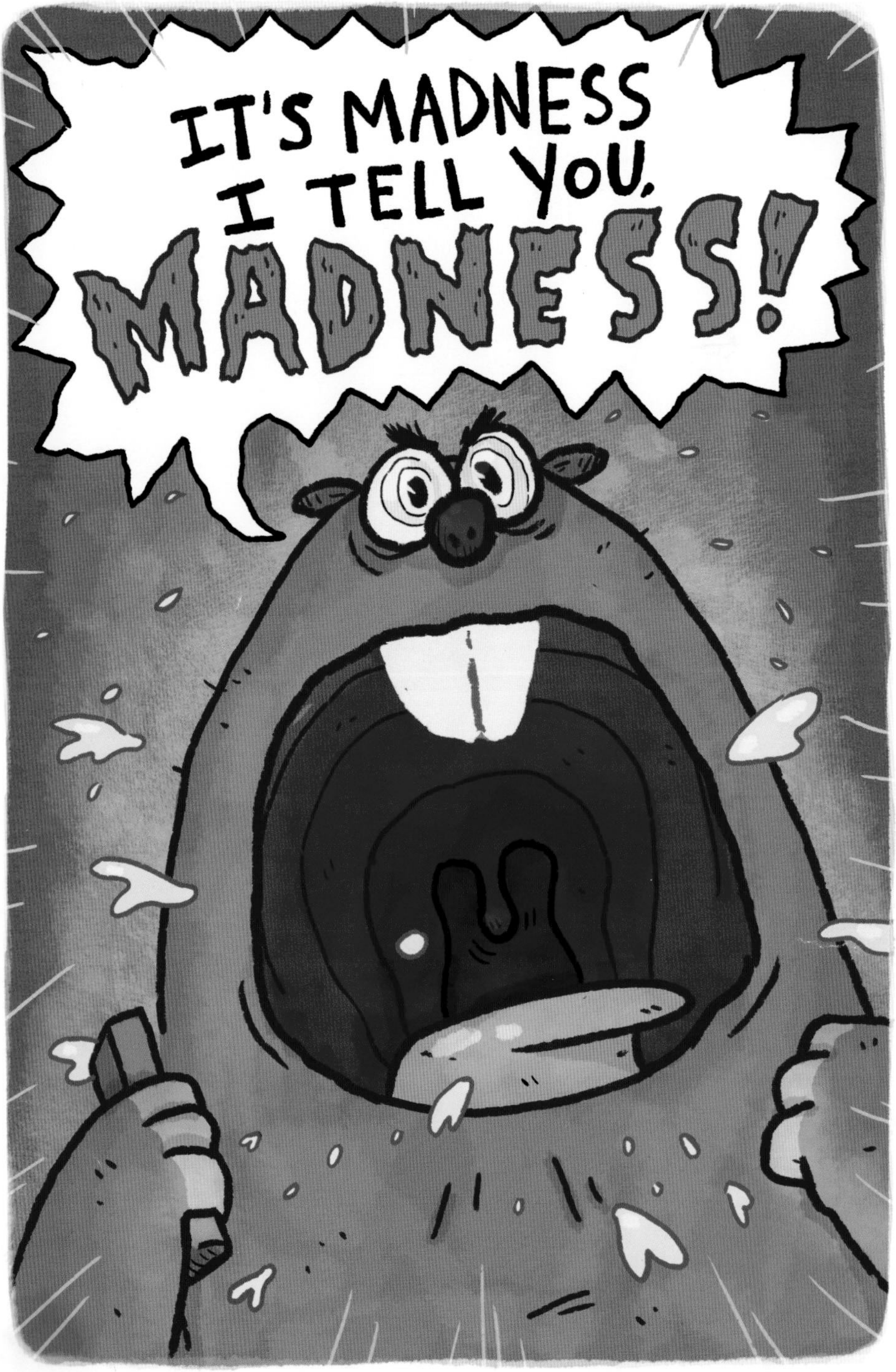
IT'S MADNESS I TELL YOU, MADNESS!

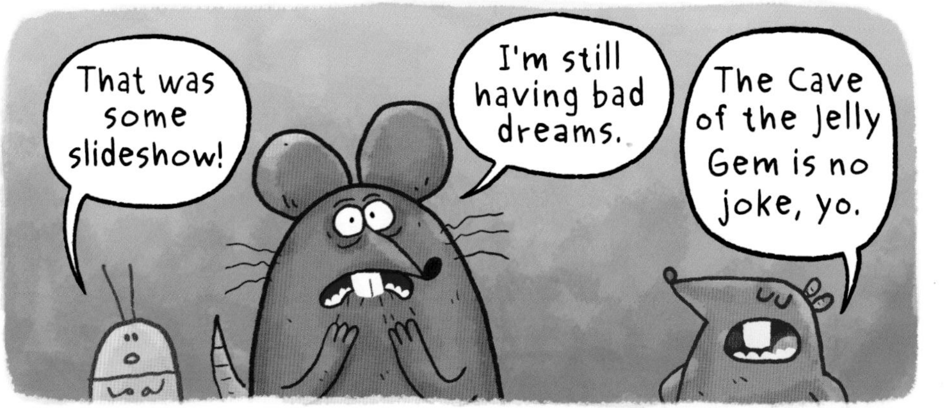
That was some slideshow!
I'm still having bad dreams.
The Cave of the Jelly Gem is no joke, yo.

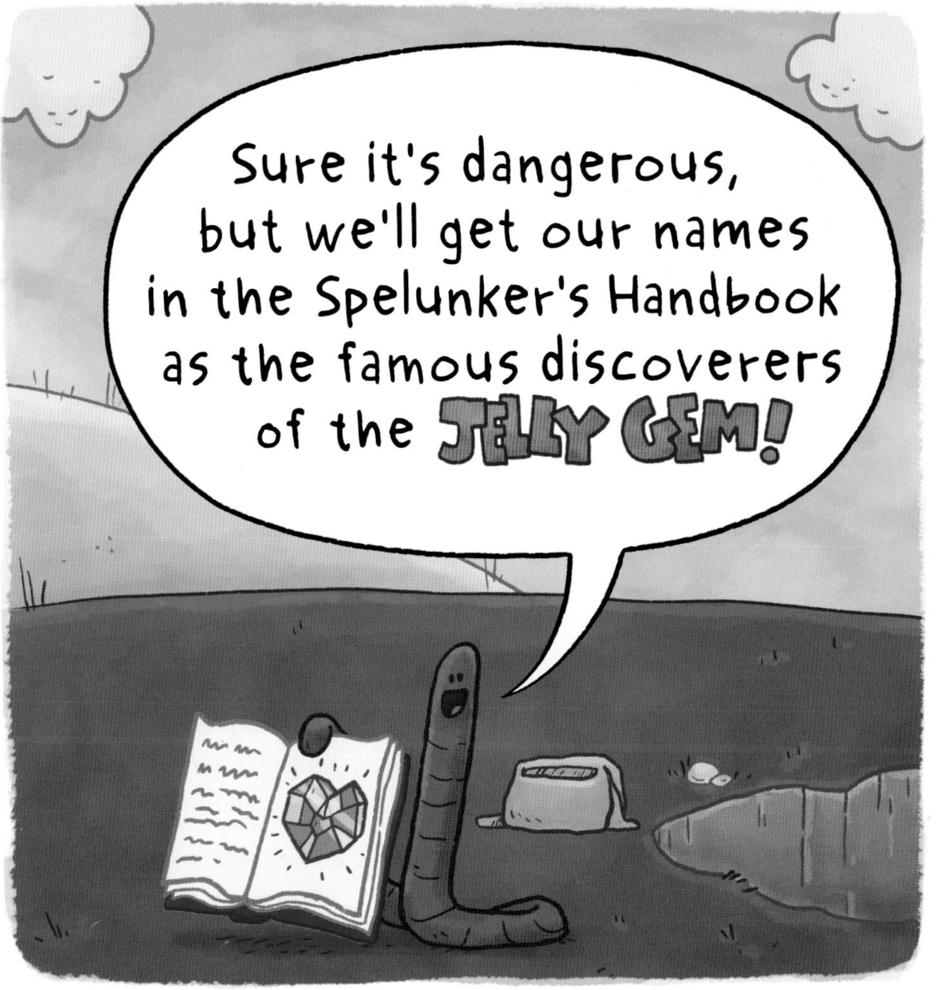
Sure it's dangerous, but we'll get our names in the Spelunker's Handbook as the famous discoverers of the JELLY GEM!

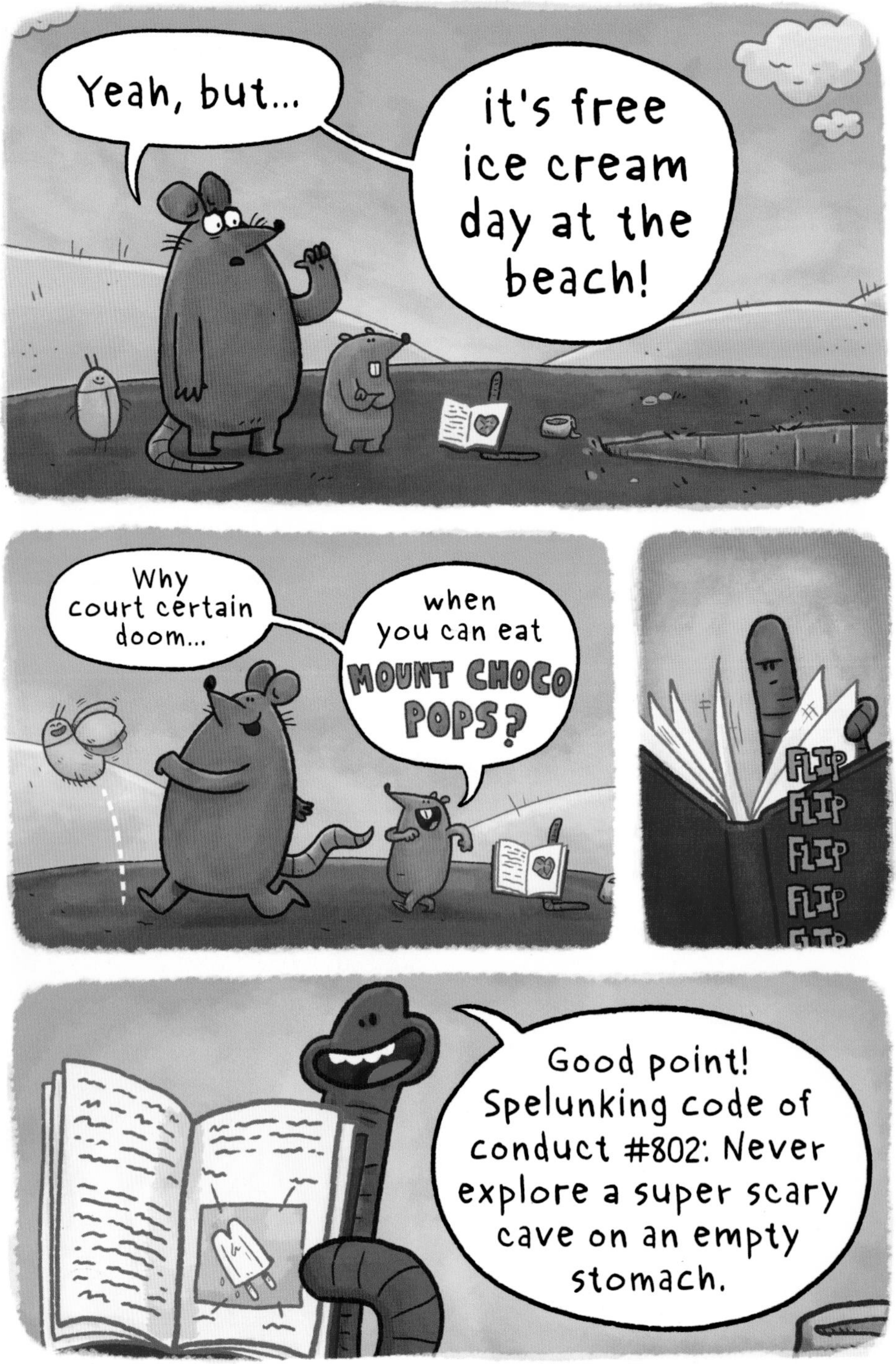
Yeah, but...
it's free ice cream day at the beach!
Why court certain doom...
when you can eat MOUNT CHOCO POPS?
FLIP
FLIP
FLIP
FLIP
Good point! Spelunking code of conduct #802: Never explore a super scary cave on an empty stomach.

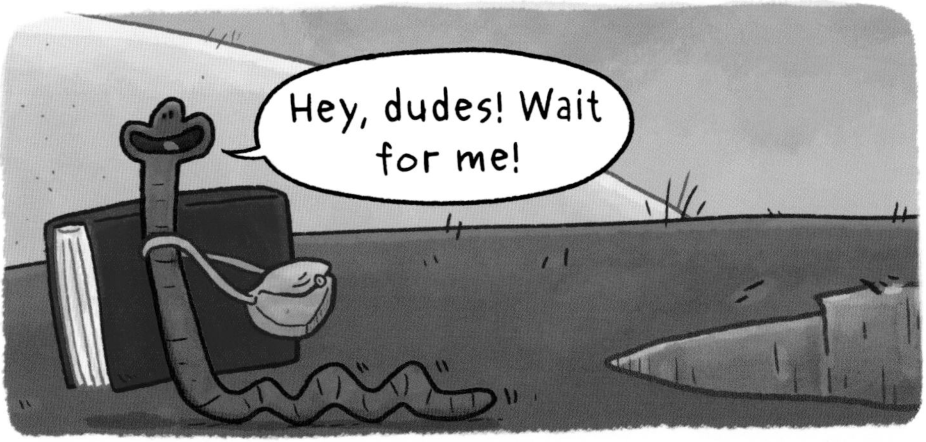
Hey, dudes! Wait for me!

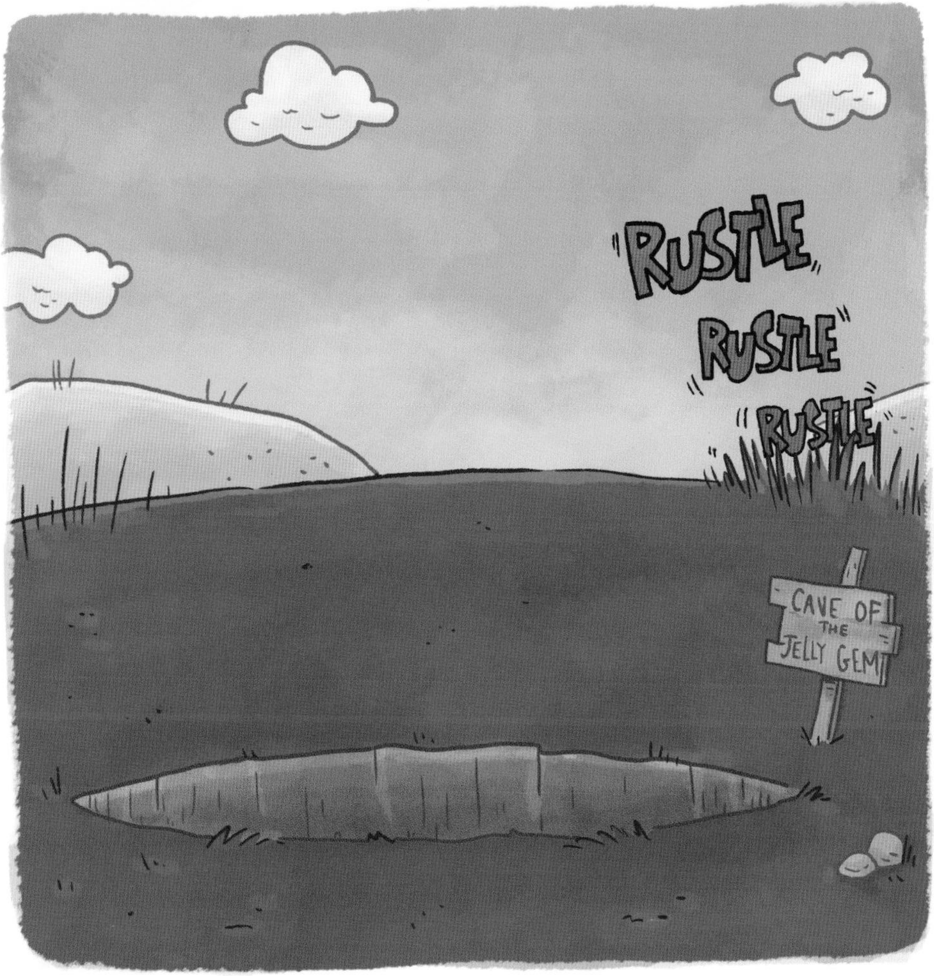
RUSTLE
RUSTLE
RUSTLE
CAVE OF THE JELLY GEM

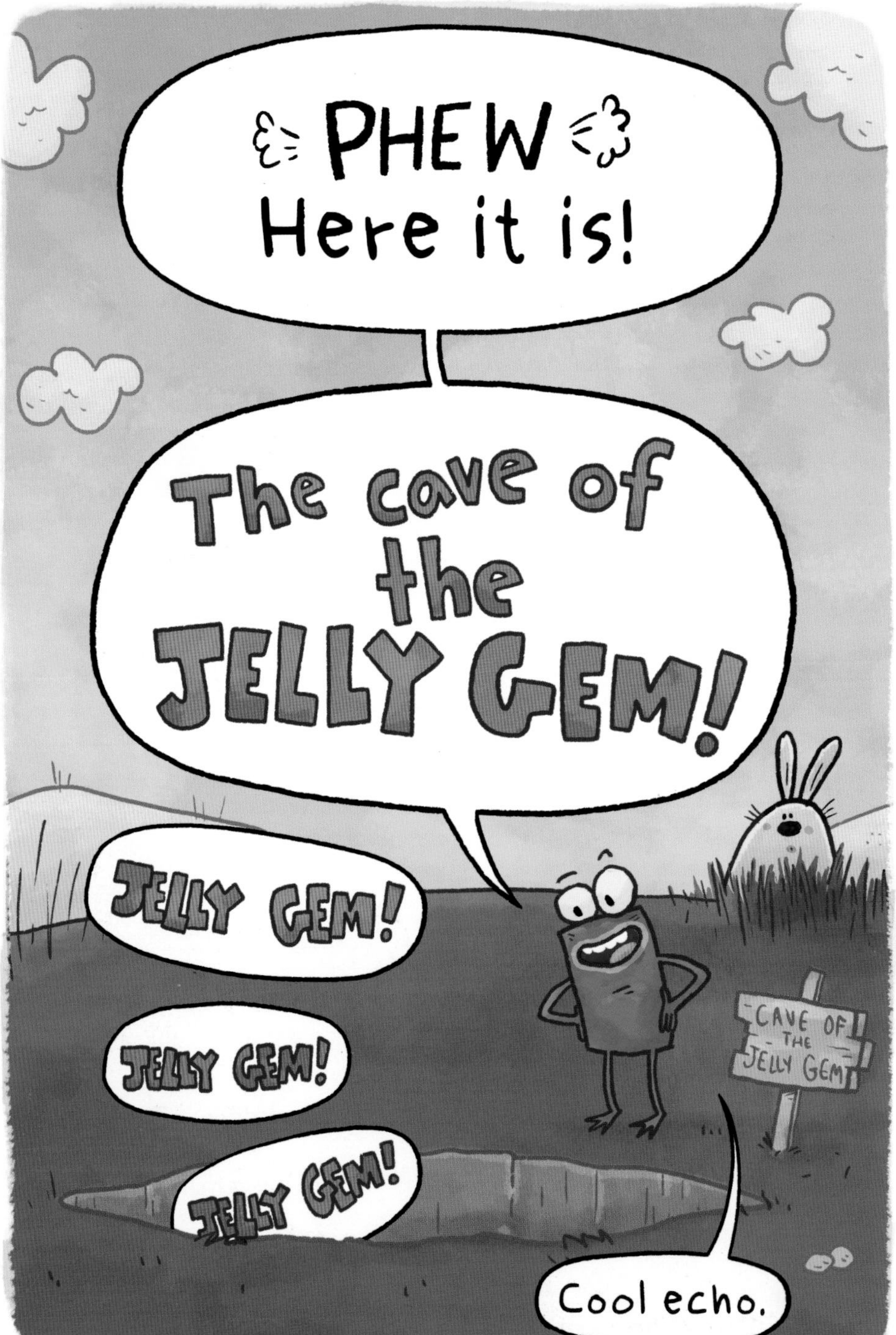
PHEW
Here it is!
The cave of the JELLY GEM!
JELLY GEM!
JELLY GEM!
JELLY GEM!
CAVE OF THE JELLY GEM
Cool echo.

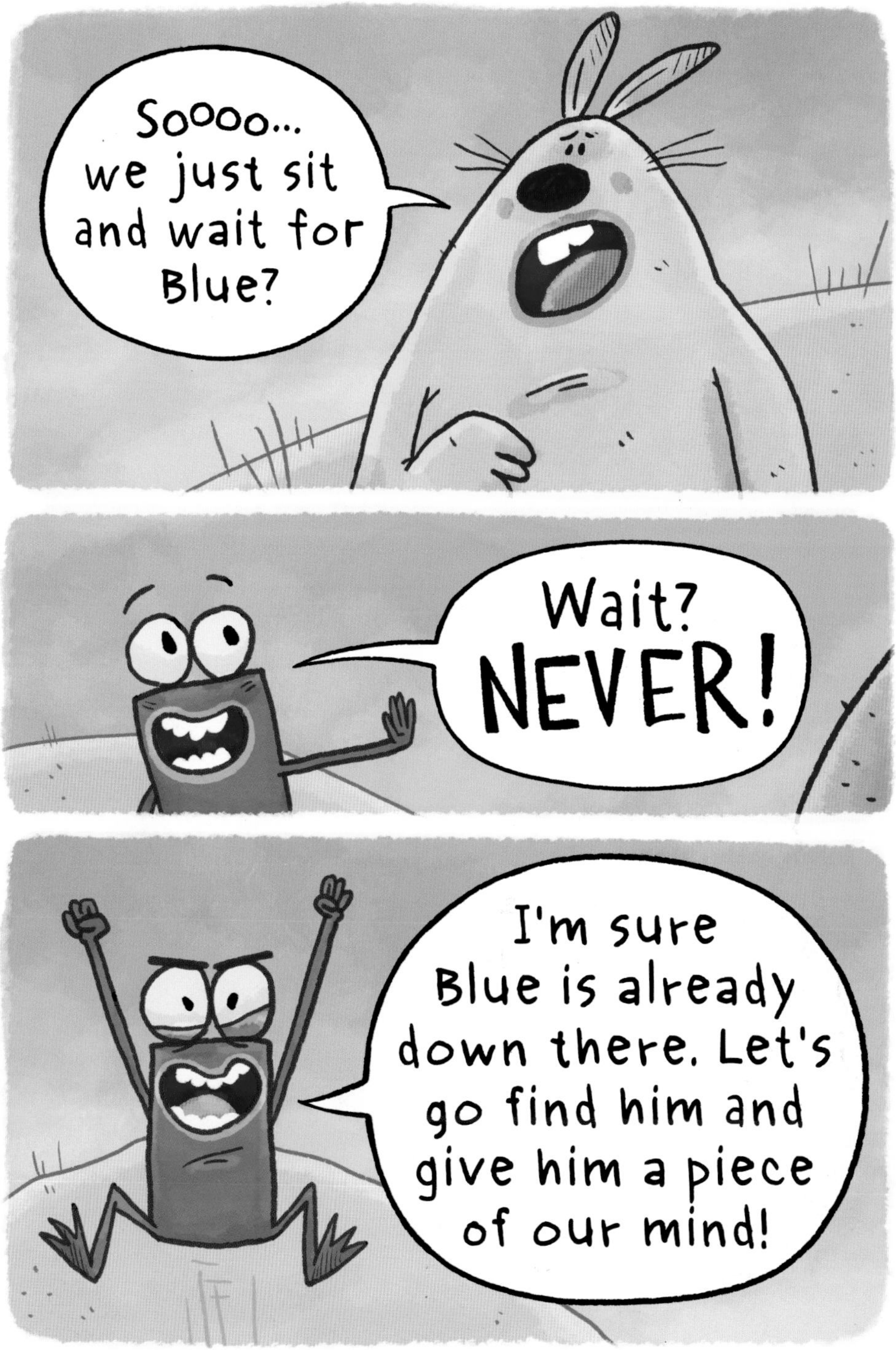
Soooo...
we just sit
and wait for
Blue?
Wait?
NEVER!
I'm sure
Blue is already
down there. Let's
go find him and
give him a piece
of our mind!

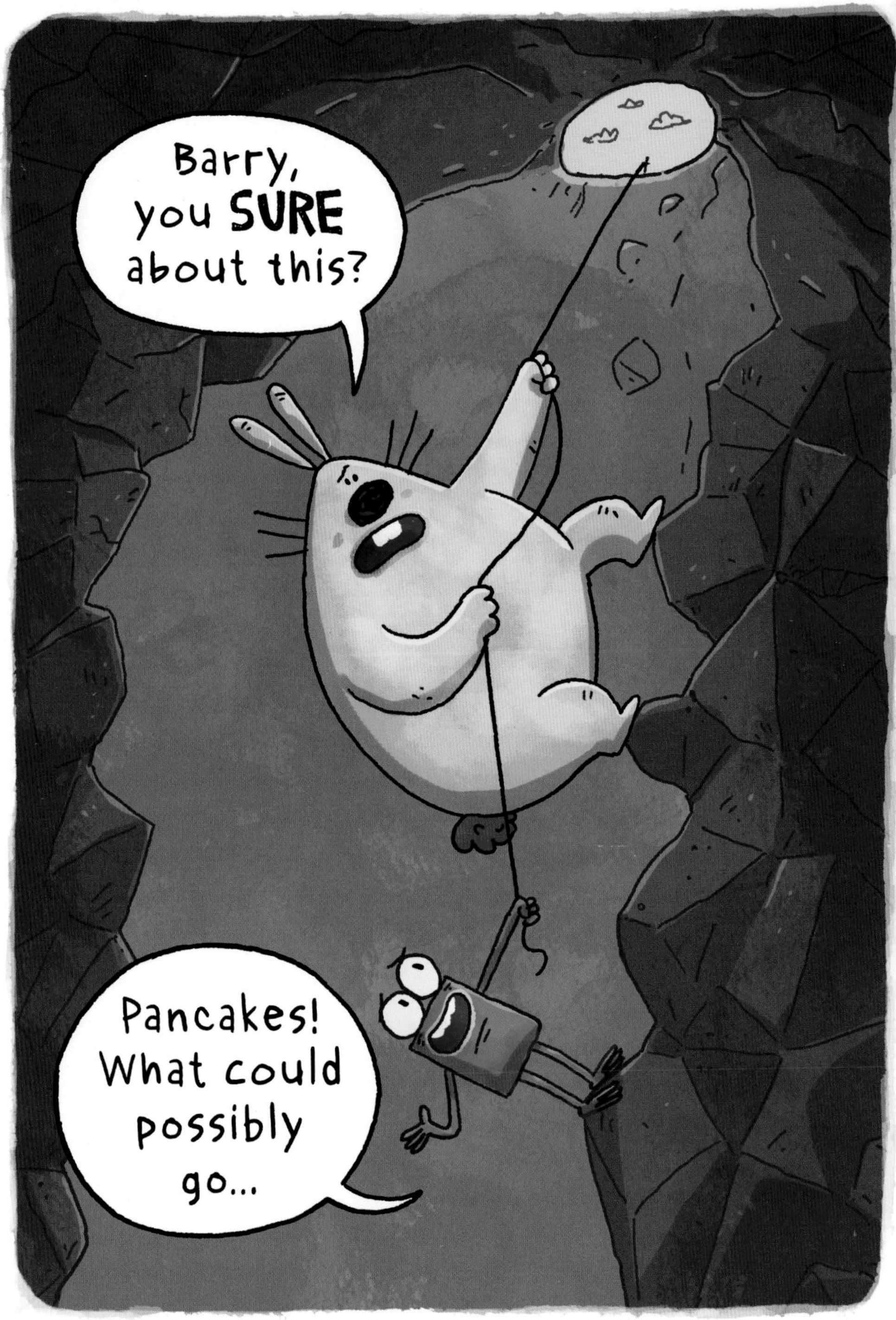
Barry, you **SURE** about this?
Pancakes! What could possibly go...

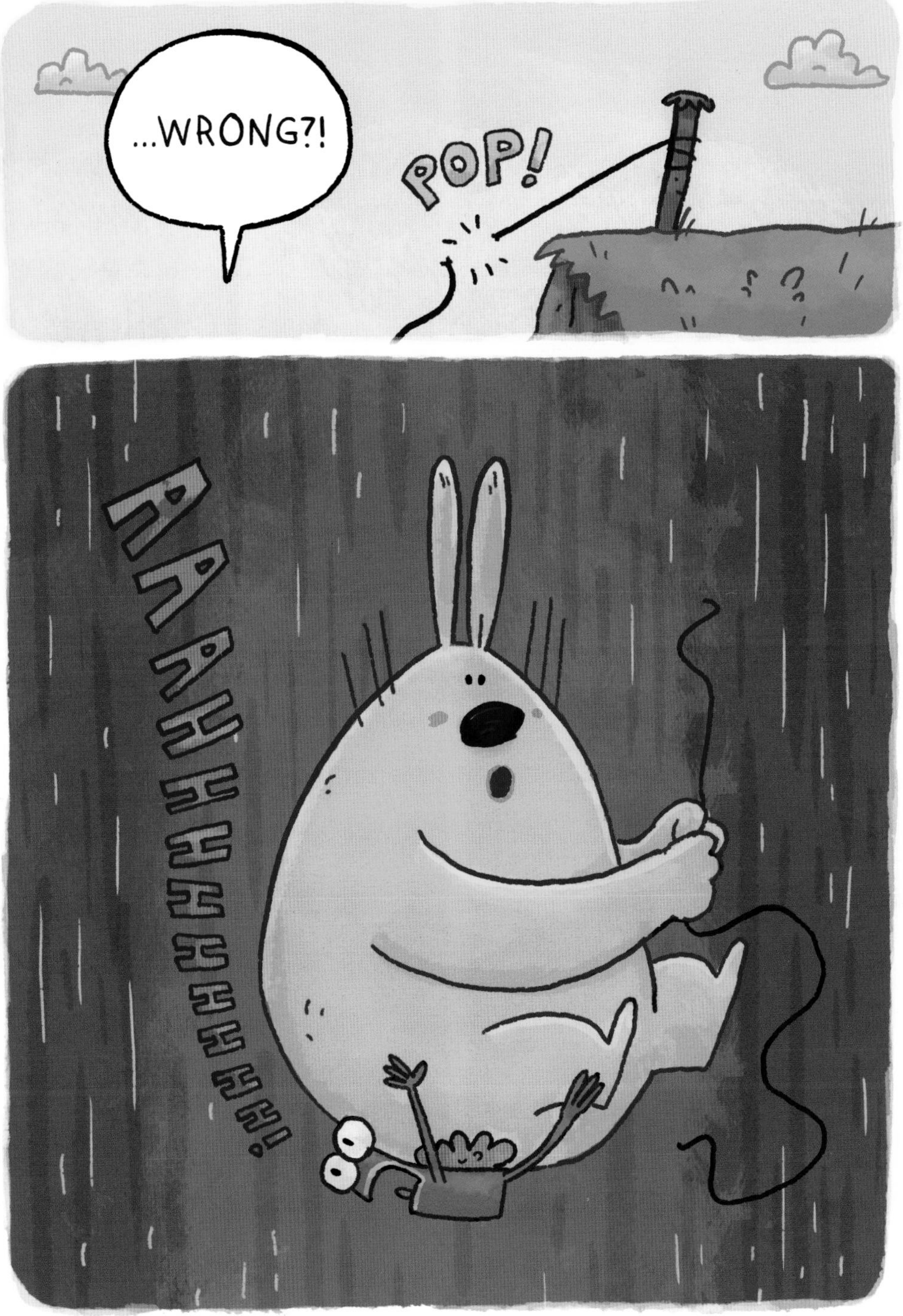
...WRONG?!
POP!
AAAAHHHHHHHH!

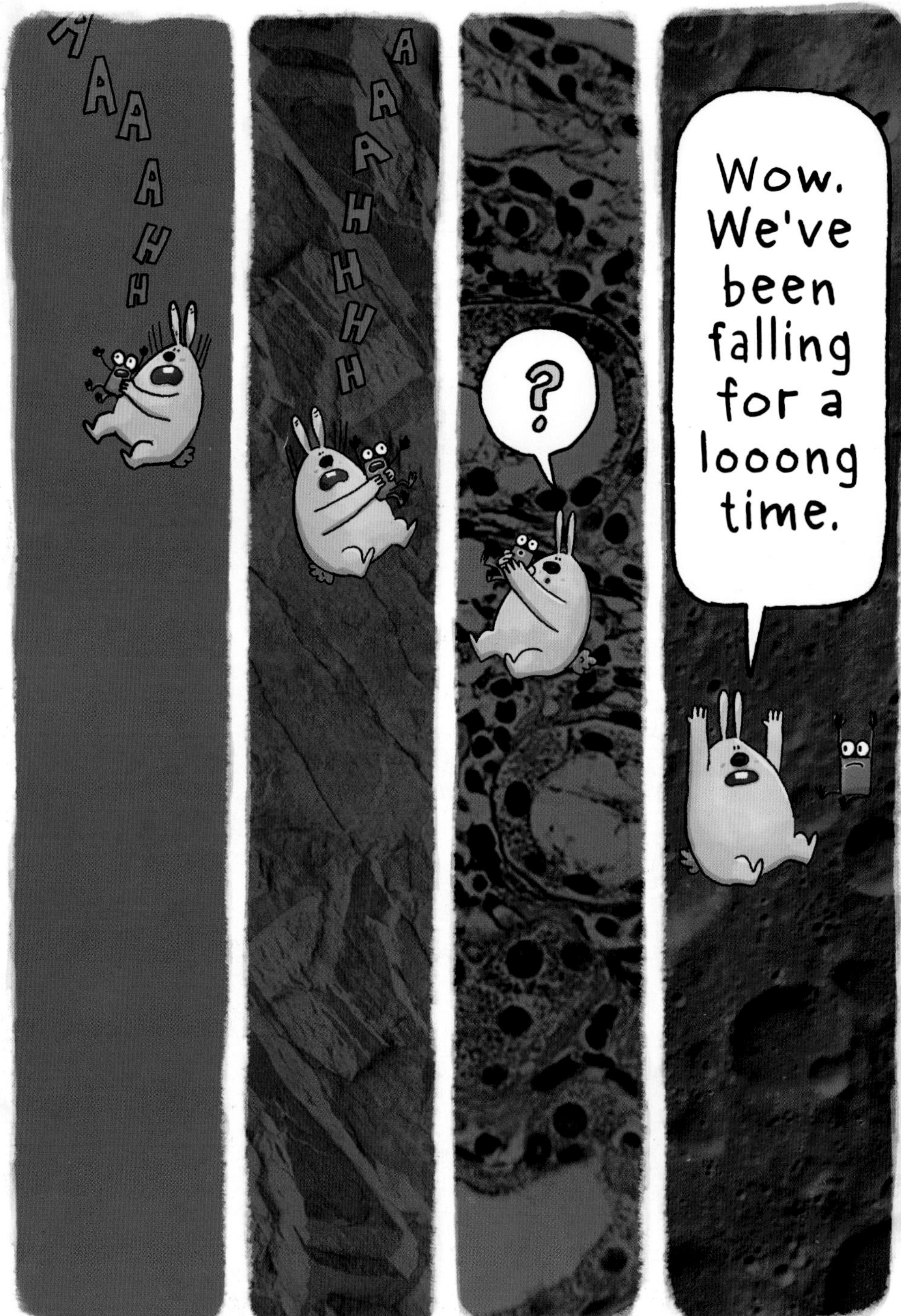
AAAAHHH
AAAHHHHH
?
Wow. We've been falling for a looong time.

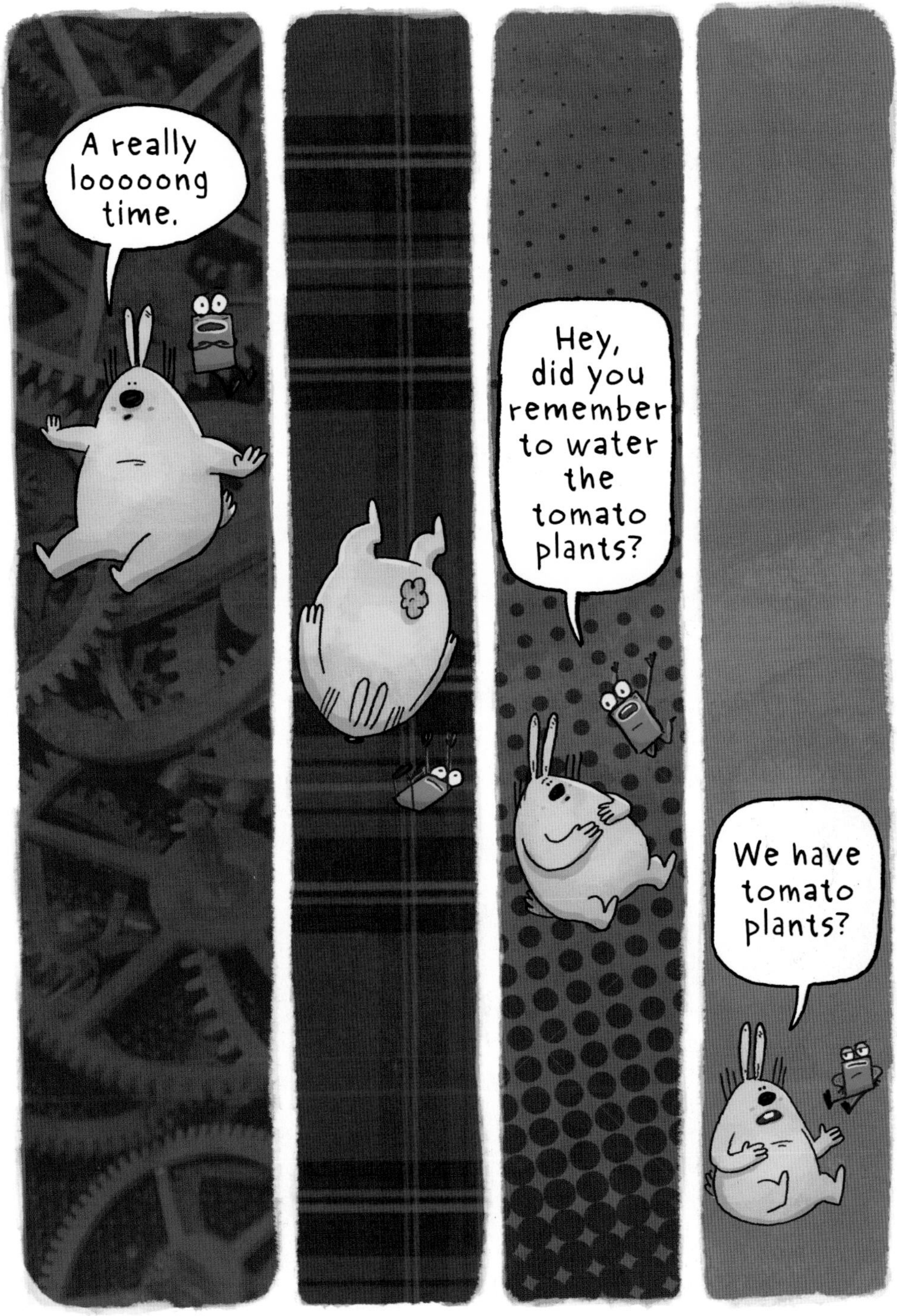
A really loooooong time.
Hey, did you remember to water the tomato plants?
We have tomato plants?

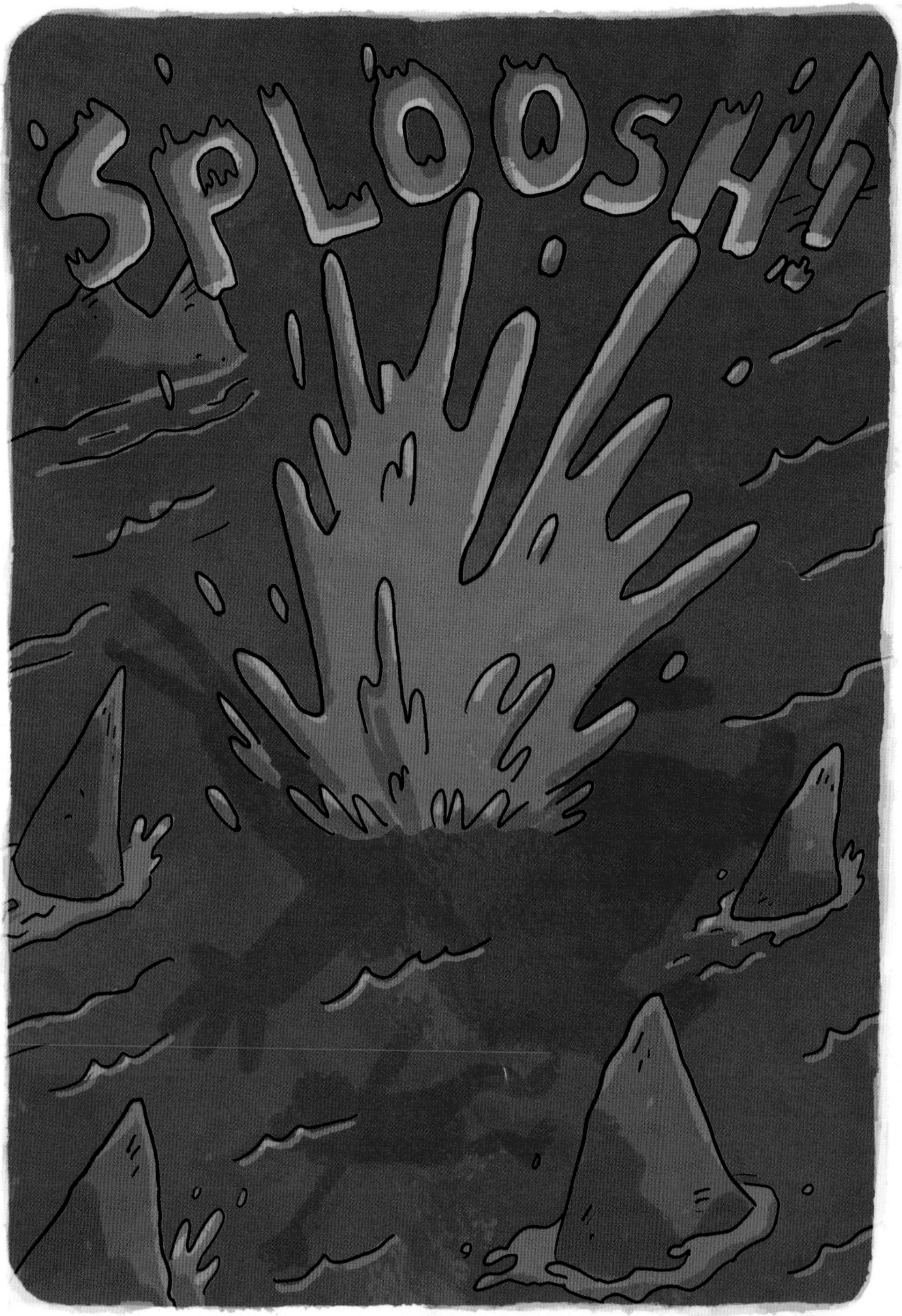
SPLOOSH!

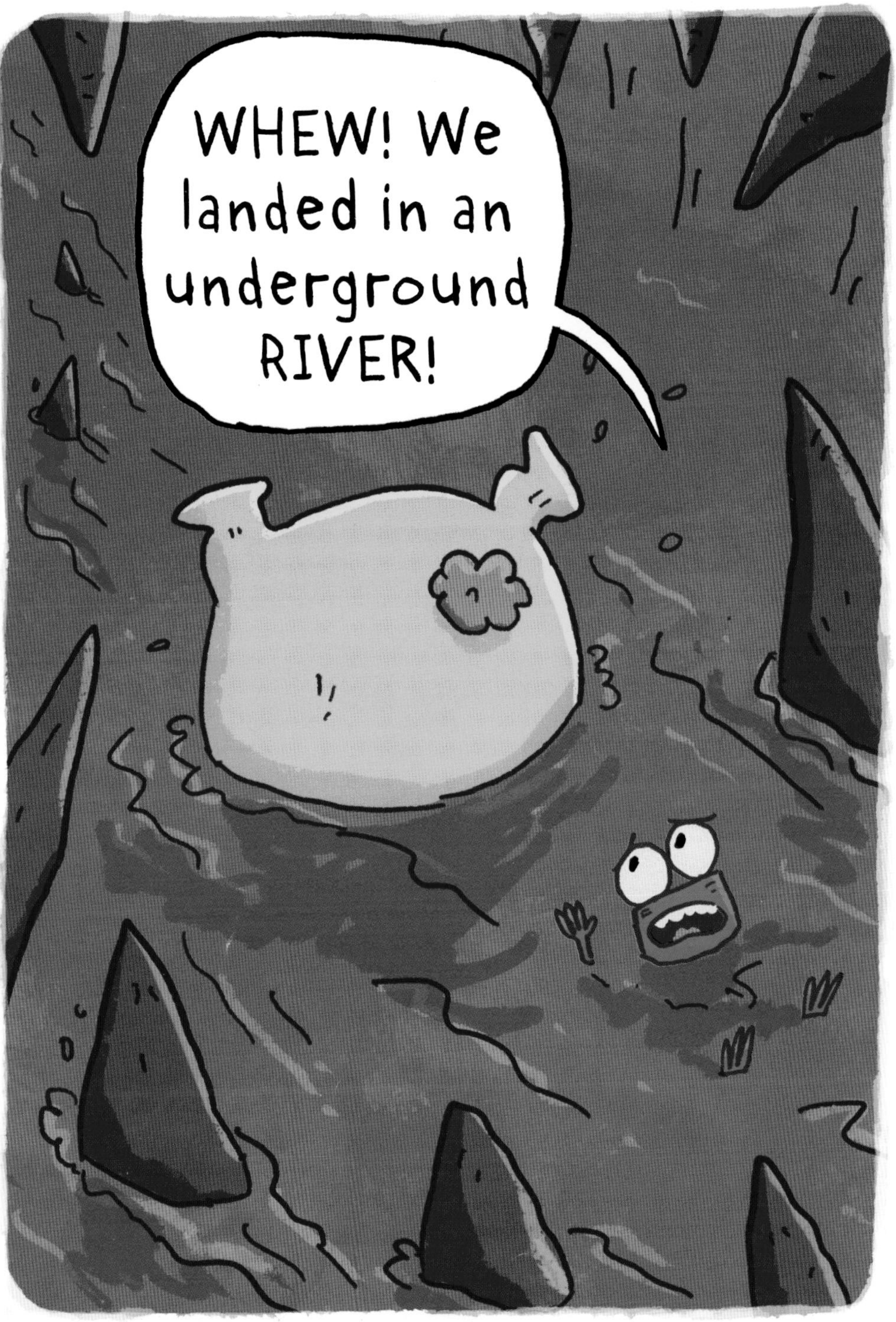
WHEW! We landed in an underground RIVER!

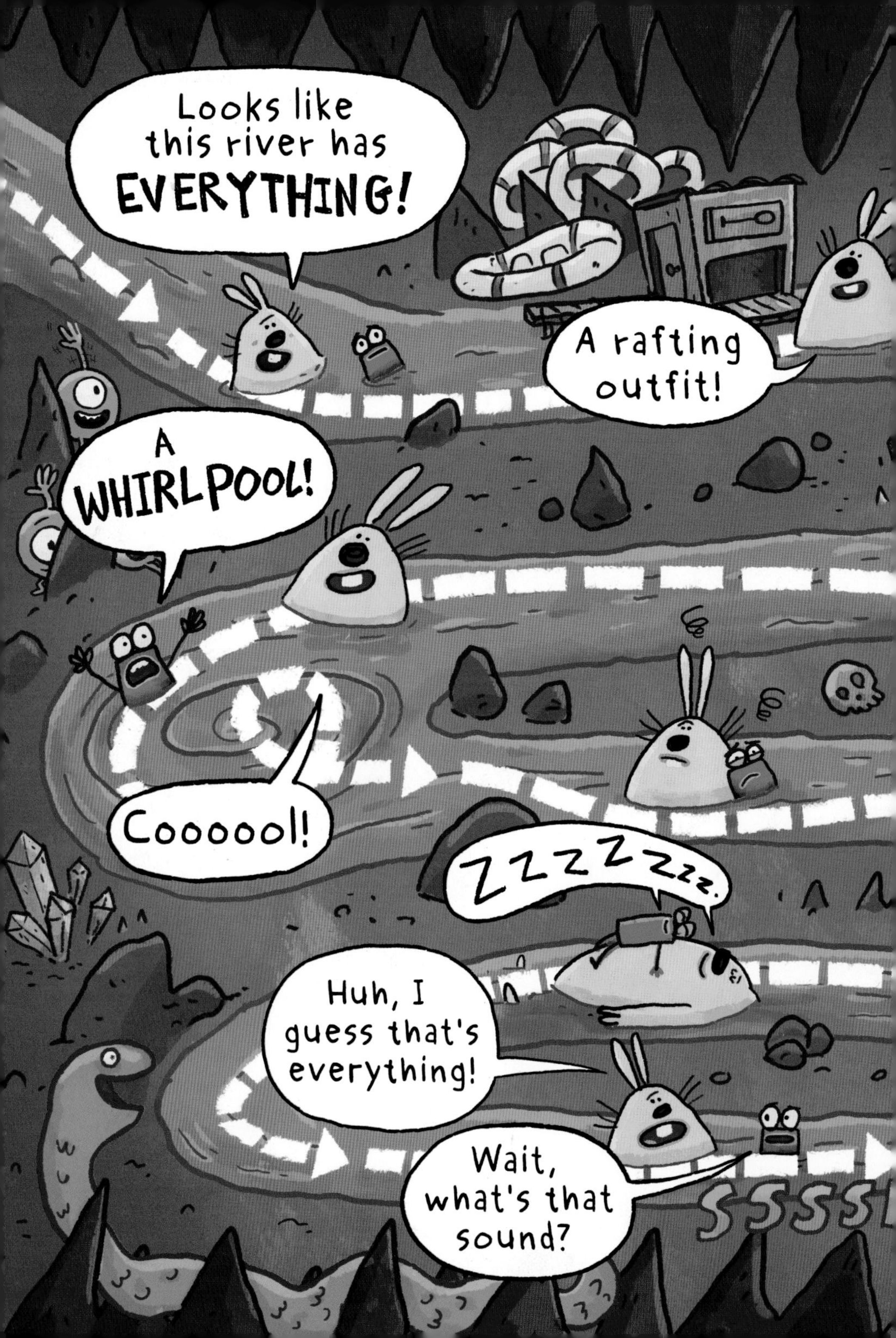
Looks like this river has EVERYTHING!
A rafting outfit!
A WHIRLPOOL!
Coooool!
ZZZZZzz.
Huh, I guess that's everything!
Wait, what's that sound?
SSSS

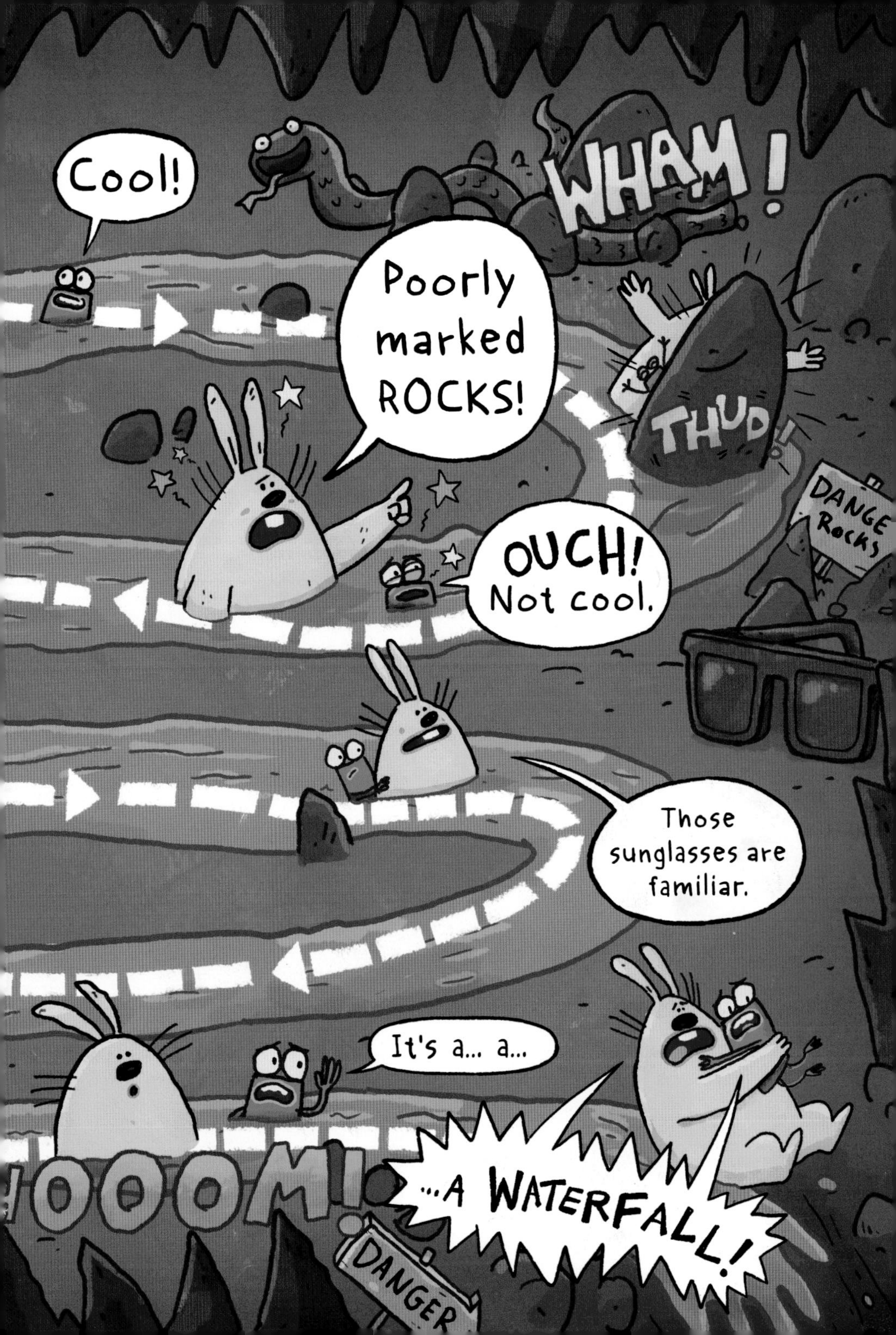
Cool!
WHAM!
Poorly marked ROCKS!
THUD!
DANGER Rocks
OUCH! Not cool.
Those sunglasses are familiar.
It's a... a...
...A WATERFALL!
OOOOM!
DANGER

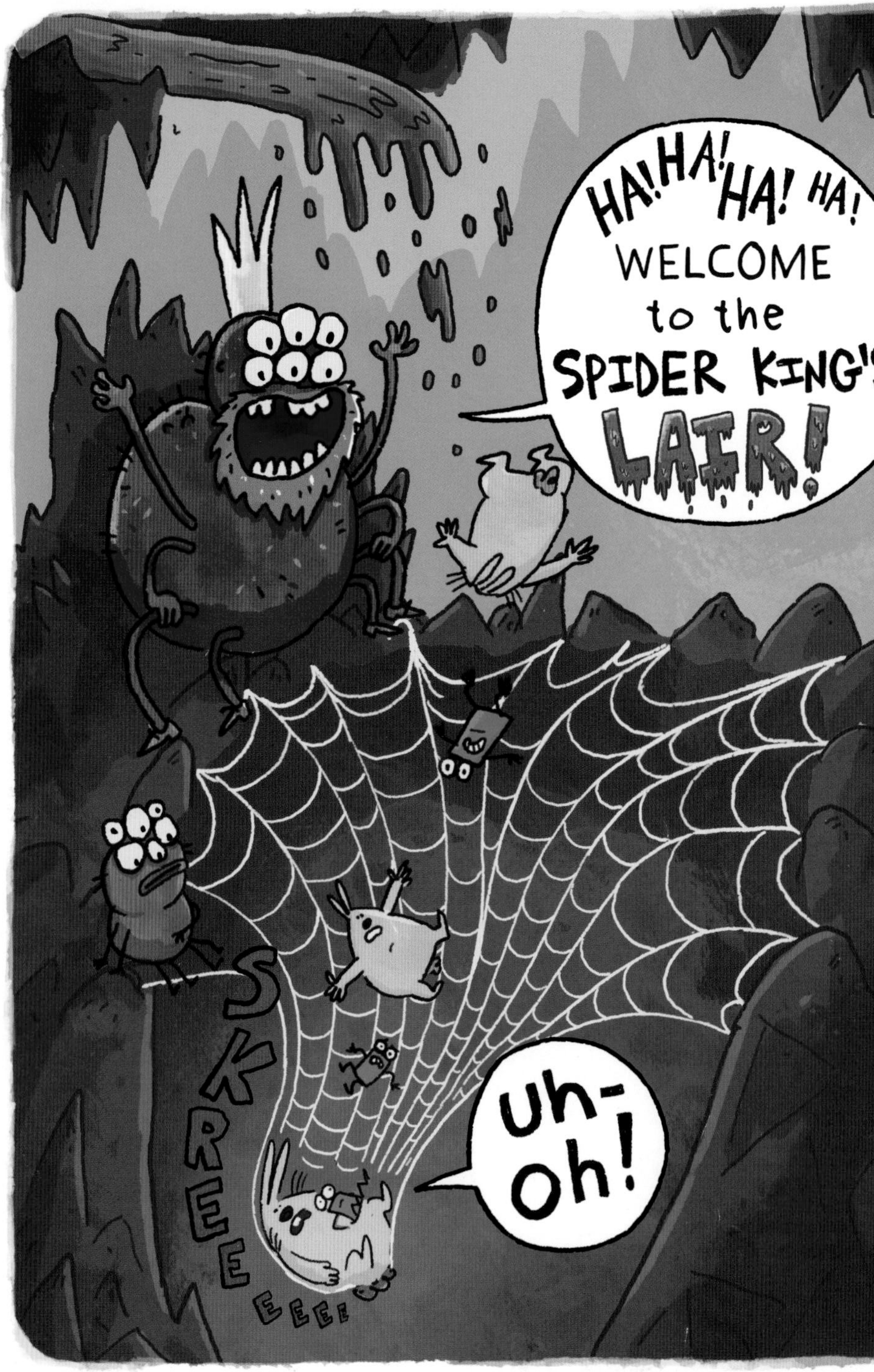
HA! HA! HA! HA!
WELCOME to the SPIDER KING'S LAIR!
SKREEEEEE
Uh-oh!

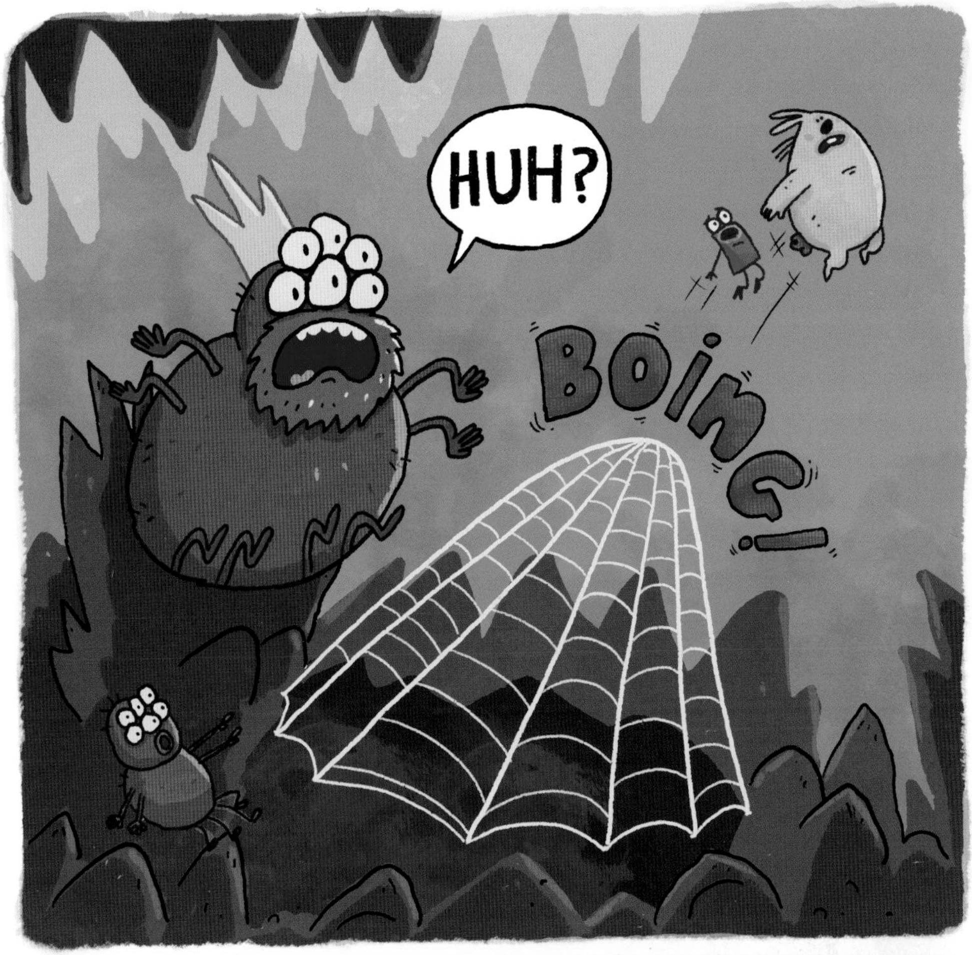
HUH?
BOING!

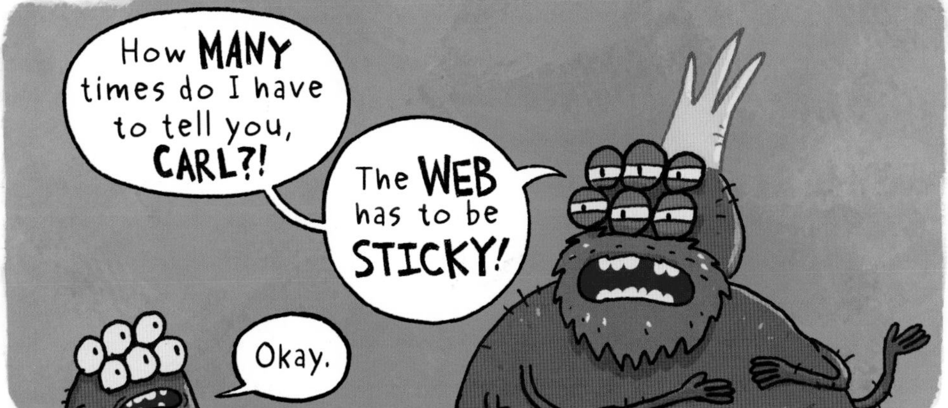
How MANY times do I have to tell you, CARL?!
The WEB has to be STICKY!
Okay.

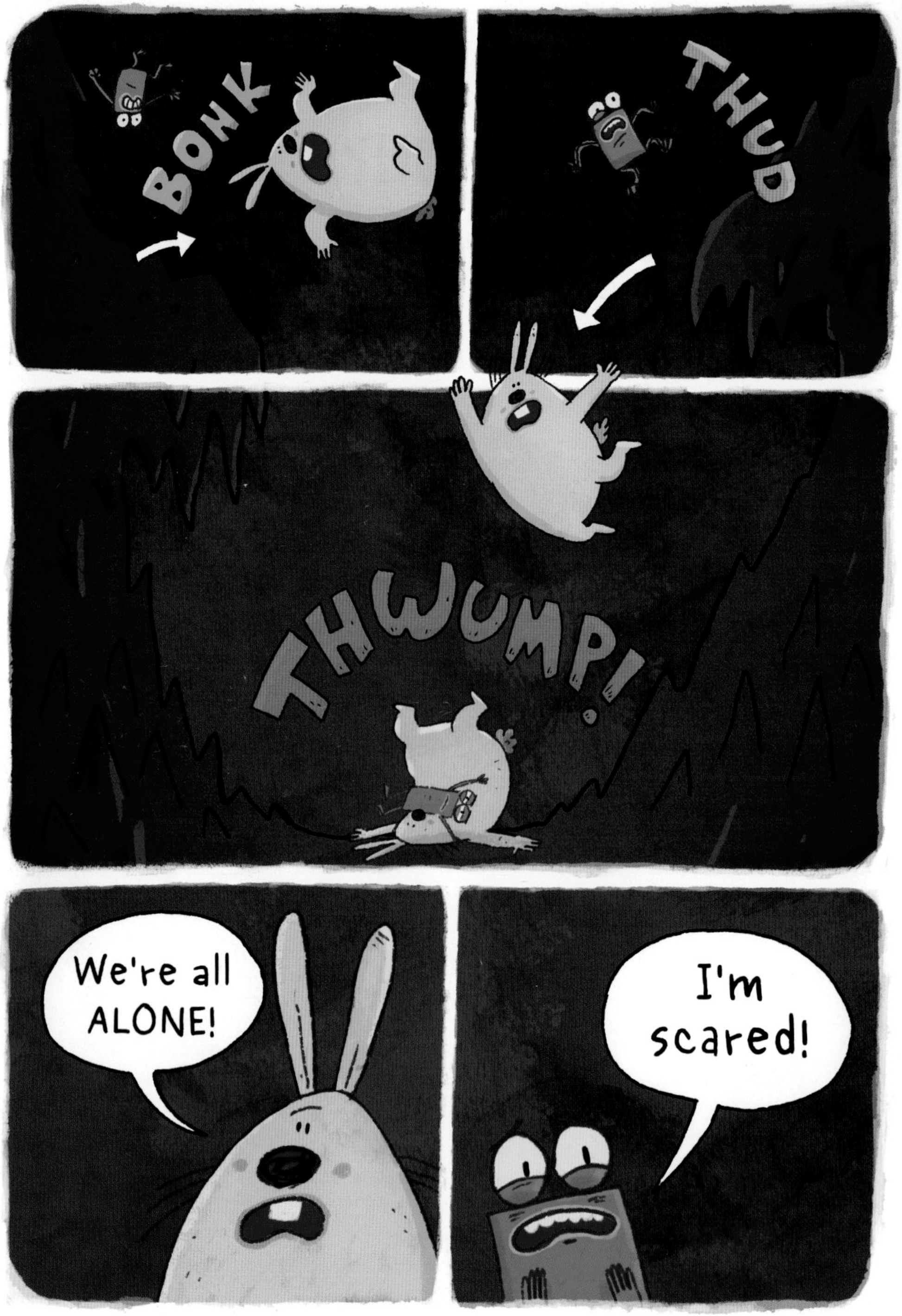
BONK
THUD
THWUMP!
We're all ALONE!
I'm scared!

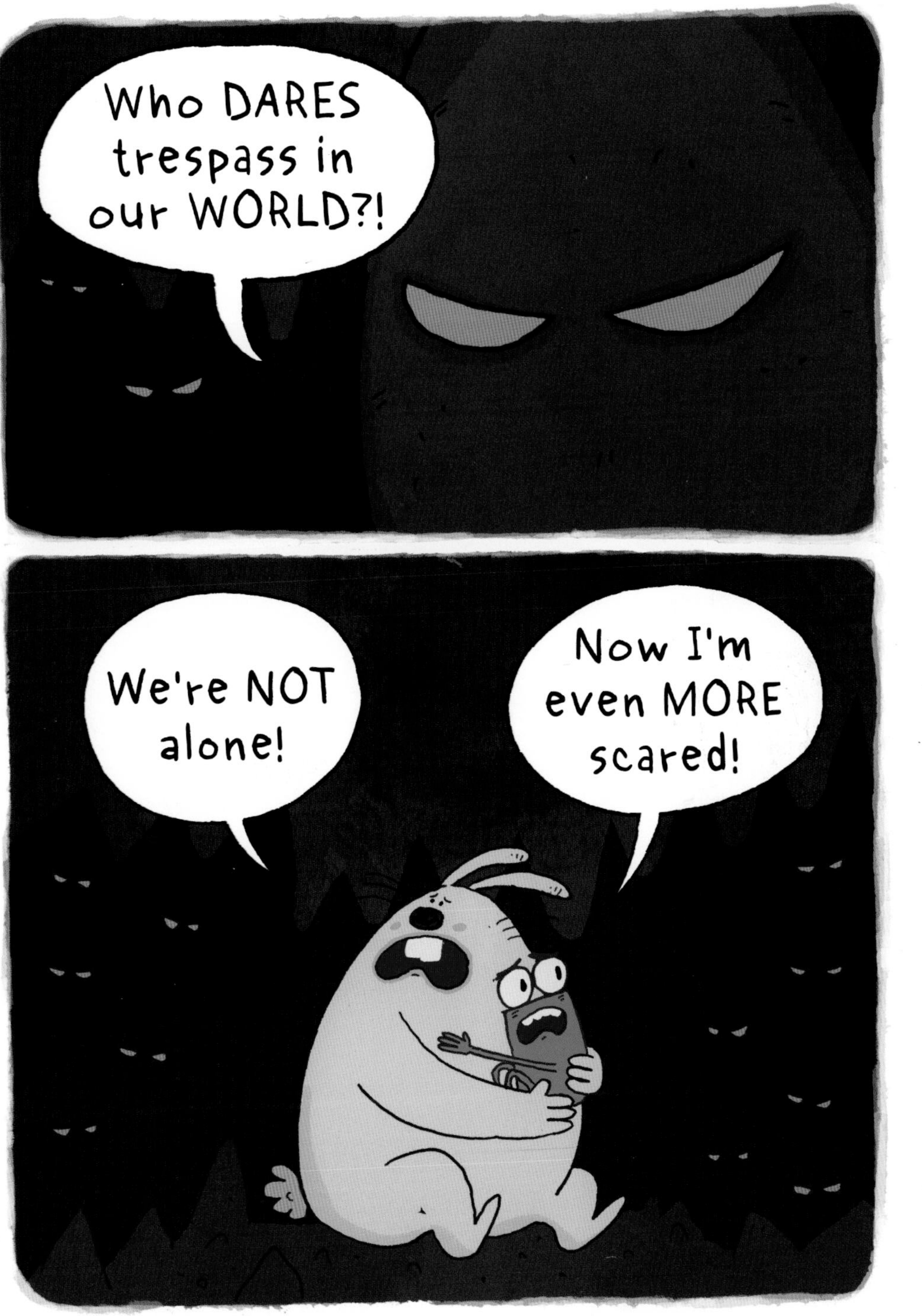
Who DARES trespass in our WORLD?!
We're NOT alone!
Now I'm even MORE scared!

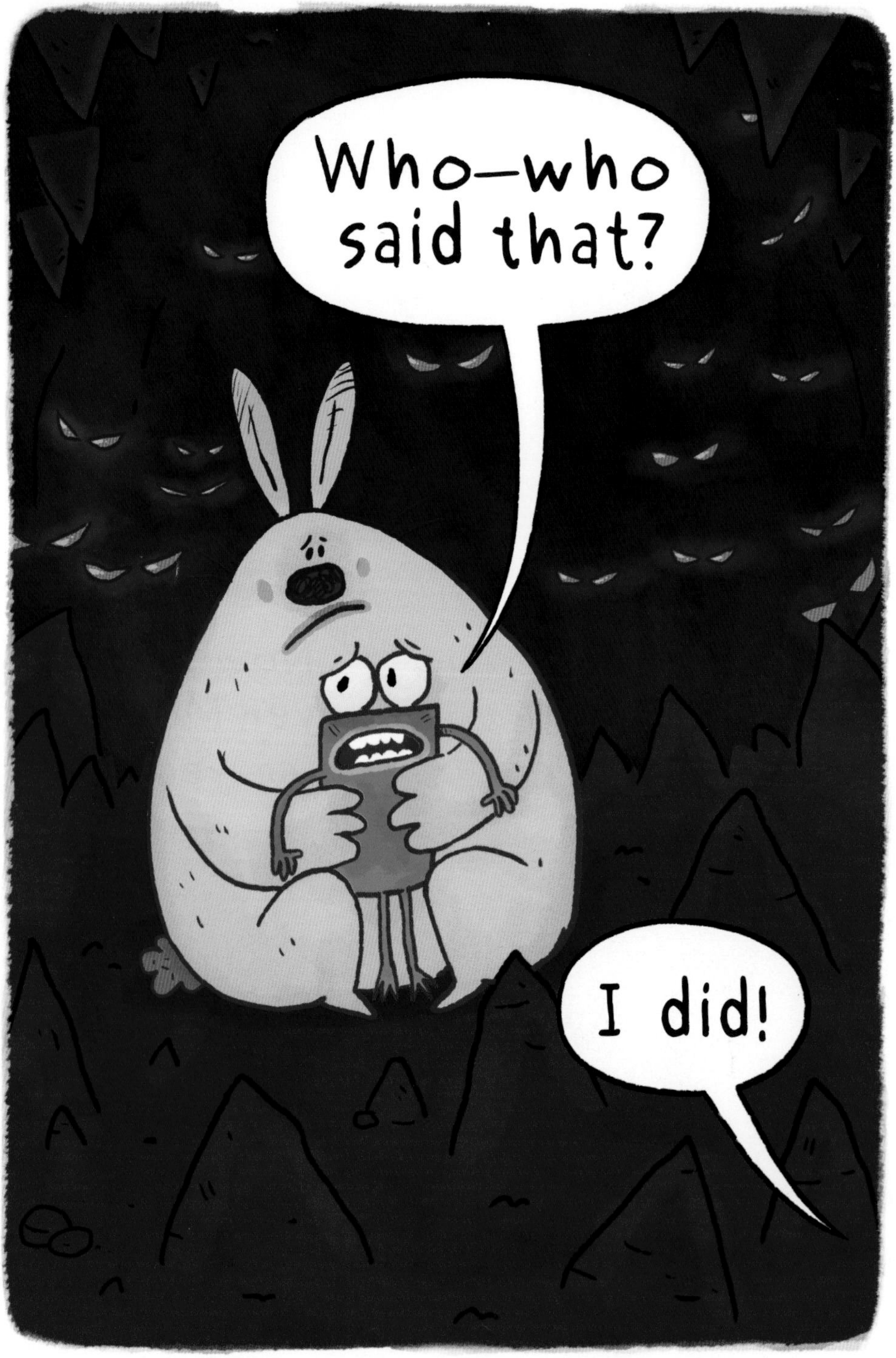
Who—who said that?
I did!

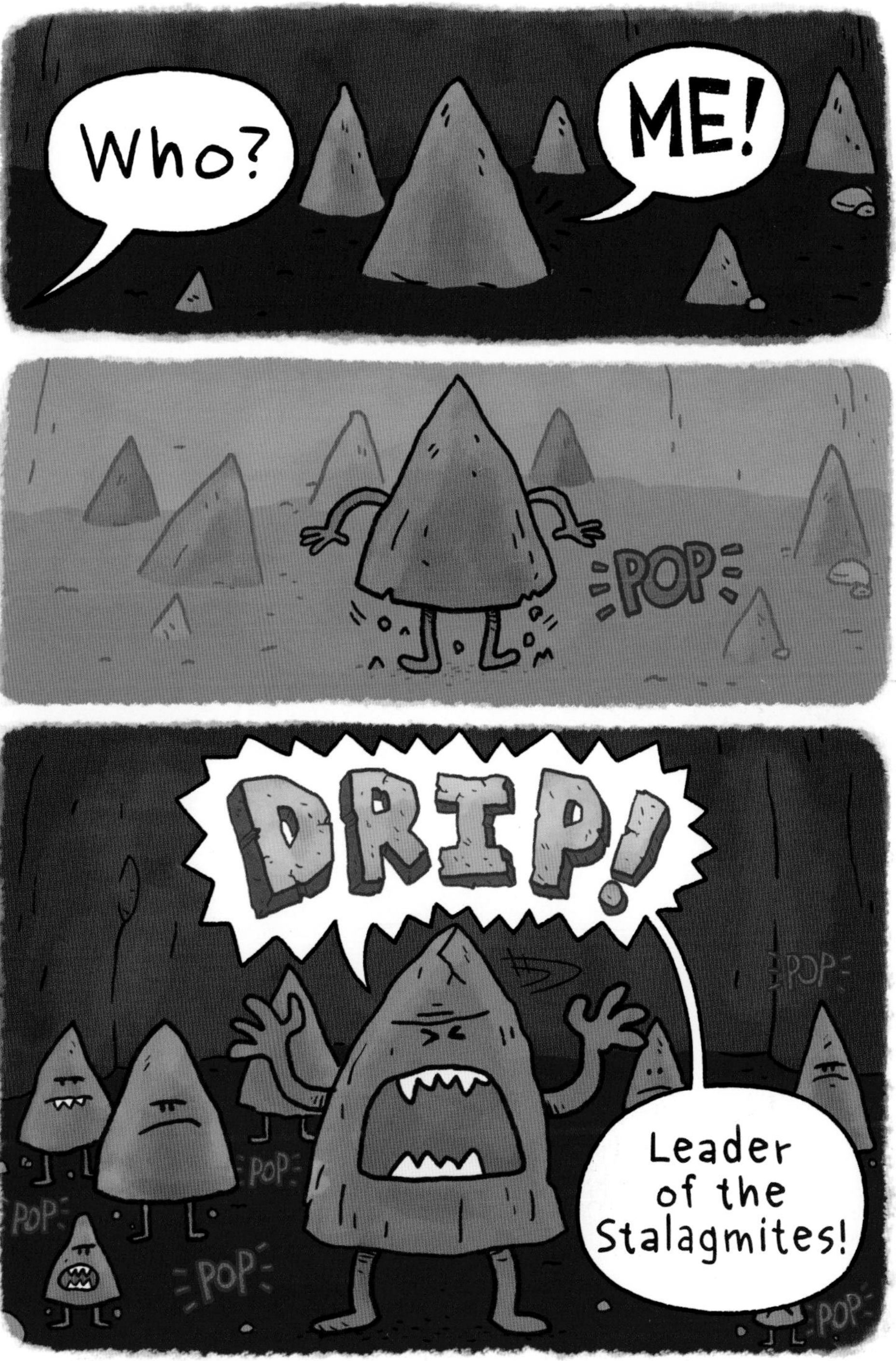
Who?
ME!
POP
DRIP!
Leader of the Stalagmites!
POP
POP
POP
POP
POP

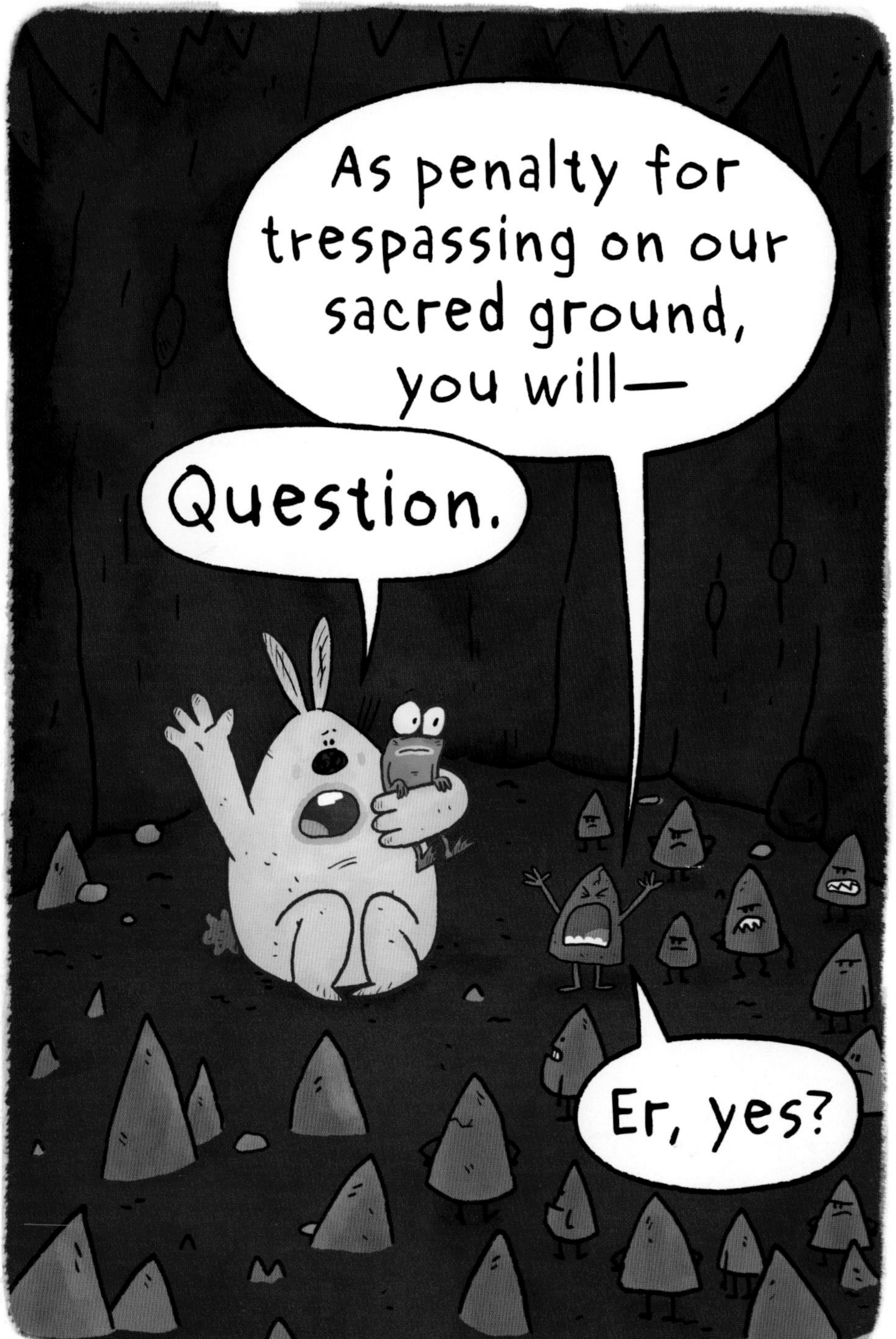
As penalty for trespassing on our sacred ground, you will—
Question.
Er, yes?

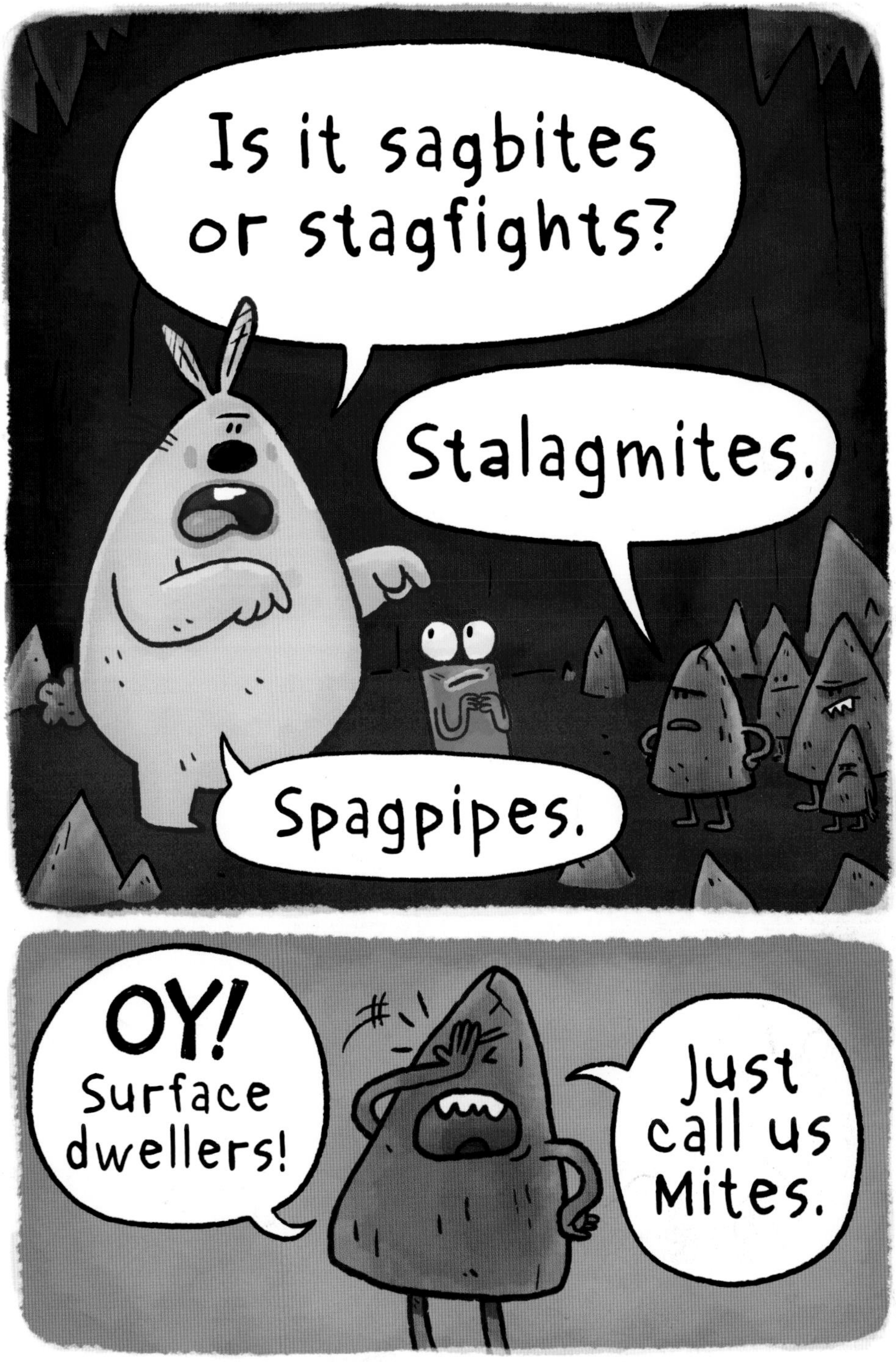
Is it sagbites or stagfights?
Stalagmites.
Spagpipes.
OY! Surface dwellers!
Just call us Mites.

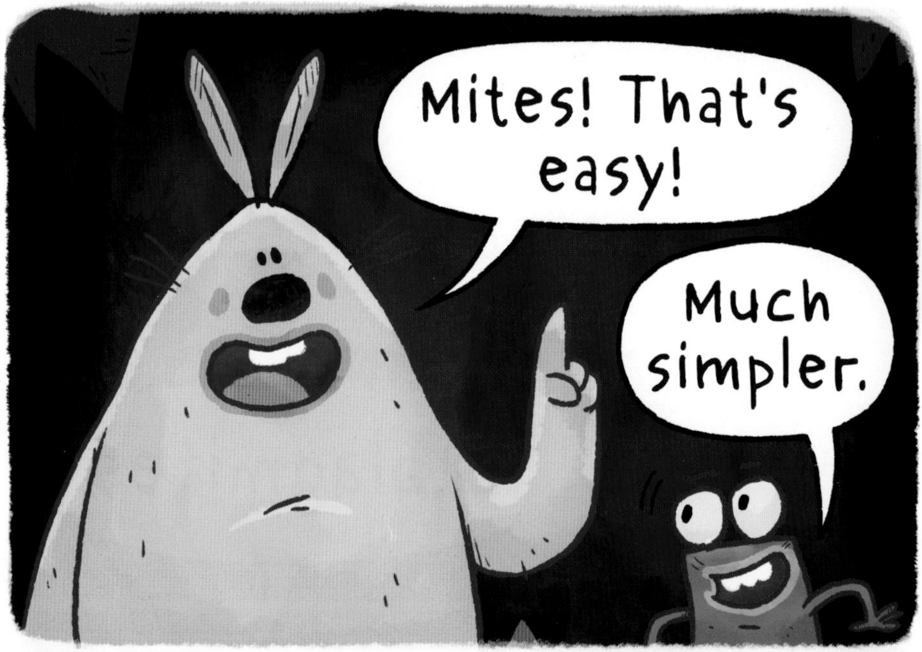
Mites! That's easy!
Much simpler.

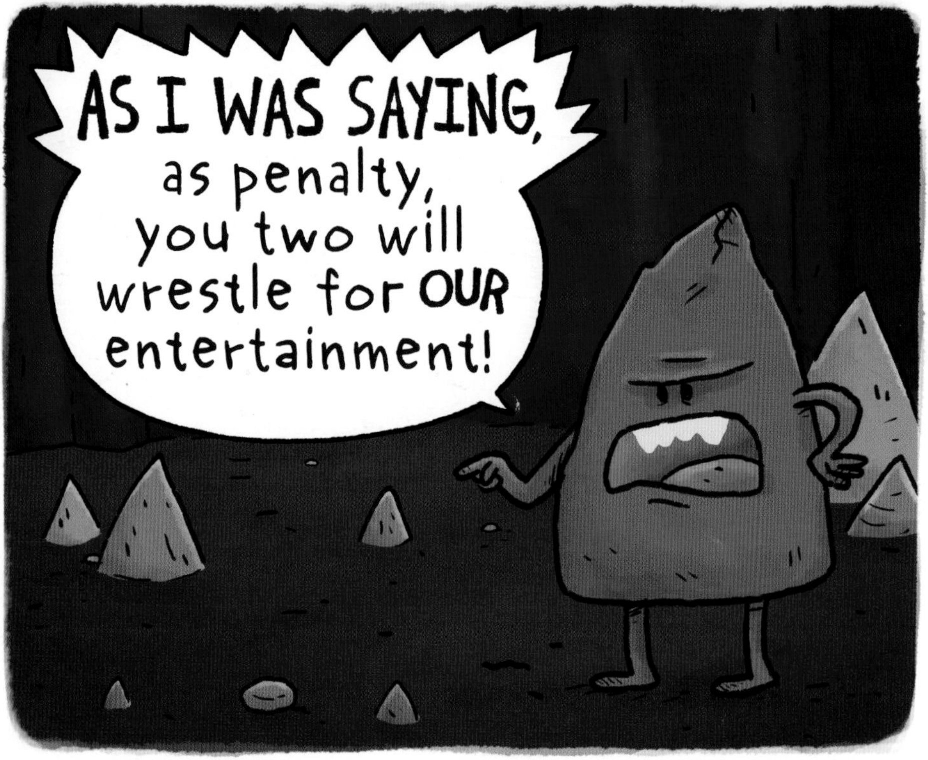
AS I WAS SAYING, as penalty, you two will wrestle for OUR entertainment!

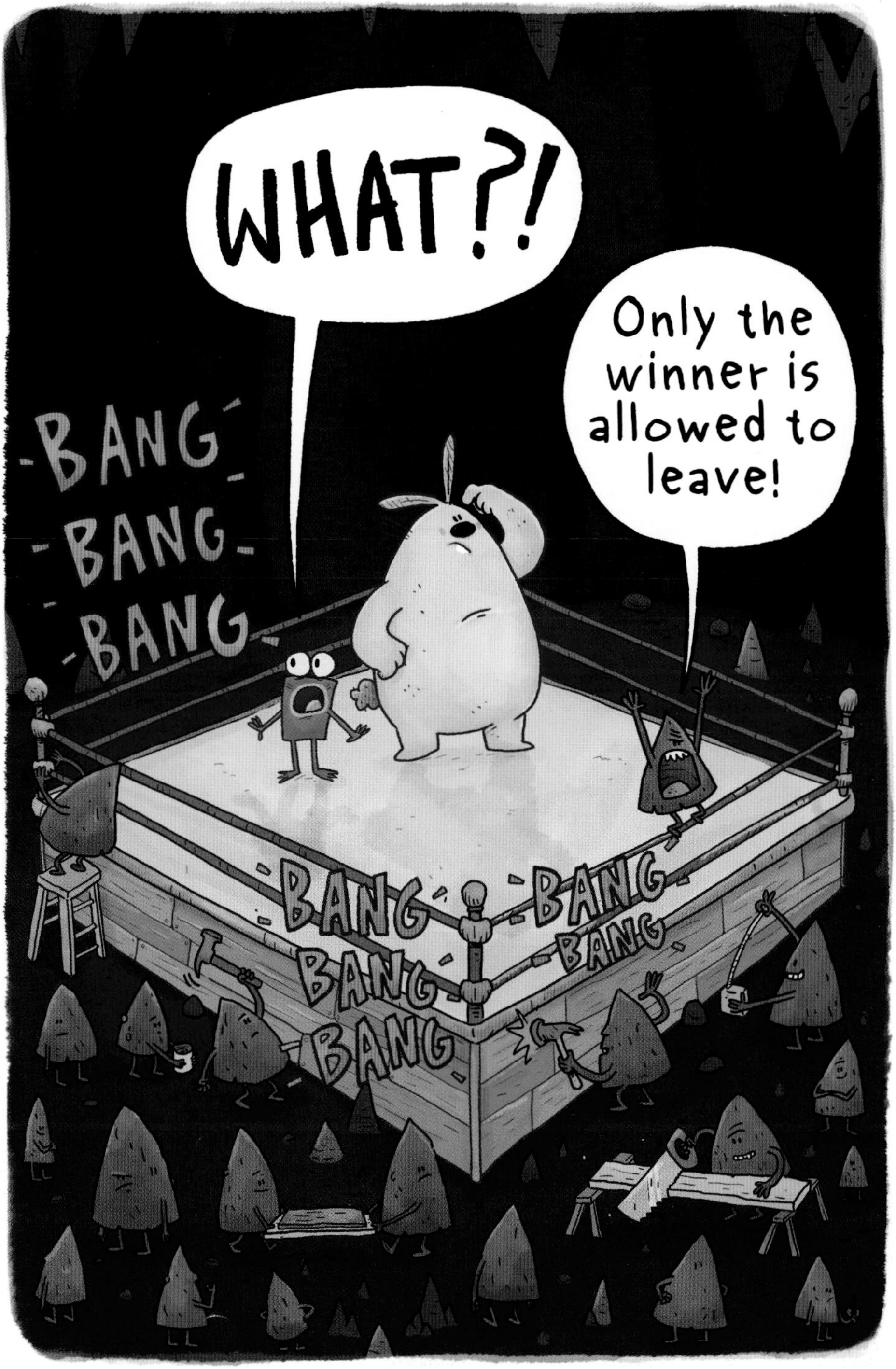
WHAT?!
Only the winner is allowed to leave!
BANG BANG BANG
BANG BANG BANG
BANG BANG

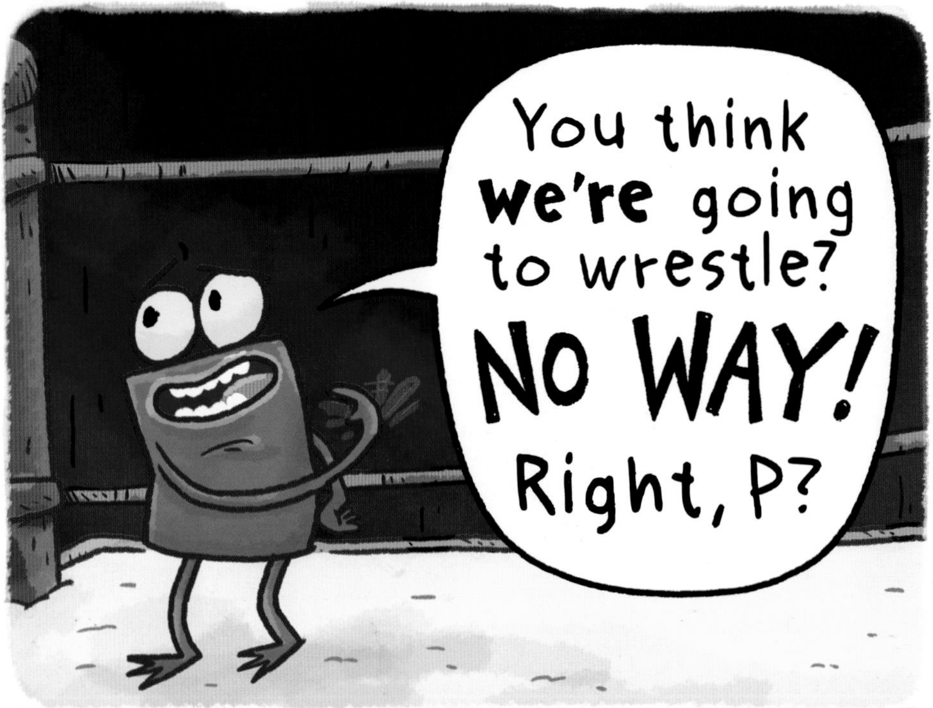
You think **we're** going to wrestle? NO WAY! Right, P?

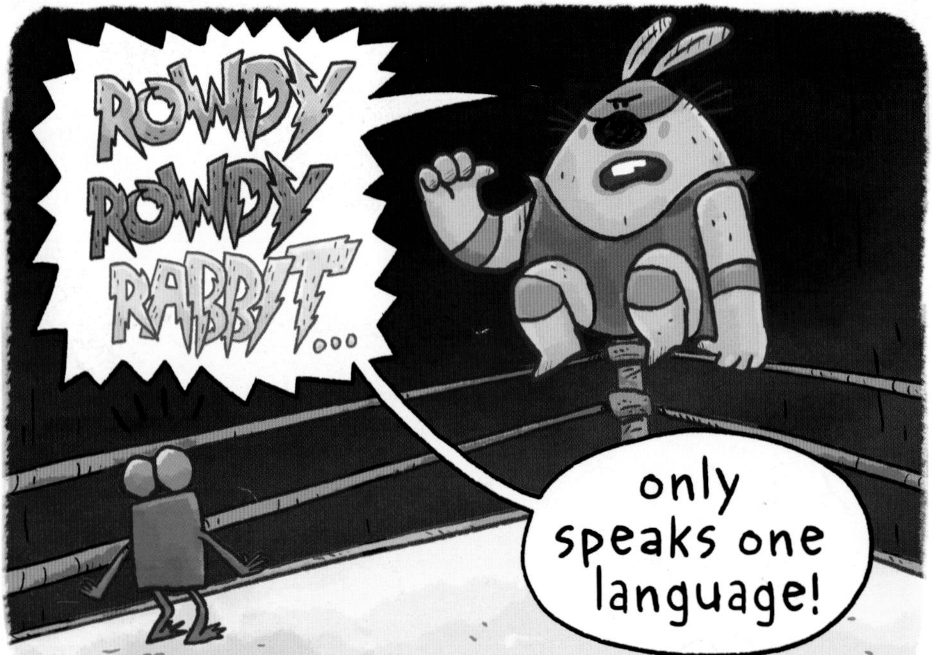
ROWDY ROWDY RABBIT...
only speaks one language!

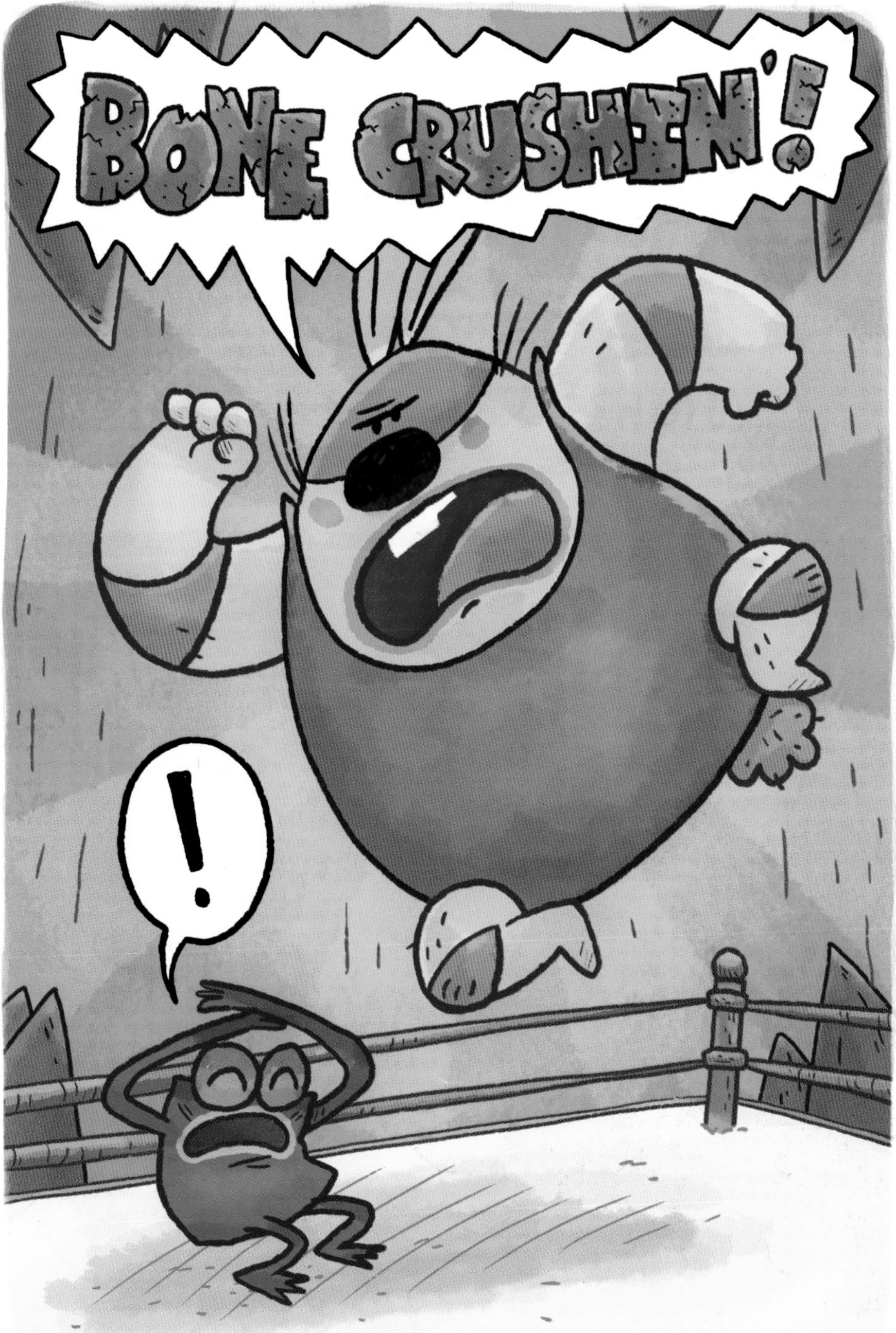
BONE CRUSHIN'!
!

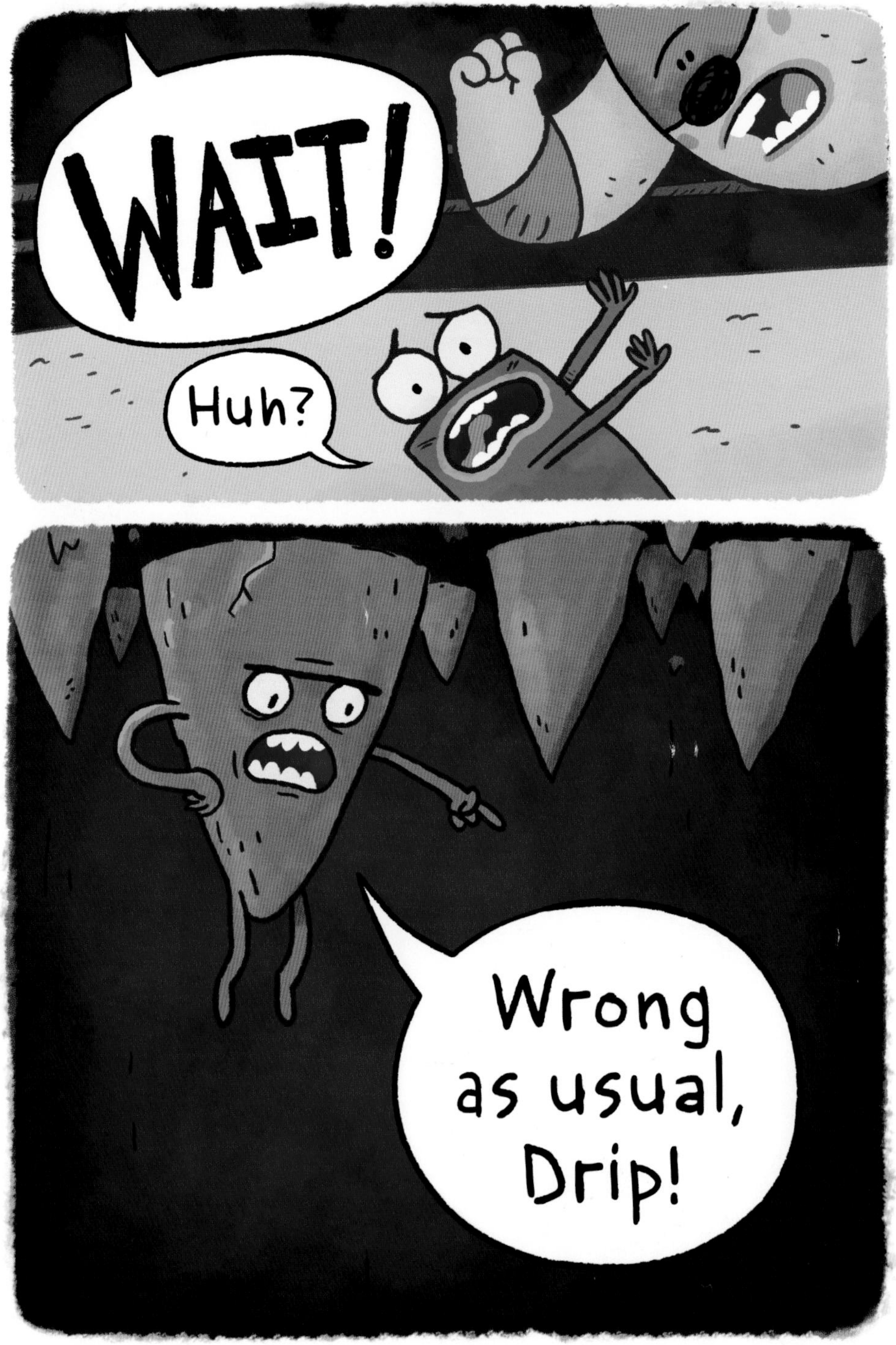
WAIT!
Huh?
Wrong as usual, Drip!

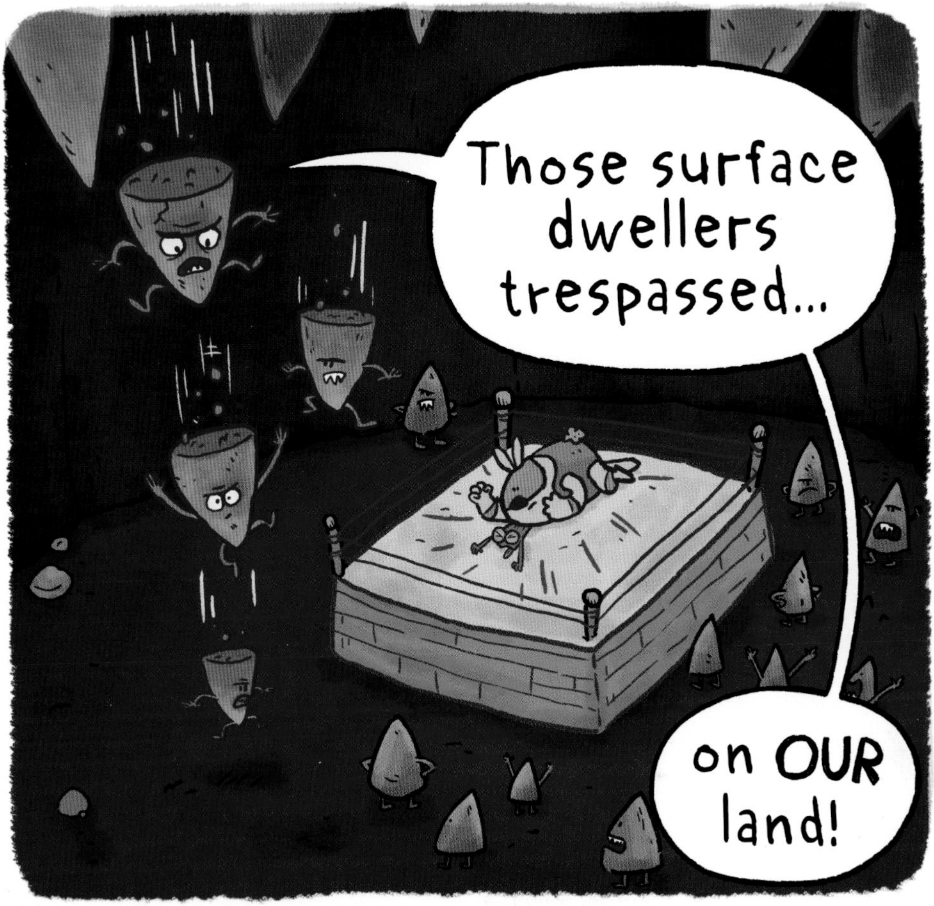
Those surface dwellers trespassed...
on OUR land!

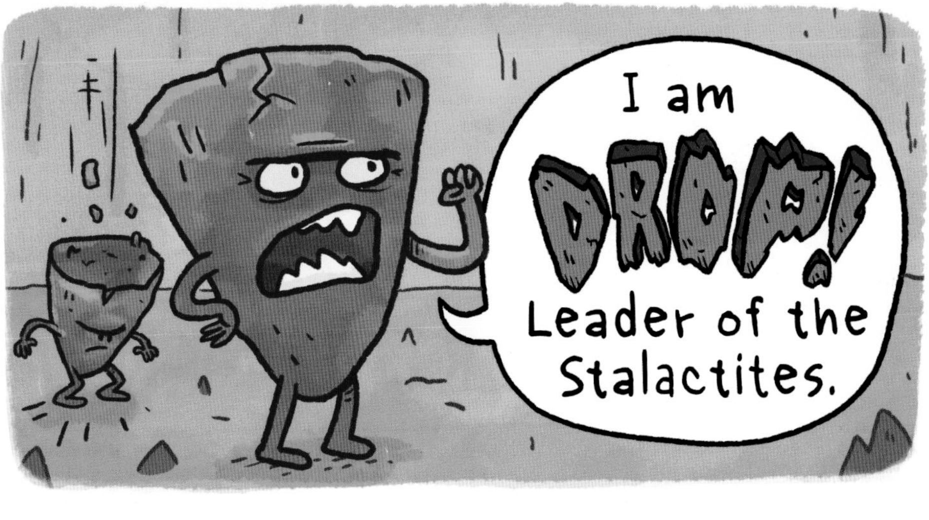
I am DROP! Leader of the Stalactites.

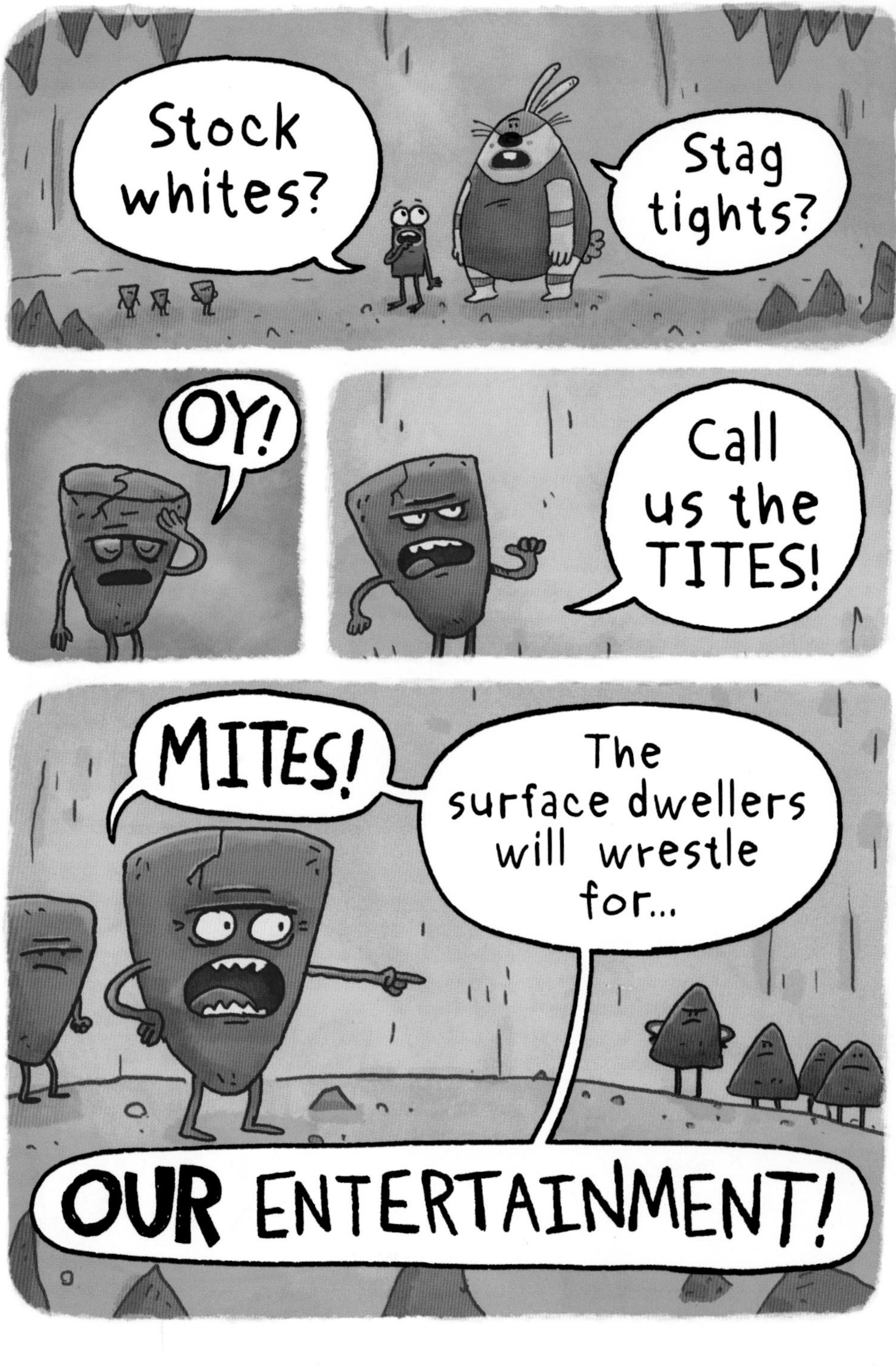
Stock whites?
Stag tights?
OY!
Call us the TITES!
MITES!
The surface dwellers will wrestle for...
OUR ENTERTAINMENT!

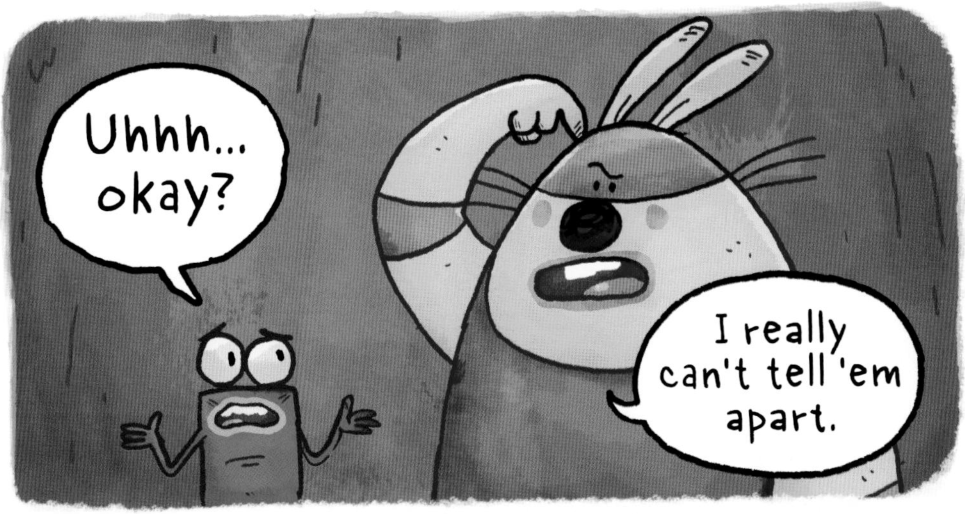
Uhhh...
okay?
I really can't tell 'em apart.

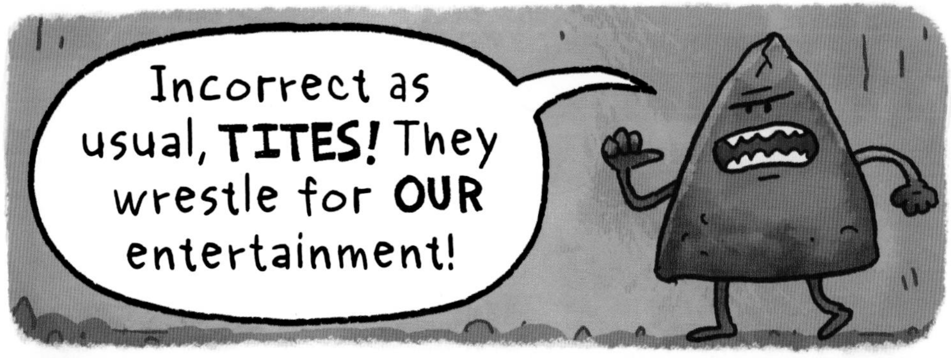
Incorrect as usual, **TITES!** They wrestle for **OUR** entertainment!

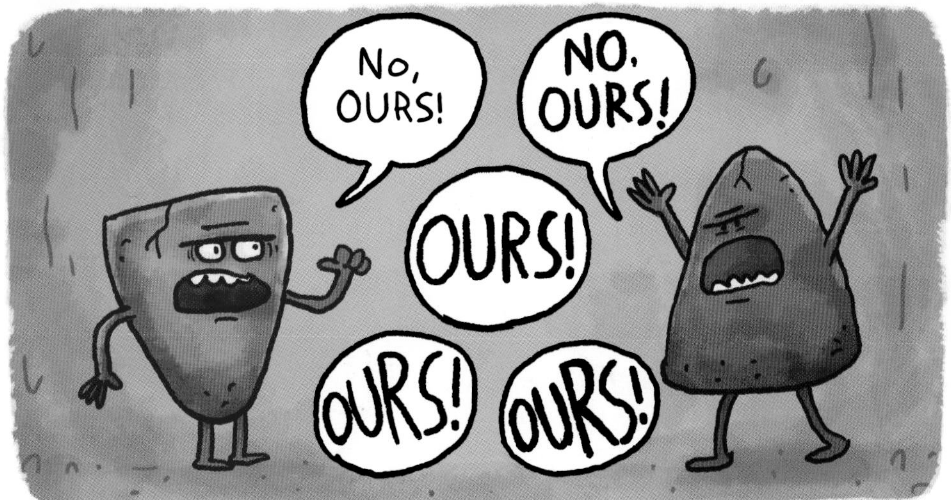
No, OURS!
NO, OURS!
OURS!
OURS!
OURS!

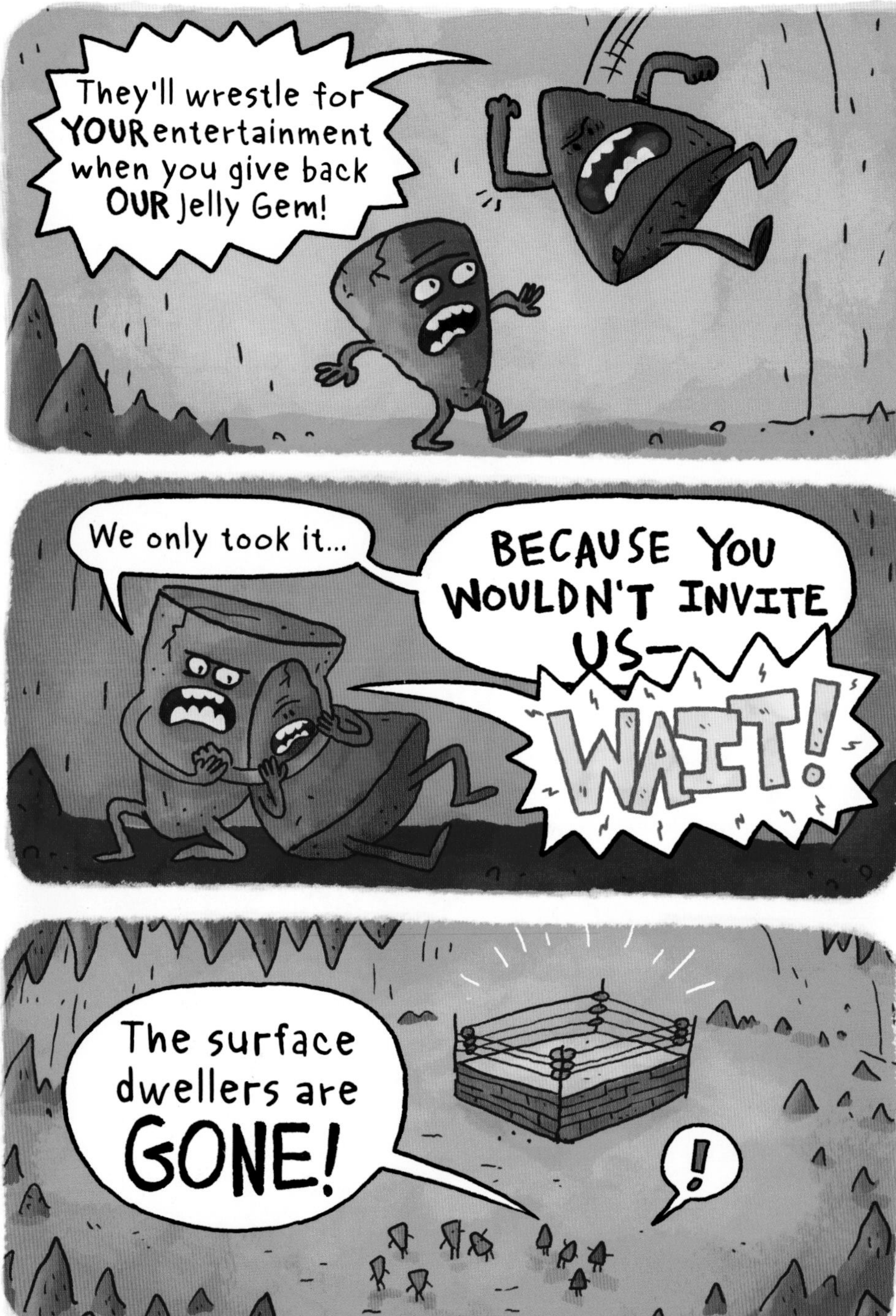
They'll wrestle for YOUR entertainment when you give back OUR Jelly Gem!
We only took it...
BECAUSE YOU WOULDN'T INVITE US—
WAIT!
The surface dwellers are GONE!
!

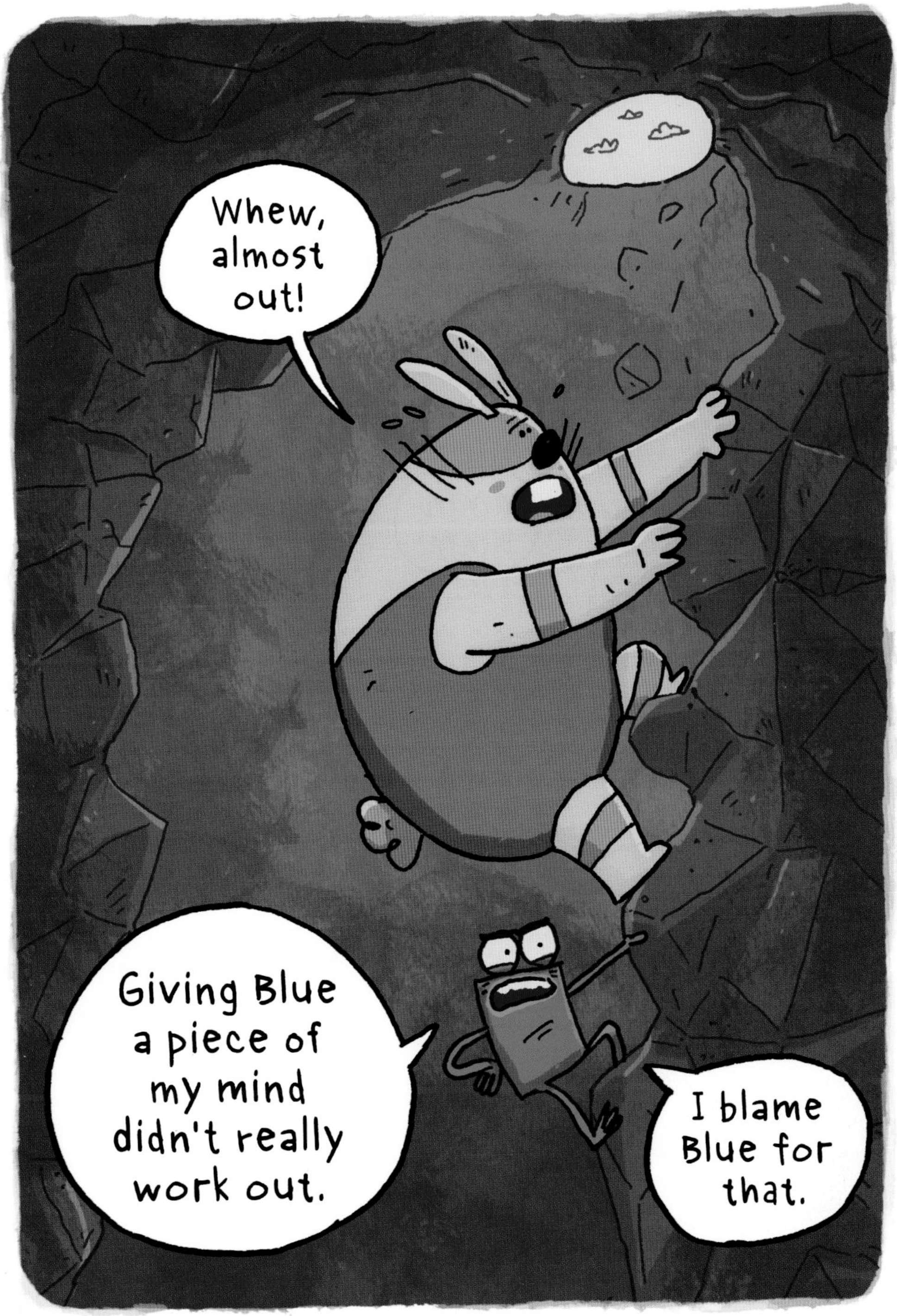
Whew, almost out!
Giving Blue a piece of my mind didn't really work out.
I blame Blue for that.

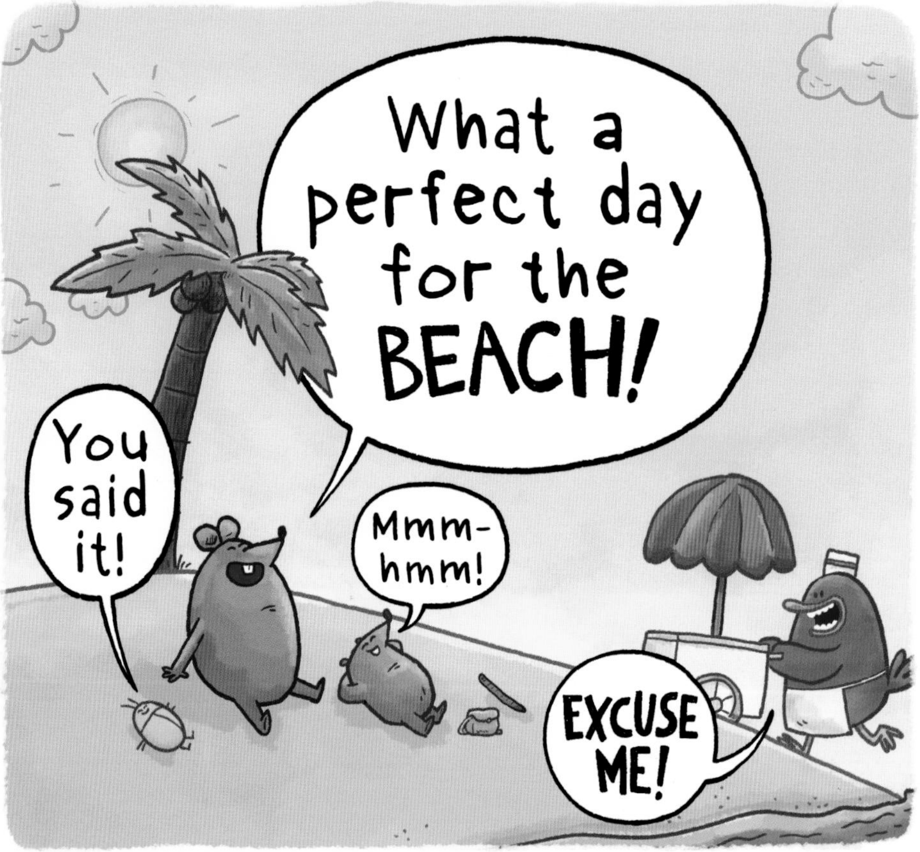
What a perfect day for the BEACH!
You said it!
Mmm-hmm!
EXCUSE ME!

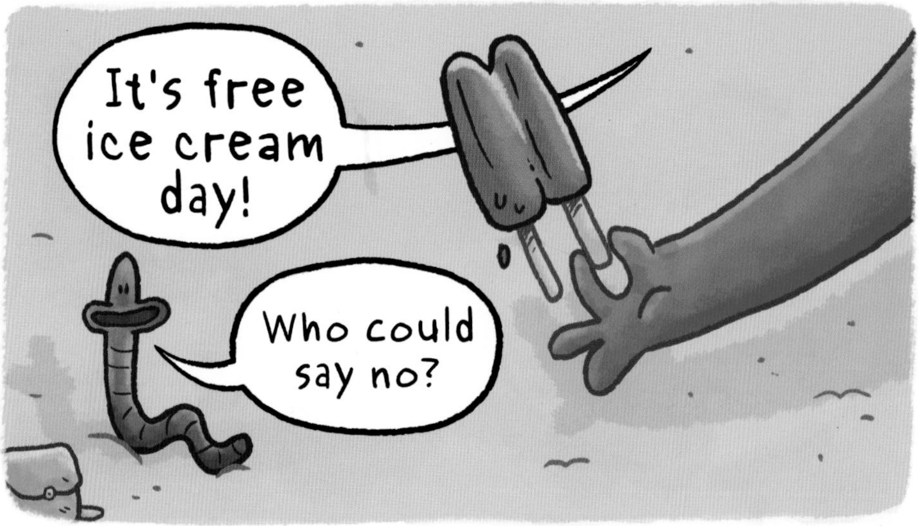
It's free ice cream day!
Who could say no?

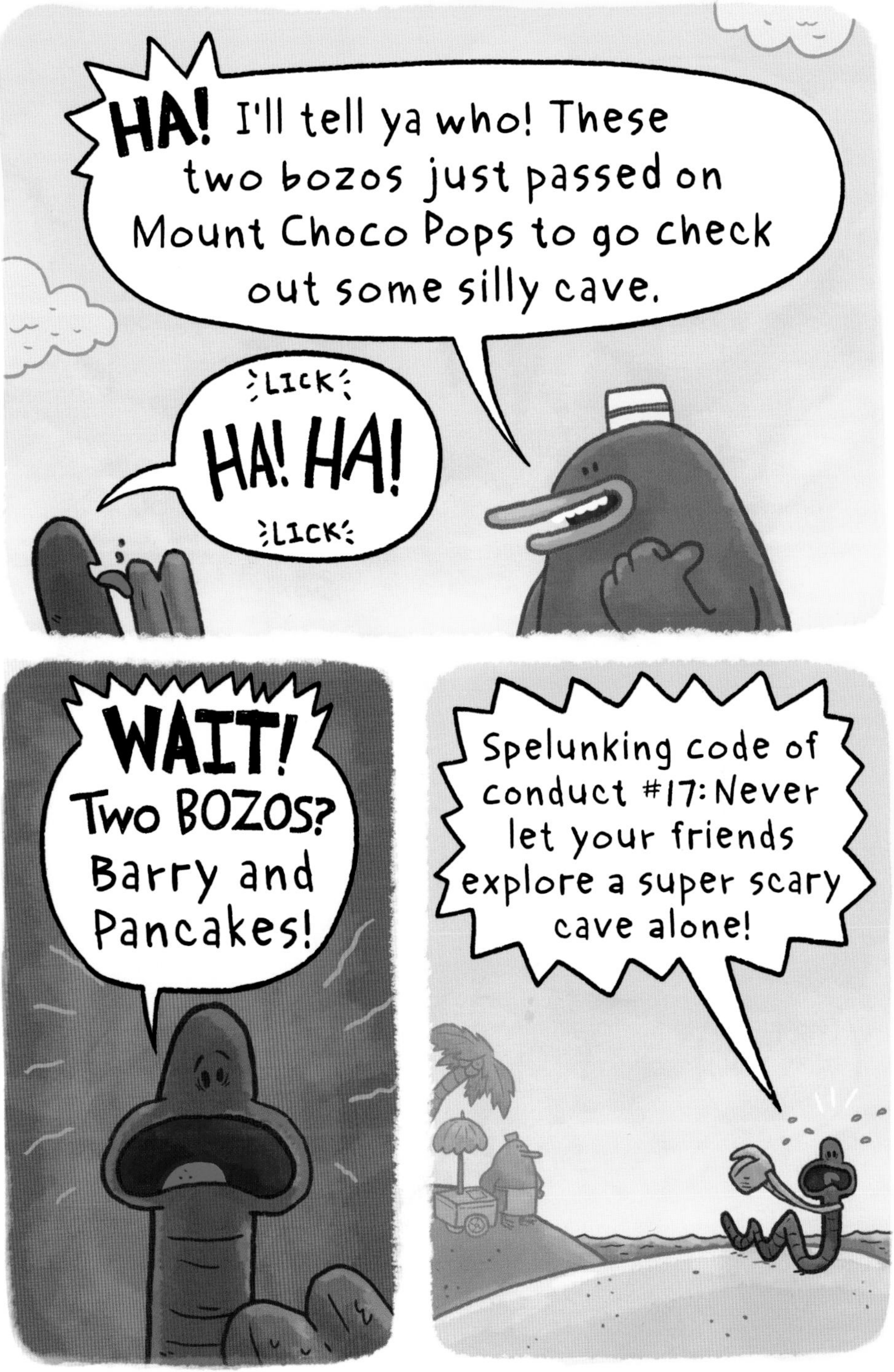
HA! I'll tell ya who! These two bozos just passed on Mount Choco Pops to go check out some silly cave.
LICK
HA! HA!
LICK
WAIT! Two BOZOS? Barry and Pancakes!
Spelunking code of conduct #17: Never let your friends explore a super scary cave alone!

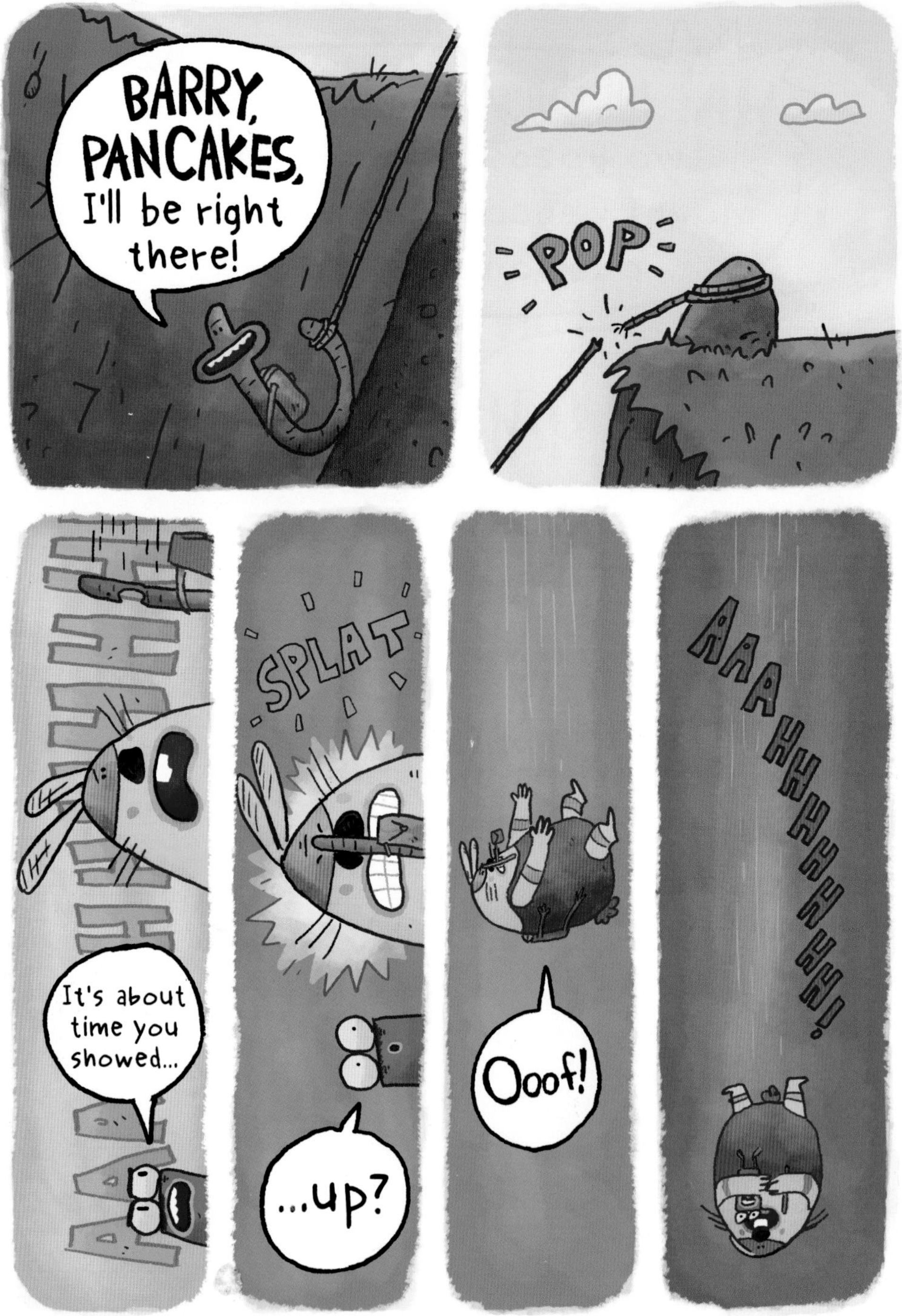
BARRY, PANCAKES, I'll be right there!
POP
SPLAT
It's about time you showed...
...up?
Ooof!

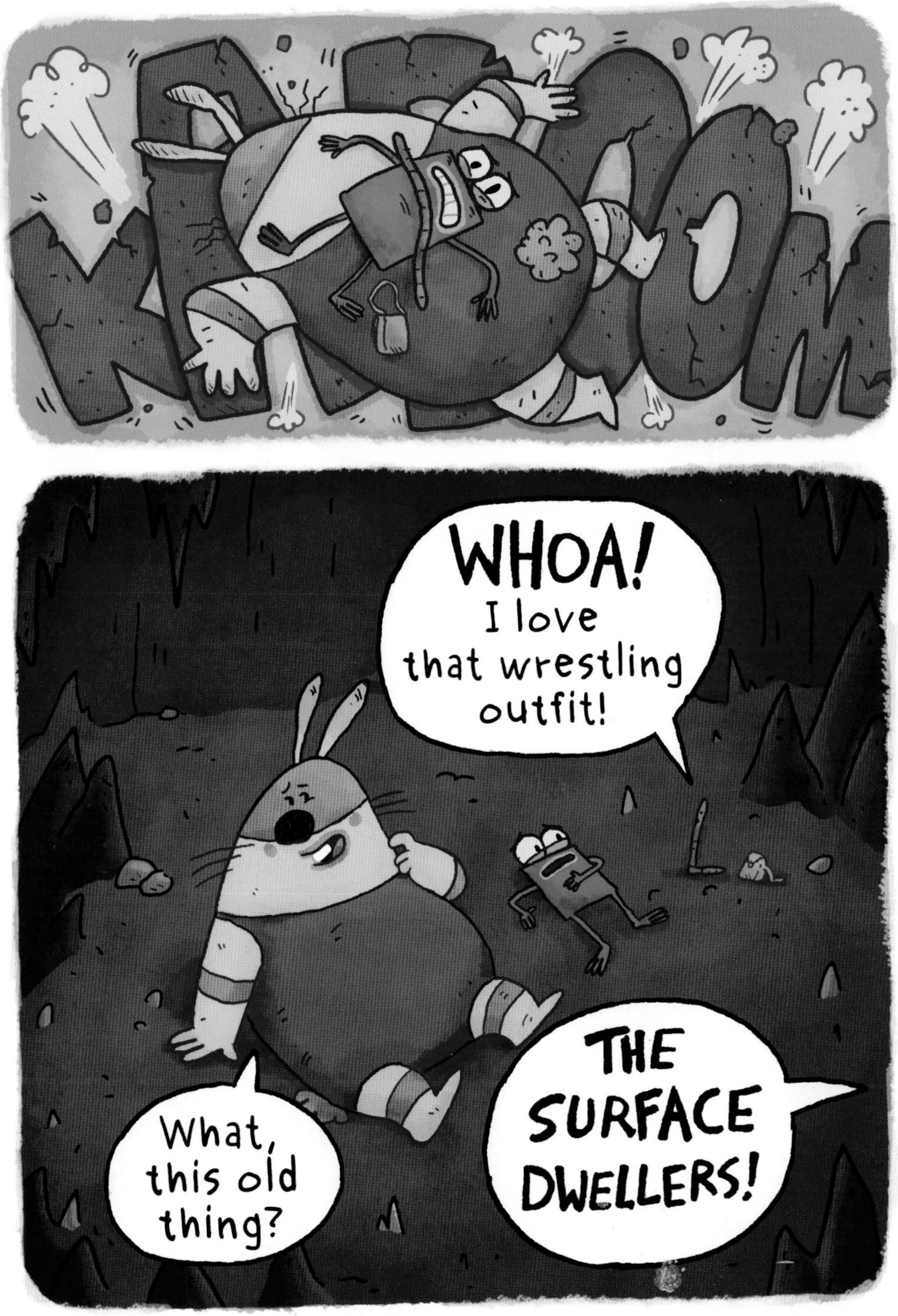
WHOA! I love that wrestling outfit!
What, this old thing?
THE SURFACE DWELLERS!

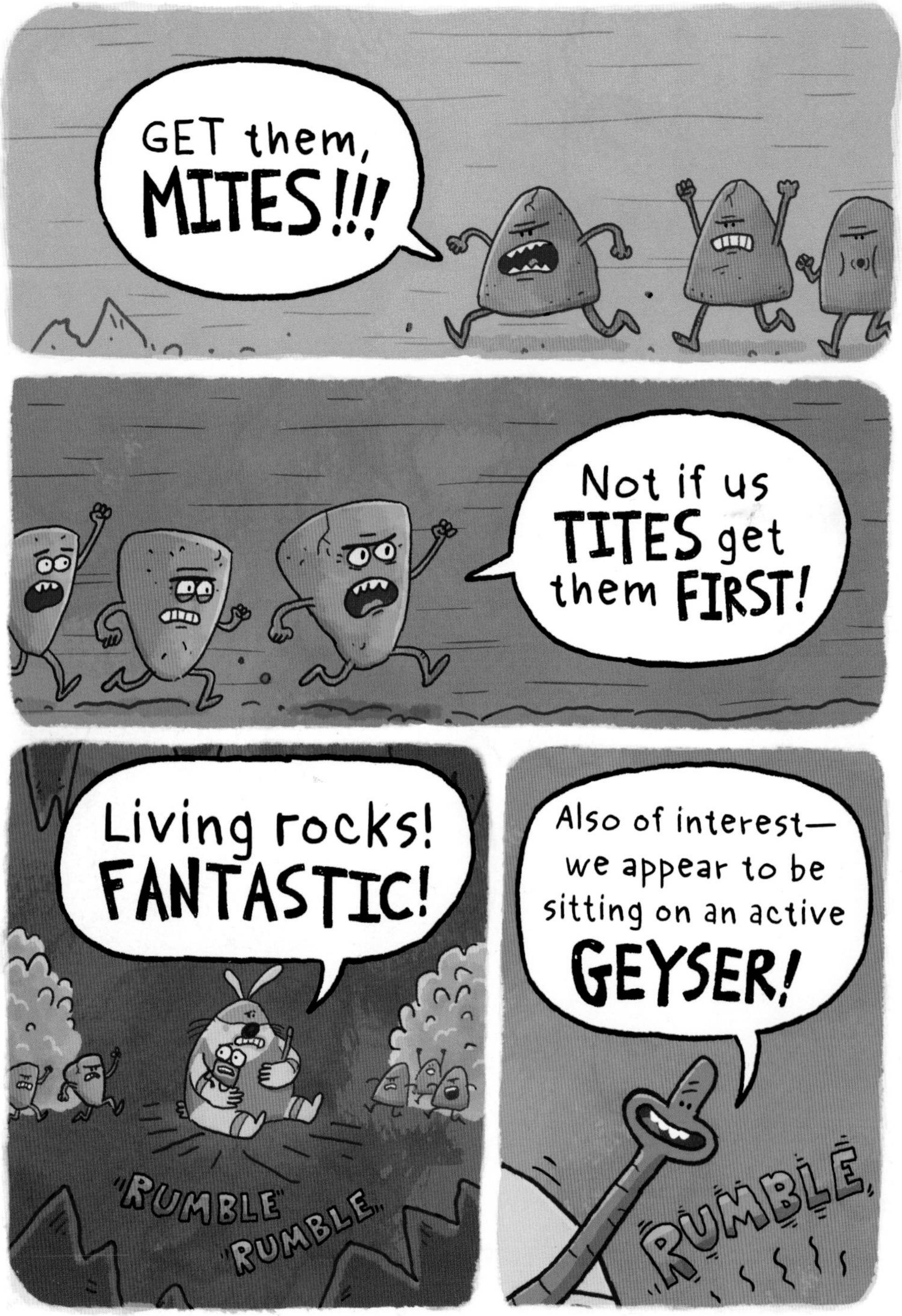
GET them, MITES!!!
Not if us TITES get them FIRST!
Living rocks! FANTASTIC!
RUMBLE
RUMBLE
Also of interest— we appear to be sitting on an active GEYSER!
RUMBLE

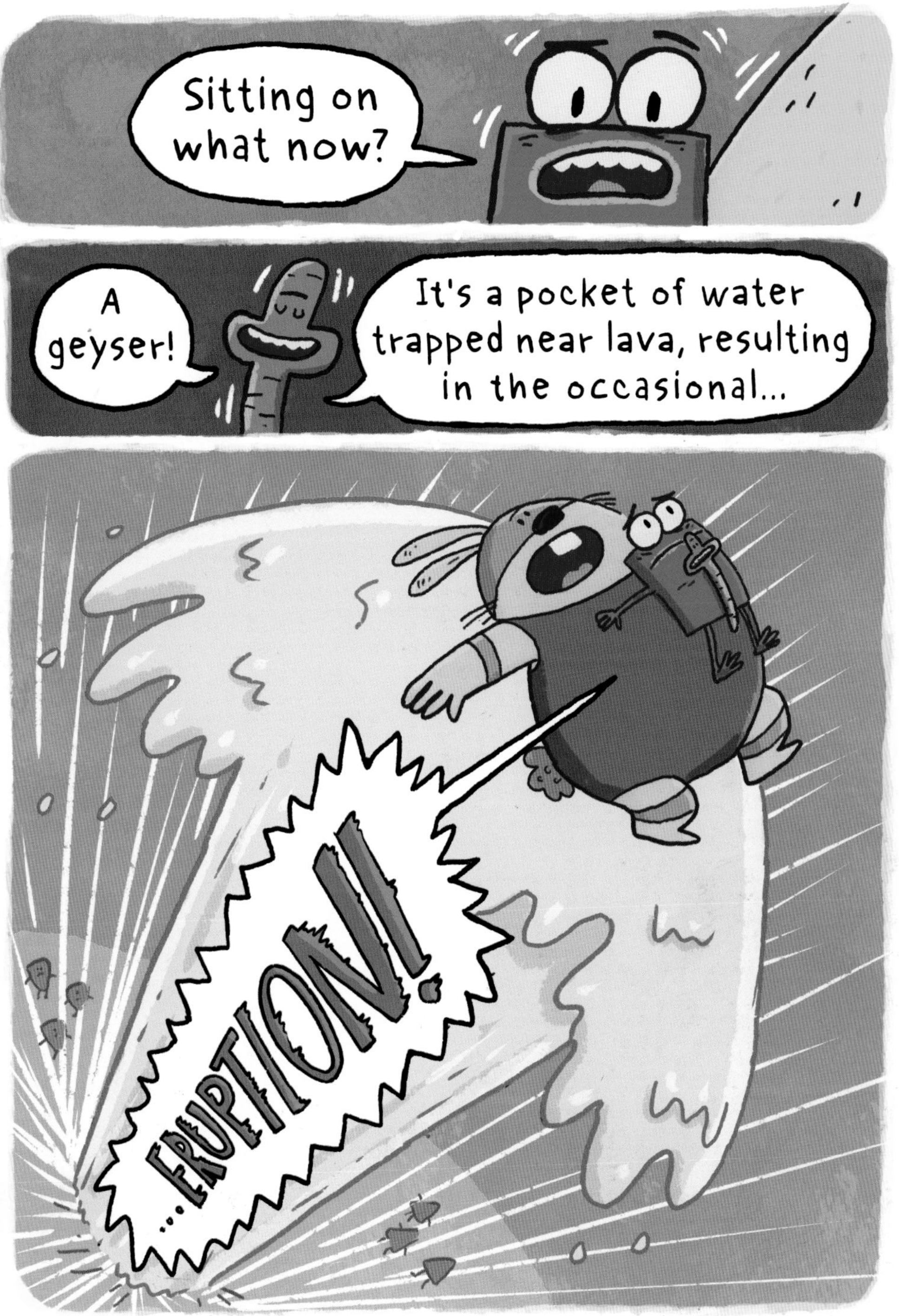
Sitting on what now?
A geyser!
It's a pocket of water trapped near lava, resulting in the occasional...
...ERUPTION!

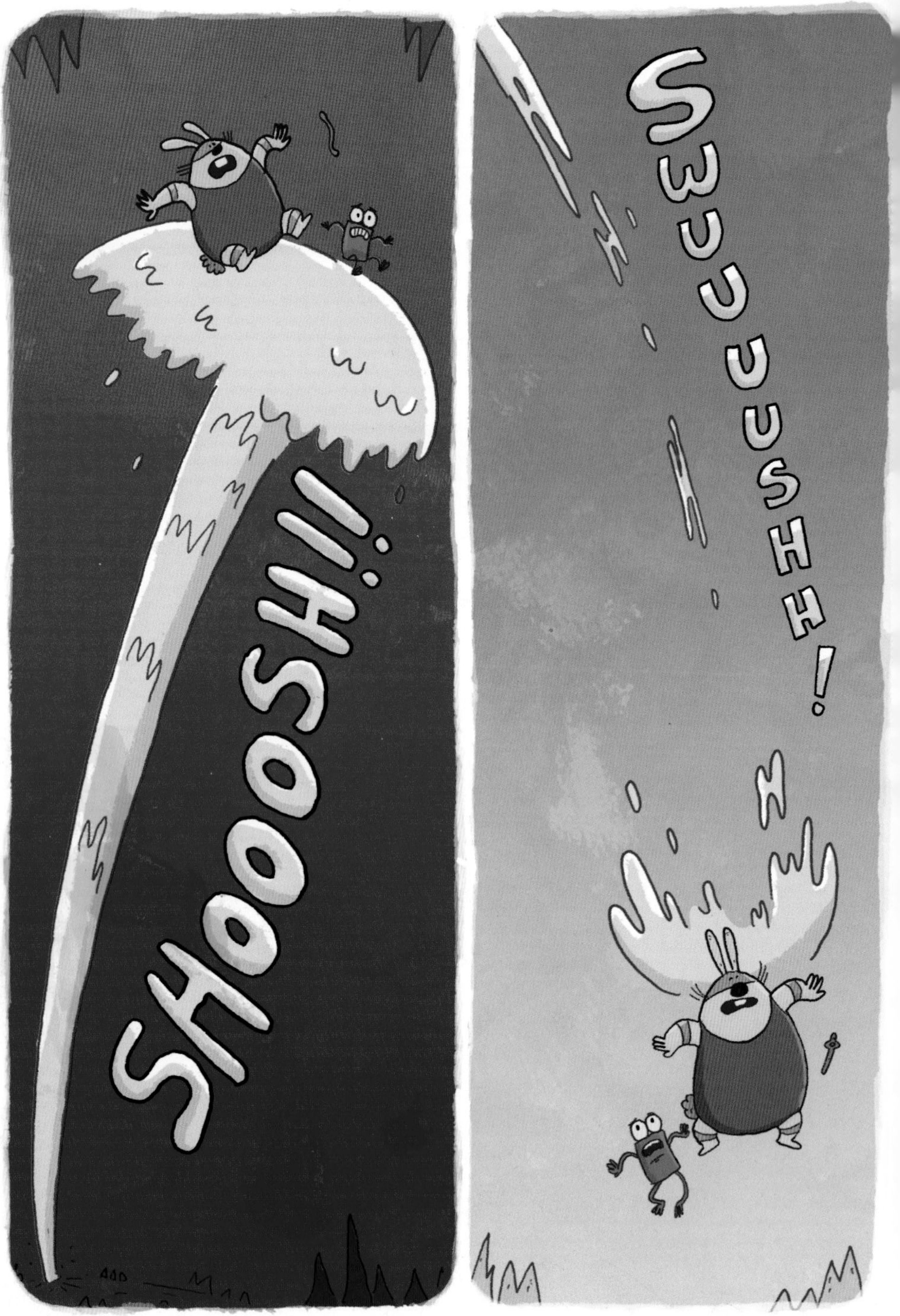
SHOOOSH!!!
SWUUUUSHH!

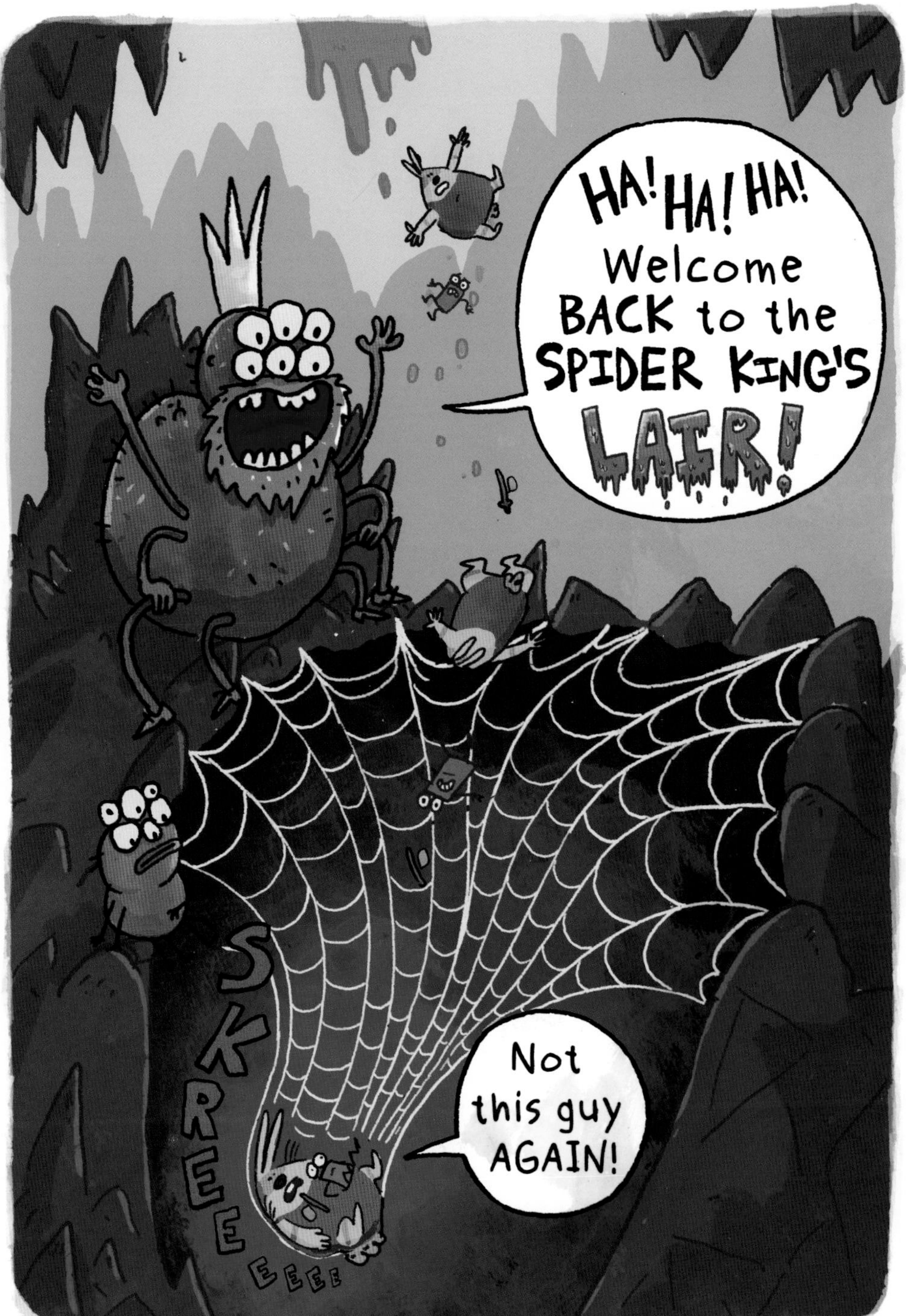
HA! HA! HA! Welcome BACK to the SPIDER KING'S LAIR!
SKREEEEEEE
Not this guy AGAIN!

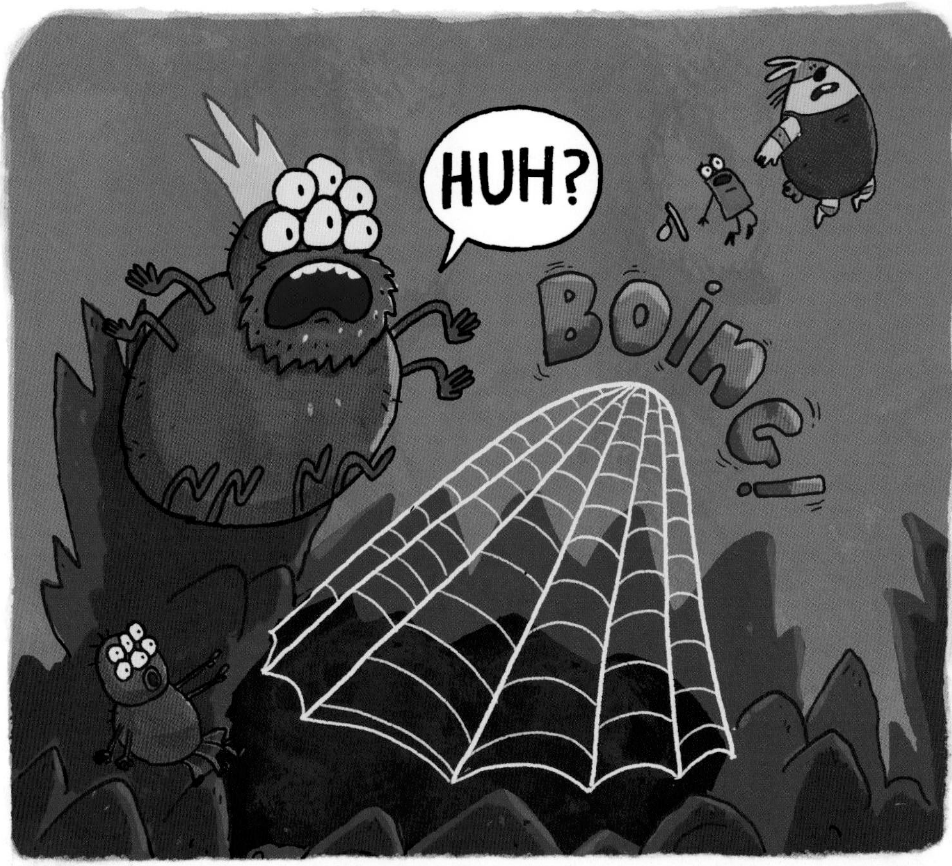

HUH?
BOING!

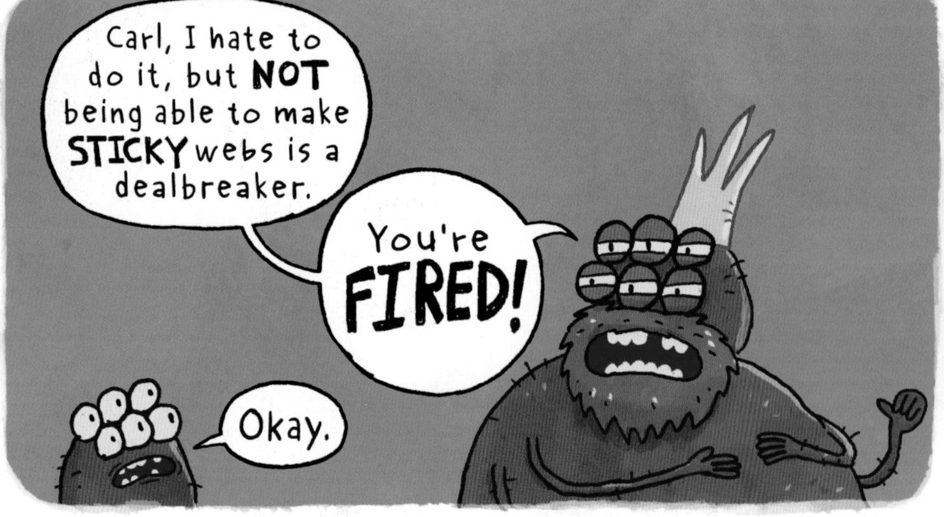

Carl, I hate to do it, but NOT being able to make STICKY webs is a dealbreaker.
You're FIRED!
Okay.

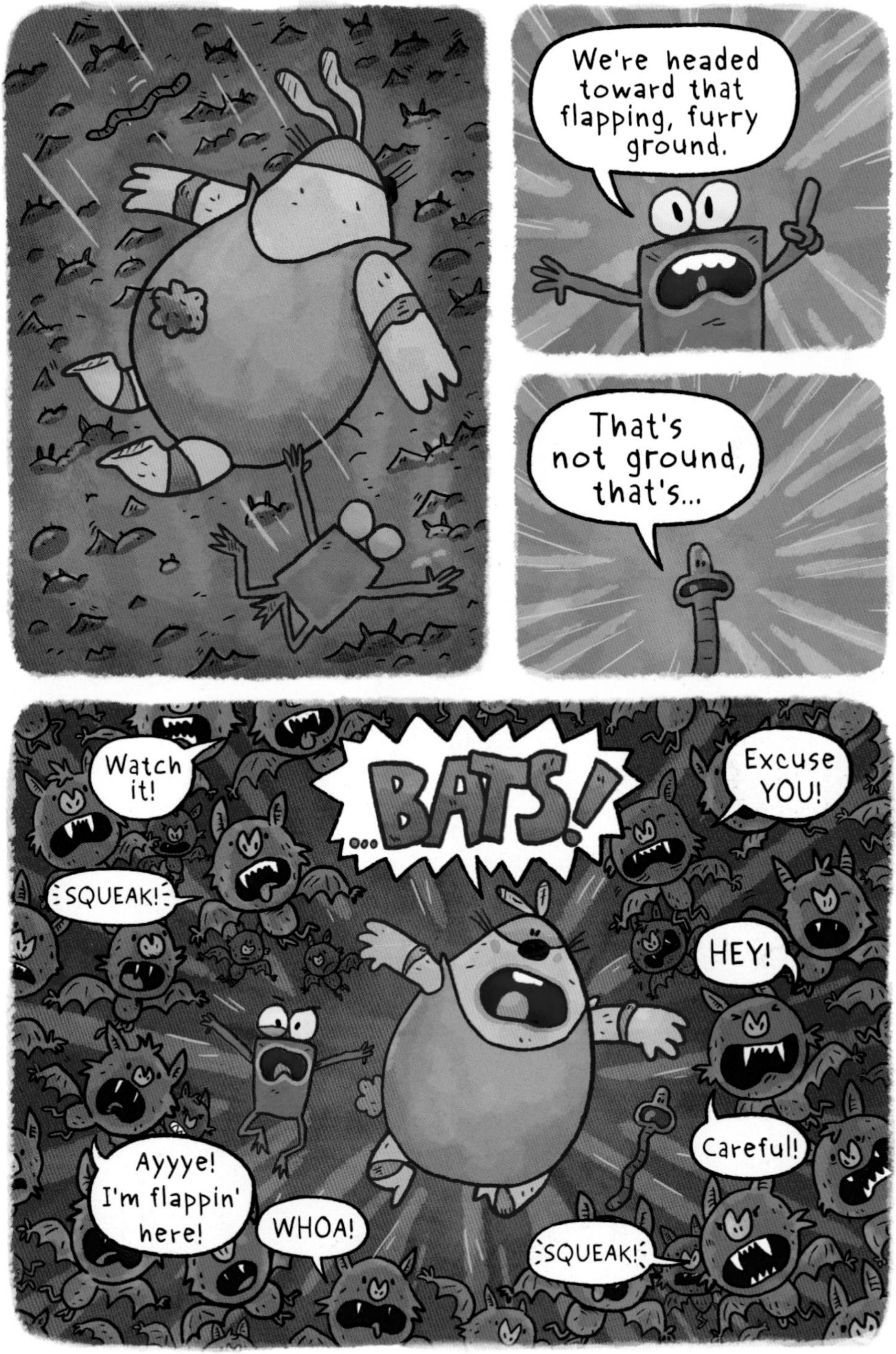
We're headed toward that flapping, furry ground.
That's not ground, that's...
Watch it!
...BATS!
Excuse YOU!
SQUEAK!
HEY!
Careful!
Ayyye! I'm flappin' here!
WHOA!
SQUEAK!

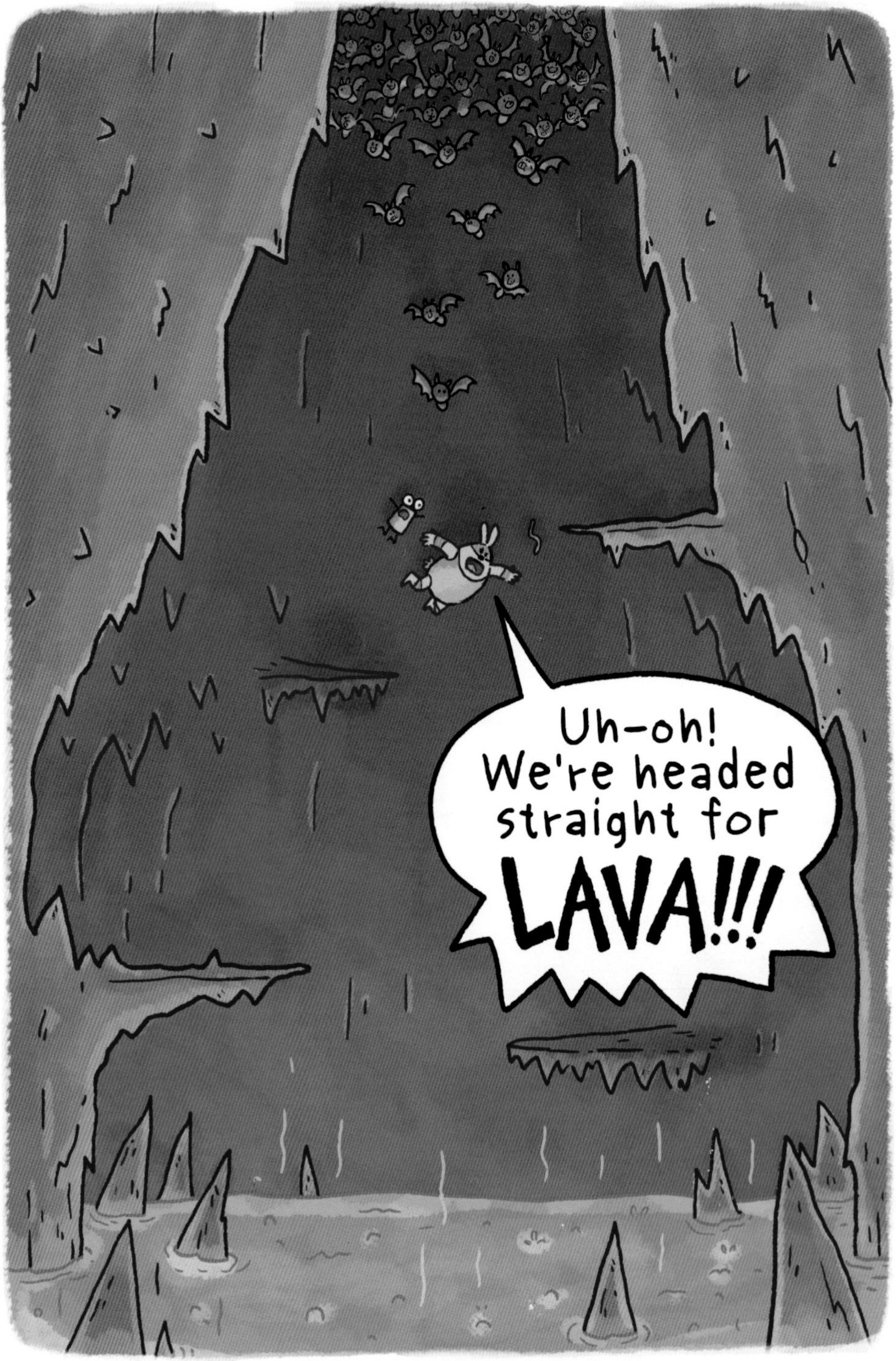
Uh-oh! We're headed straight for LAVA!!!

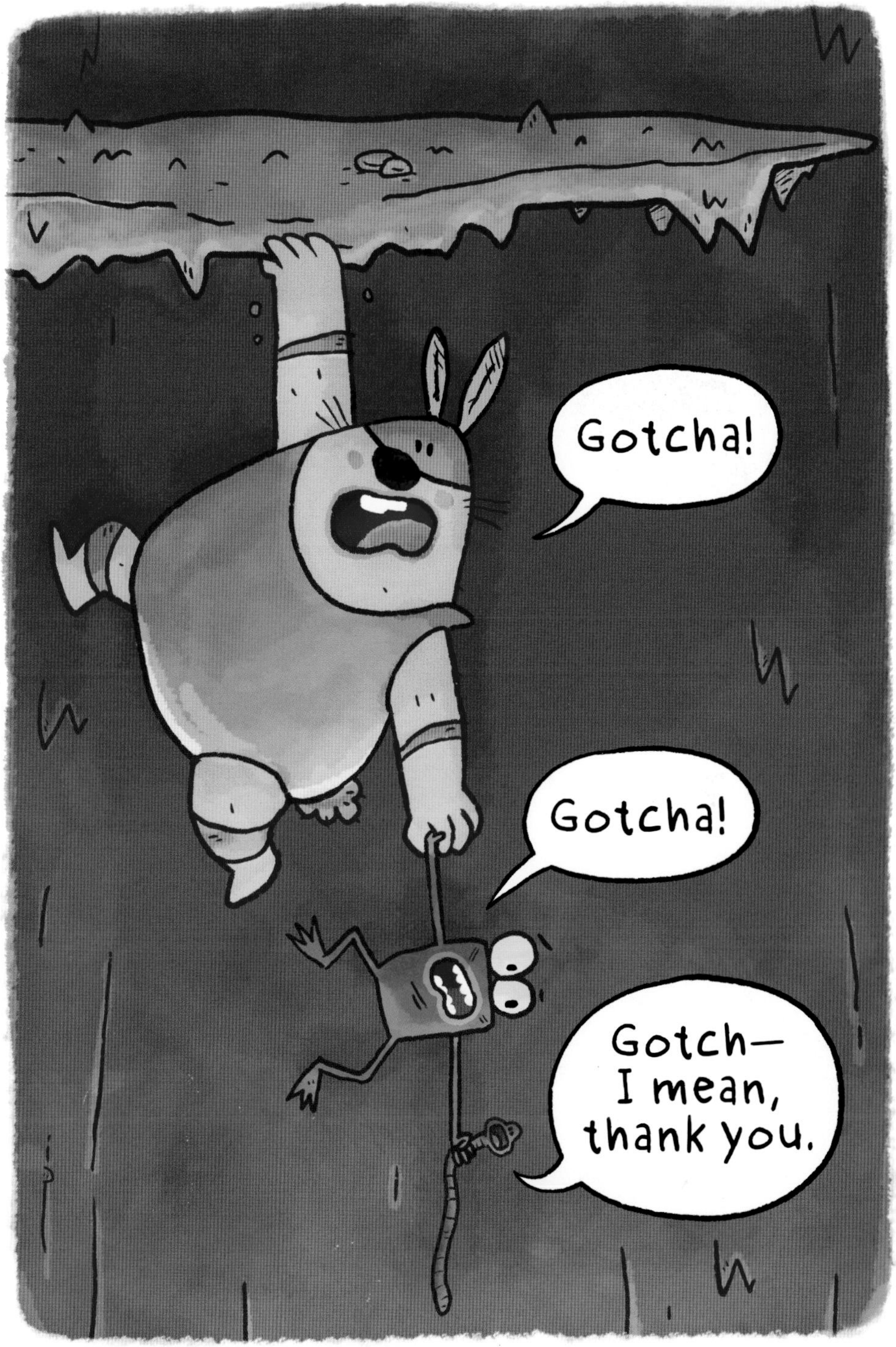
Gotcha!
Gotcha!
Gotch—
I mean,
thank you.

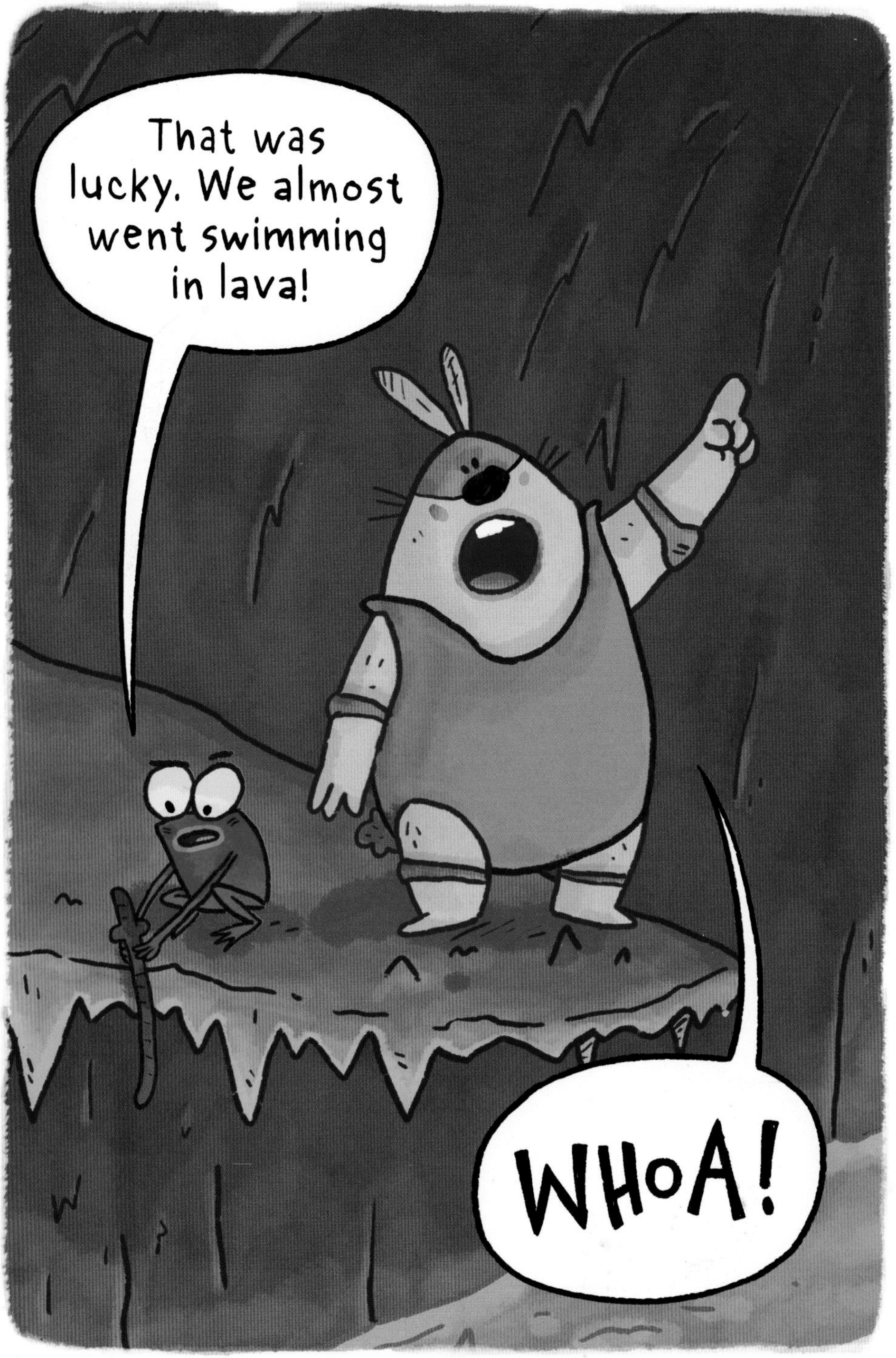
That was lucky. We almost went swimming in lava!
WHOA!

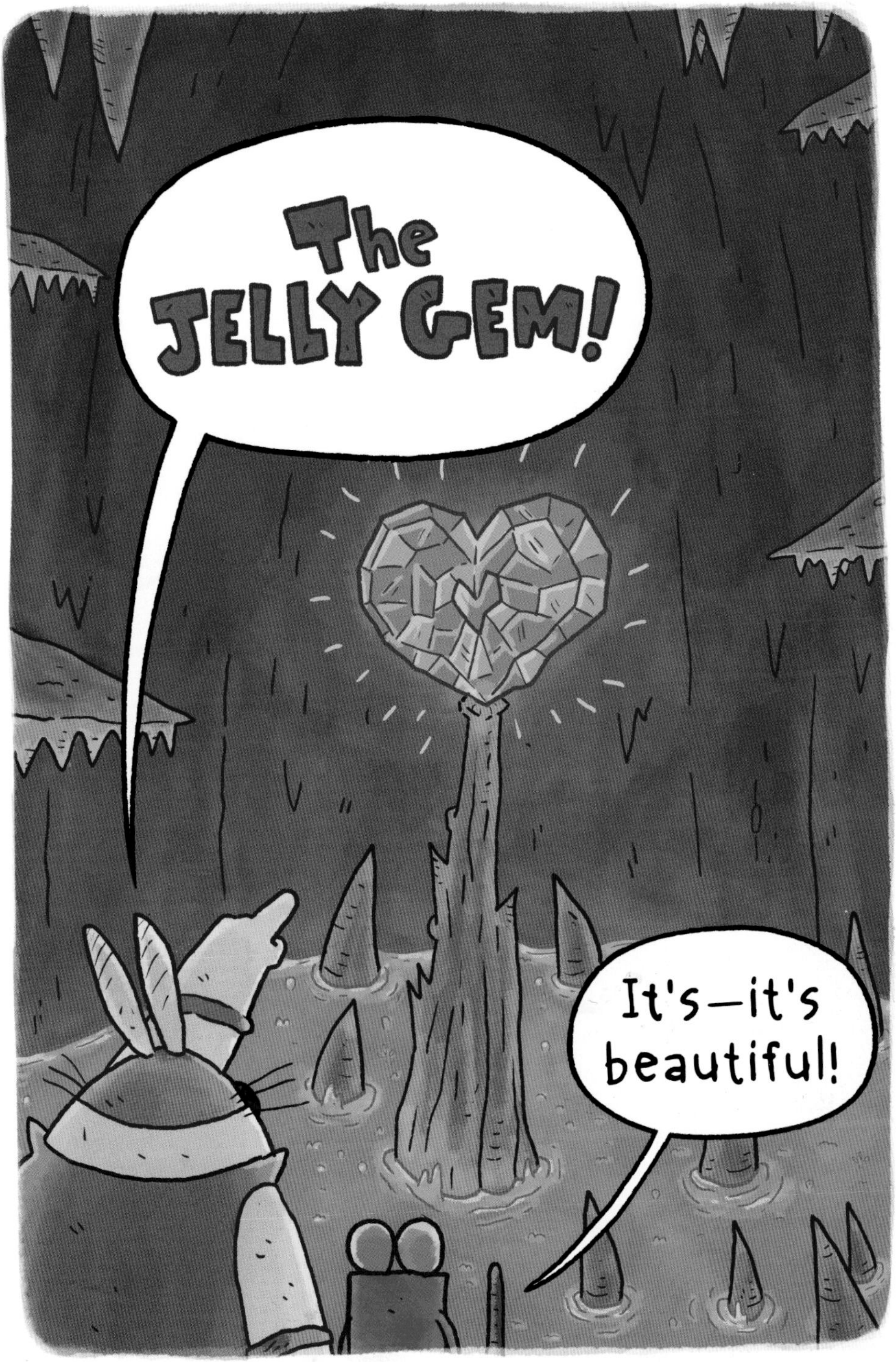
The JELLY GEM!
It's—it's beautiful!

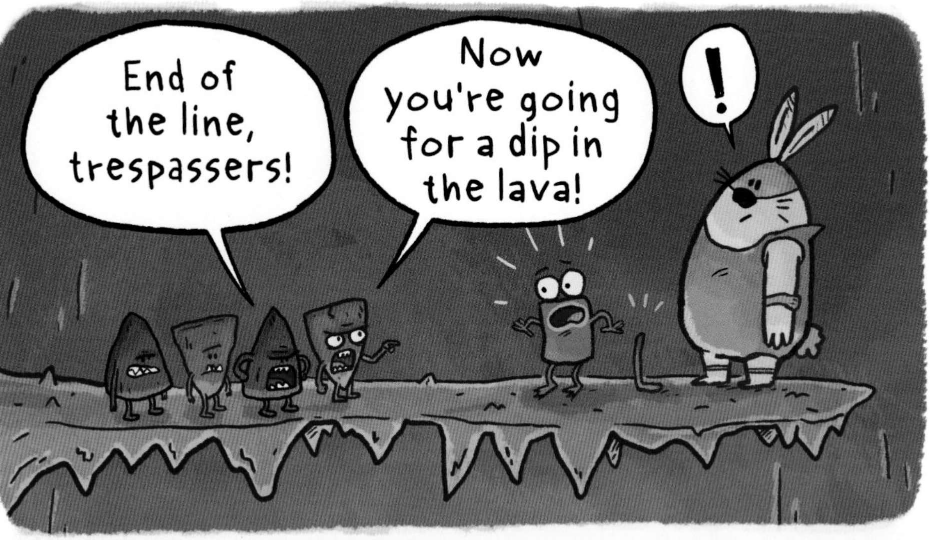
End of the line, trespassers!
Now you're going for a dip in the lava!
!

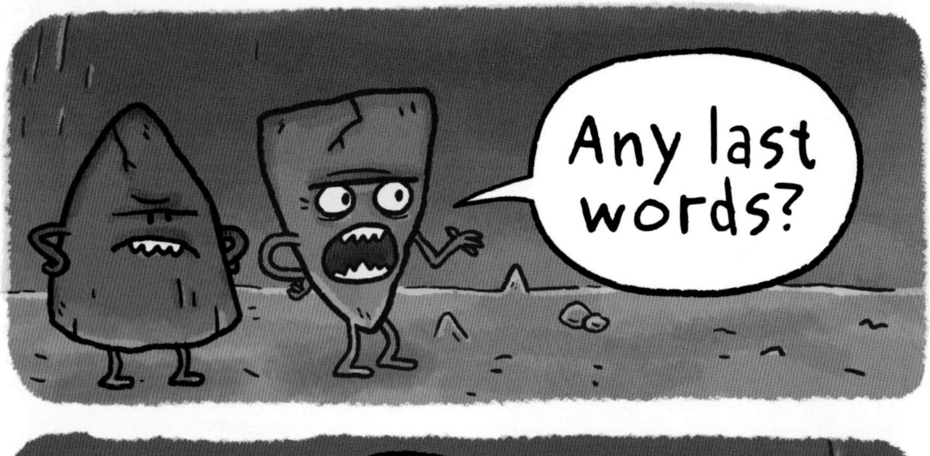
Any last words?

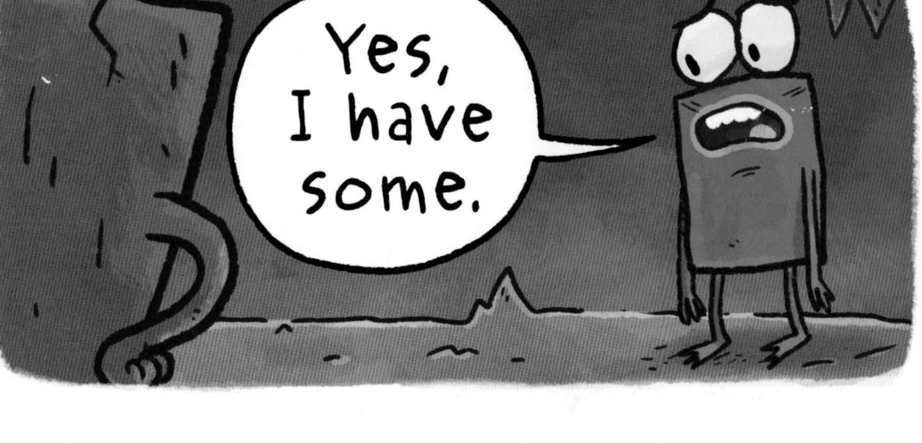
Yes, I have some.

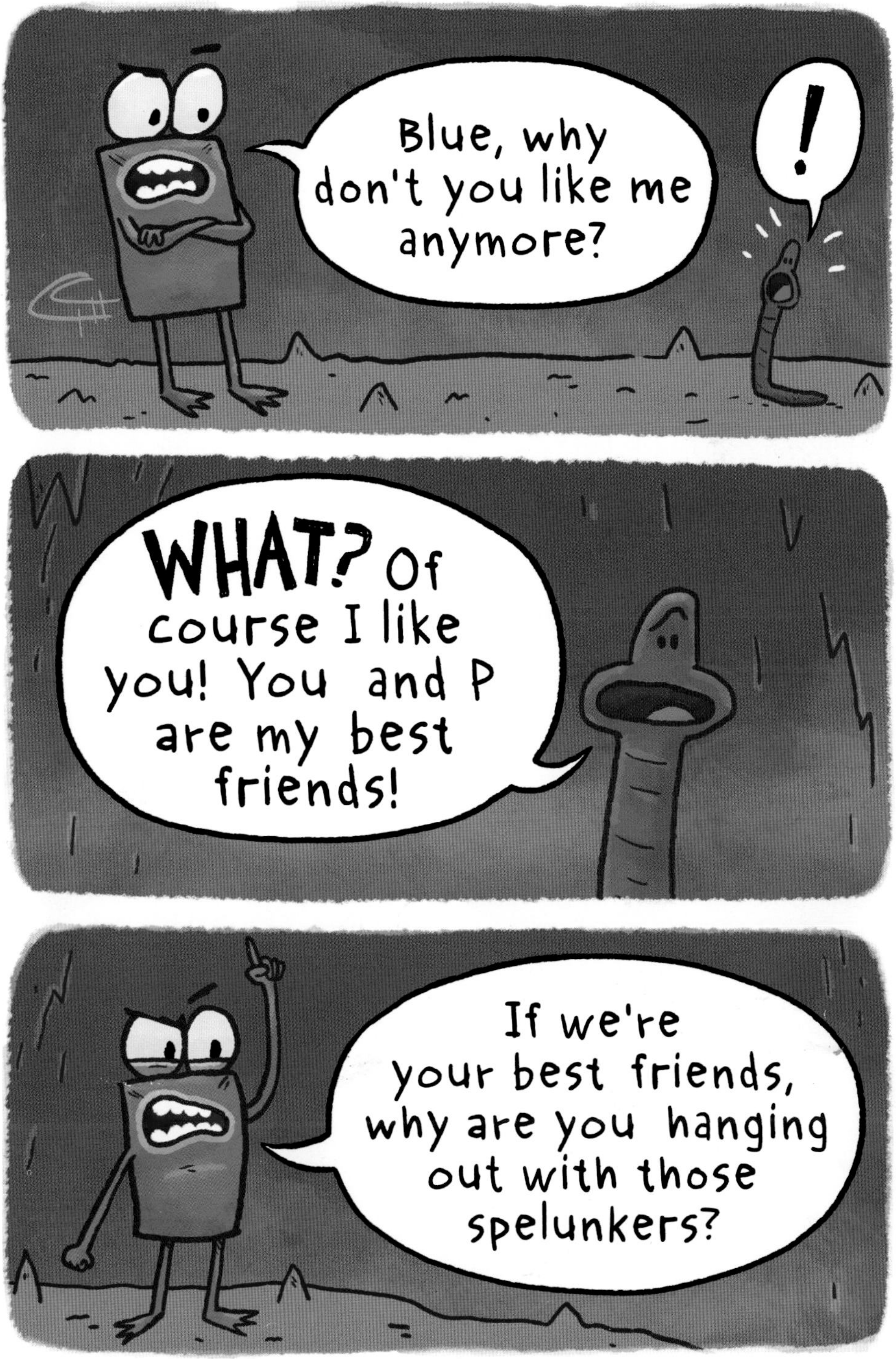
Blue, why don't you like me anymore?
!
WHAT? Of course I like you! You and P are my best friends!
If we're your best friends, why are you hanging out with those spelunkers?

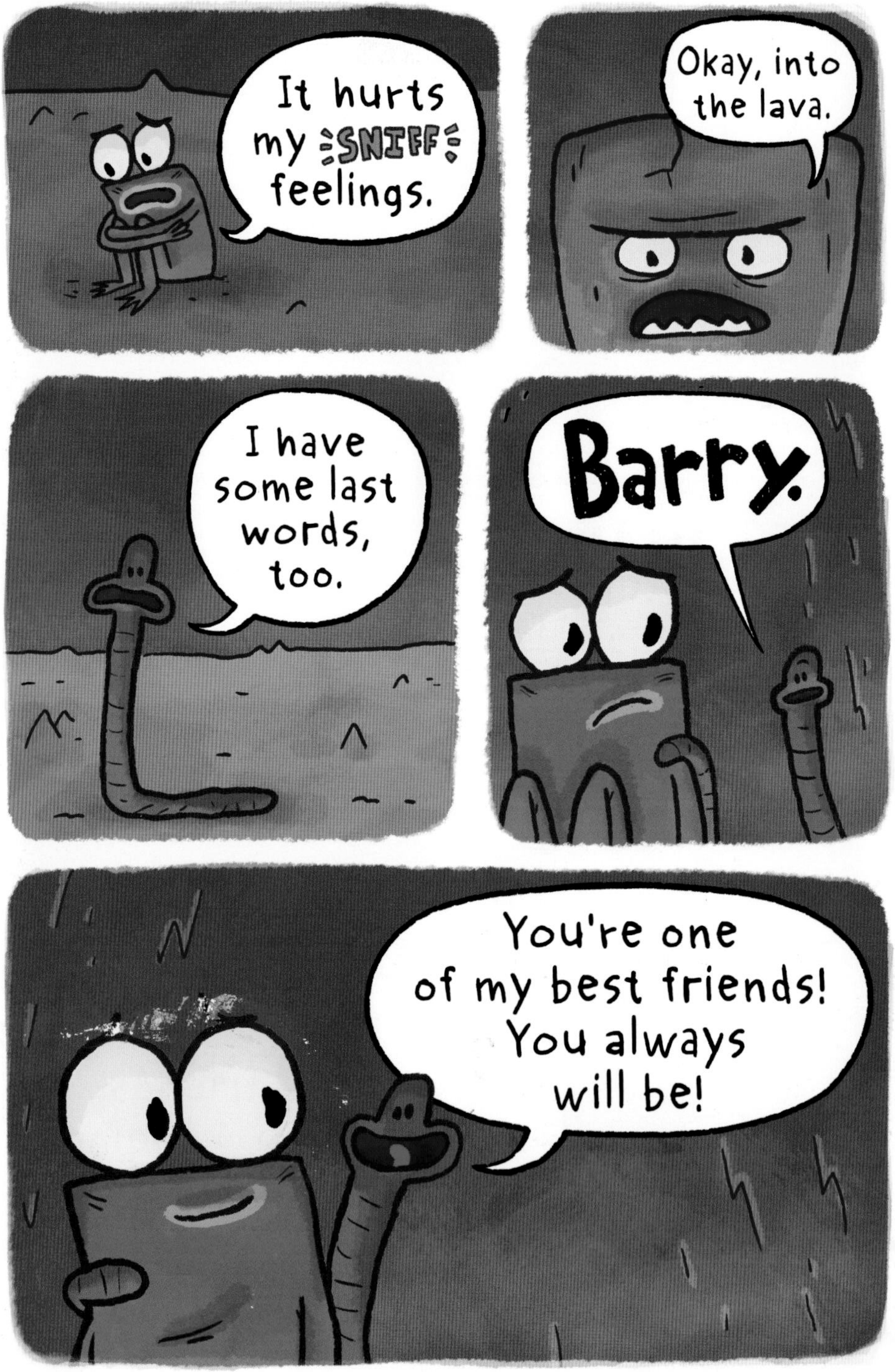
It hurts my SNIFF feelings.
Okay, into the lava.
I have some last words, too.
Barry.
You're one of my best friends! You always will be!

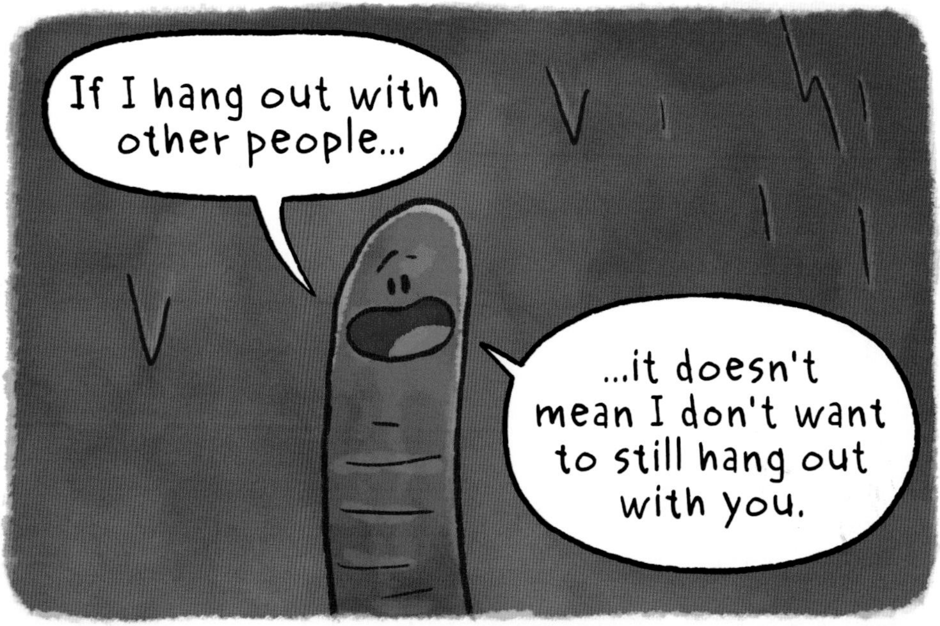
If I hang out with other people...
...it doesn't mean I don't want to still hang out with you.

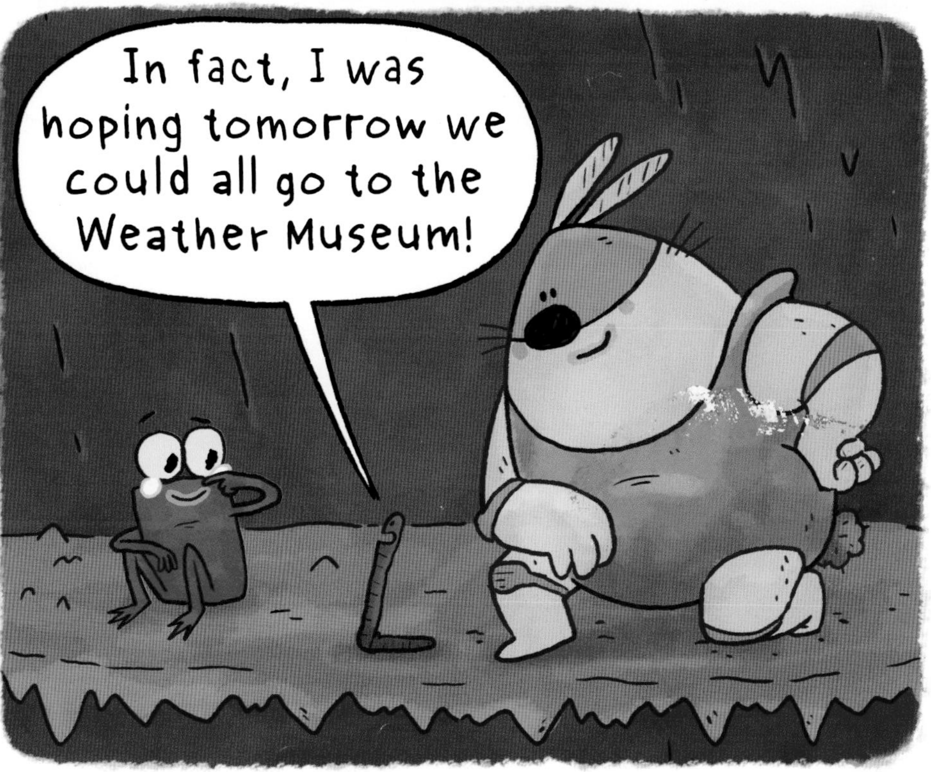
In fact, I was hoping tomorrow we could all go to the Weather Museum!

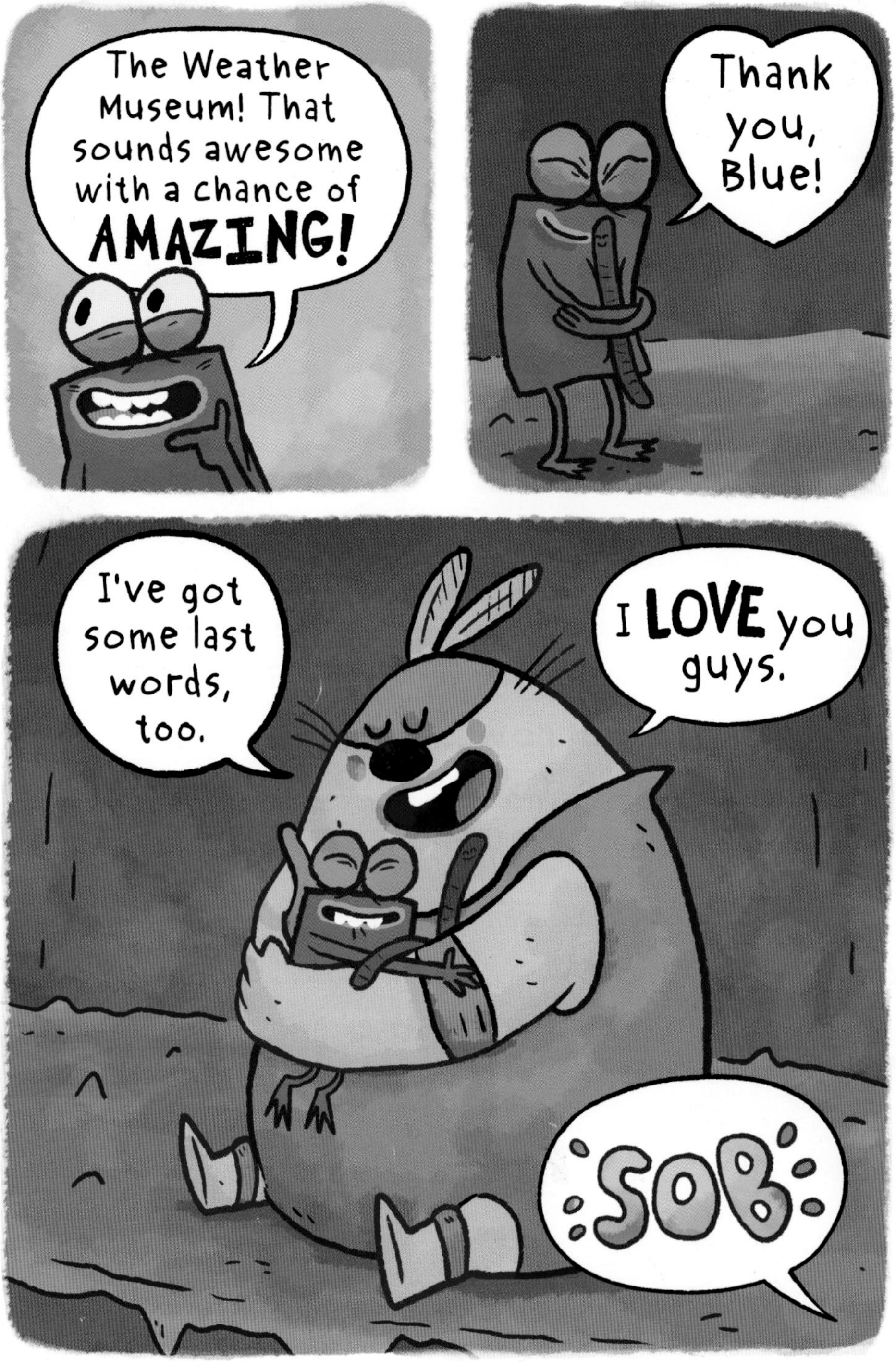

The Weather Museum! That sounds awesome with a chance of **AMAZING!**
Thank you, Blue!
I've got some last words, too.
I **LOVE** you guys.
SOB

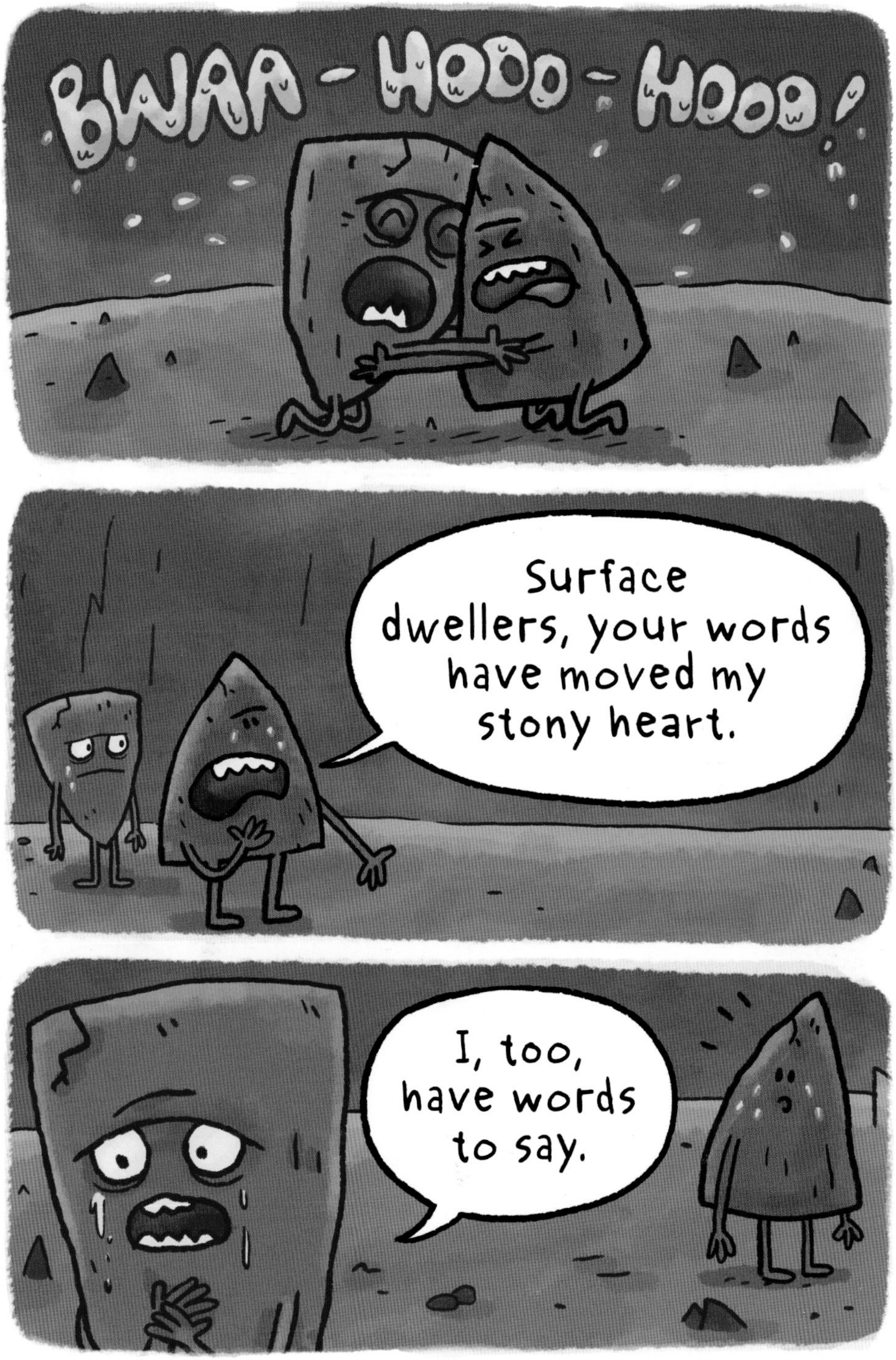
BWAA-HOOO-HOOO!
Surface dwellers, your words have moved my stony heart.
I, too, have words to say.

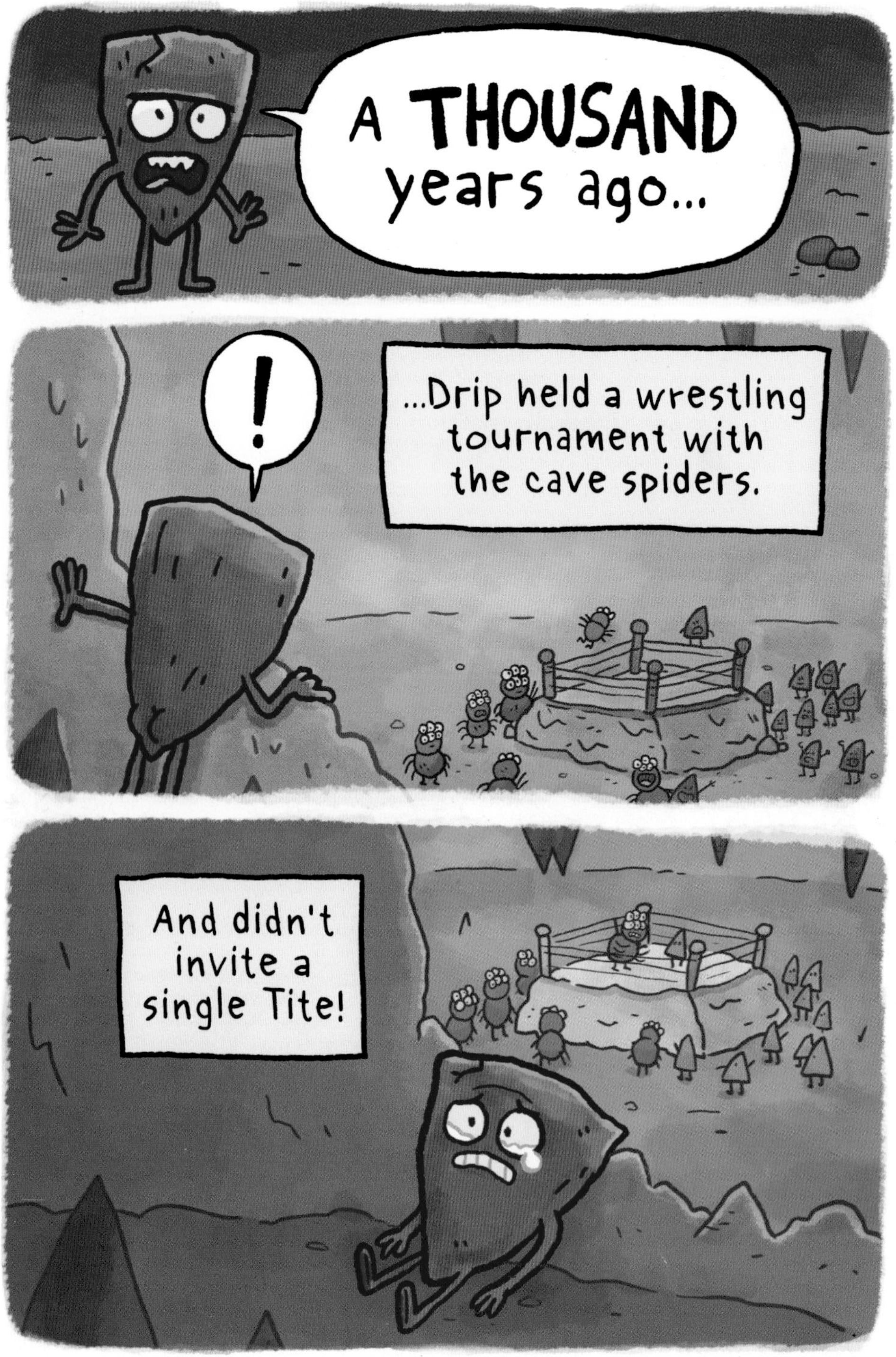
A THOUSAND years ago...
!
...Drip held a wrestling tournament with the cave spiders.
And didn't invite a single Tite!

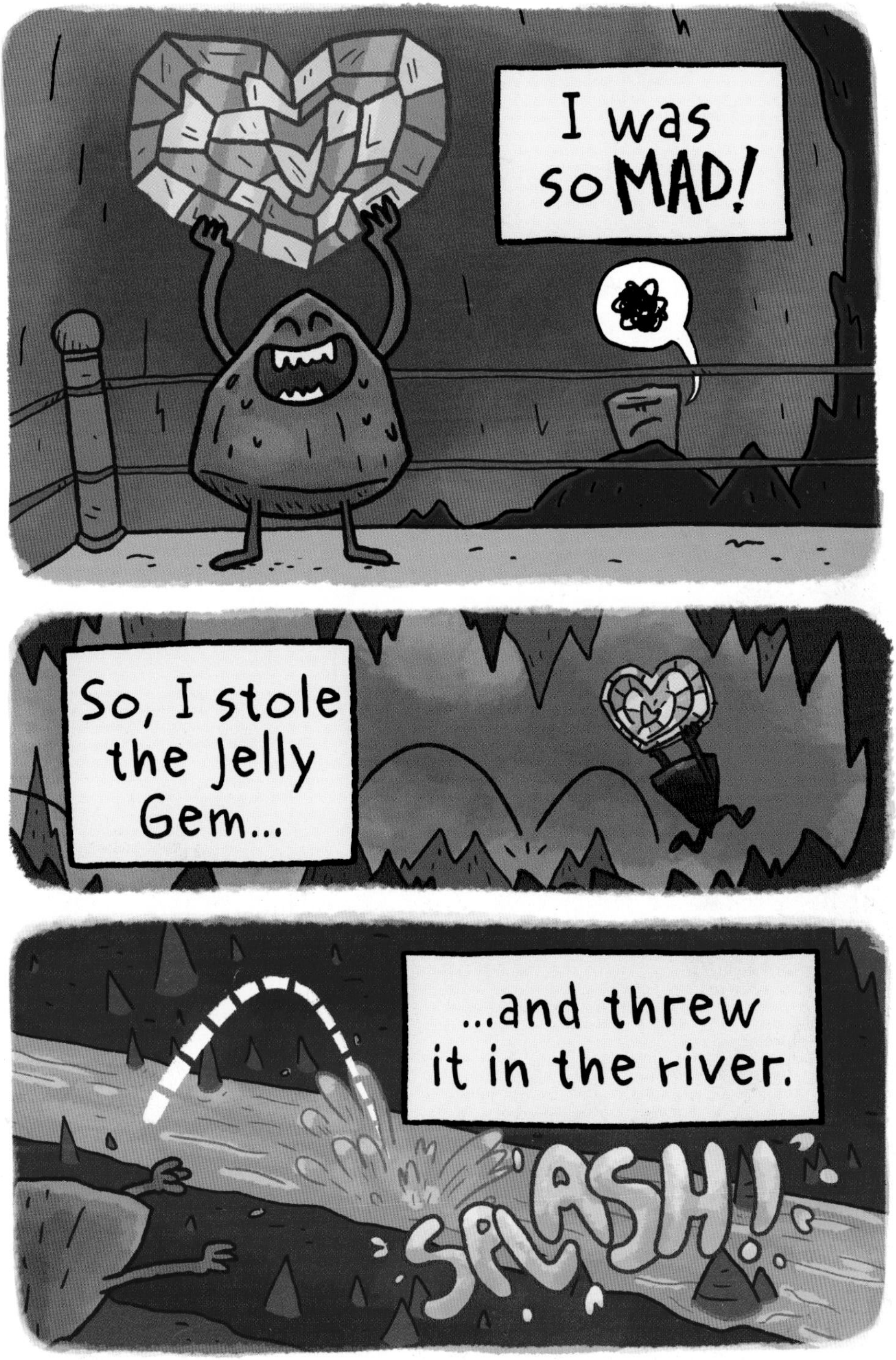
I was so MAD!
So, I stole the Jelly Gem...
...and threw it in the river.
SPLASH!

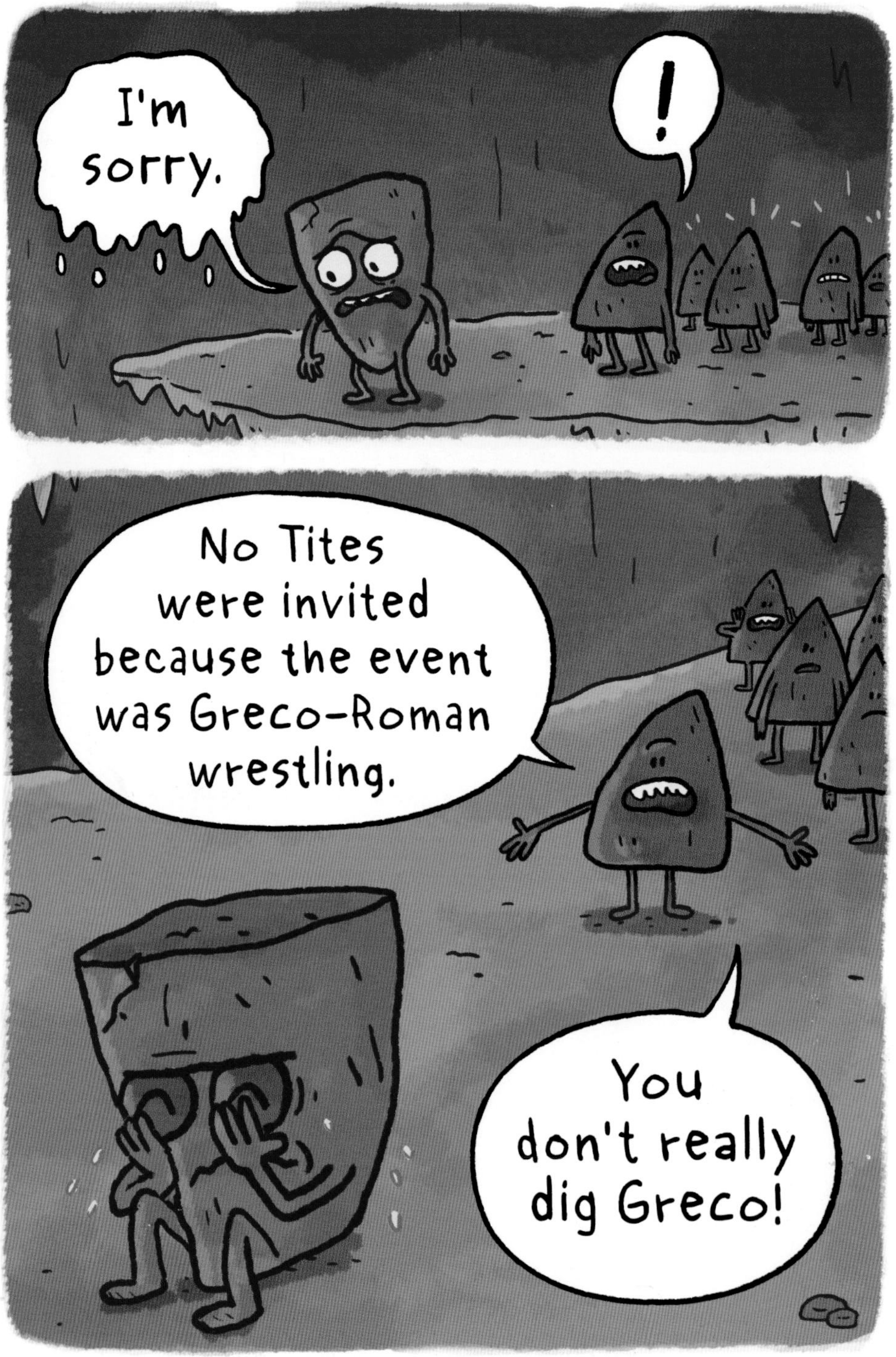
I'm sorry.
!
No Tites were invited because the event was Greco-Roman wrestling.
You don't really dig Greco!

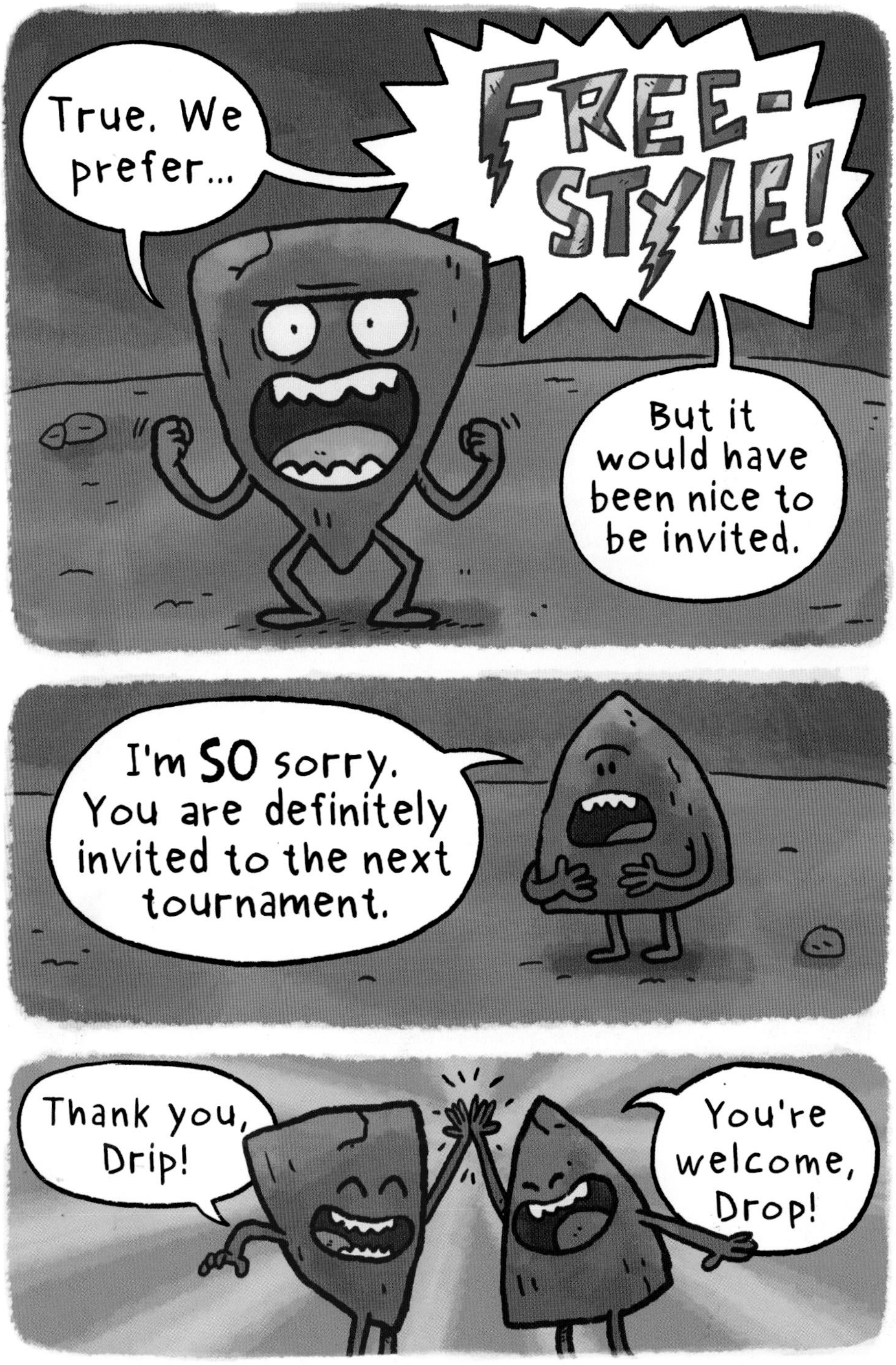
True. We prefer...
FREE-STYLE!
But it would have been nice to be invited.
I'm SO sorry. You are definitely invited to the next tournament.
Thank you, Drip!
You're welcome, Drop!

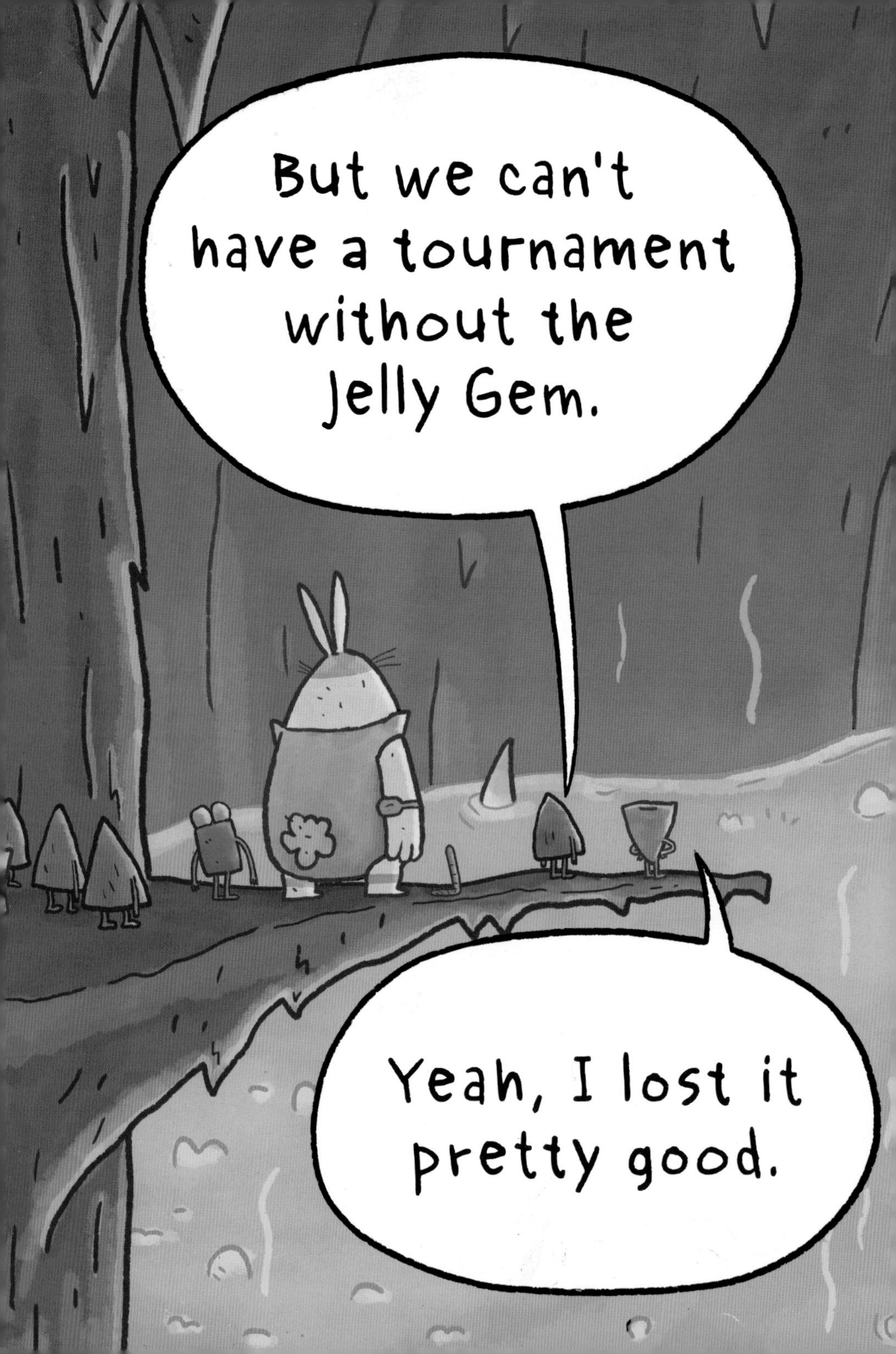
But we can't have a tournament without the Jelly Gem.
Yeah, I lost it pretty good.

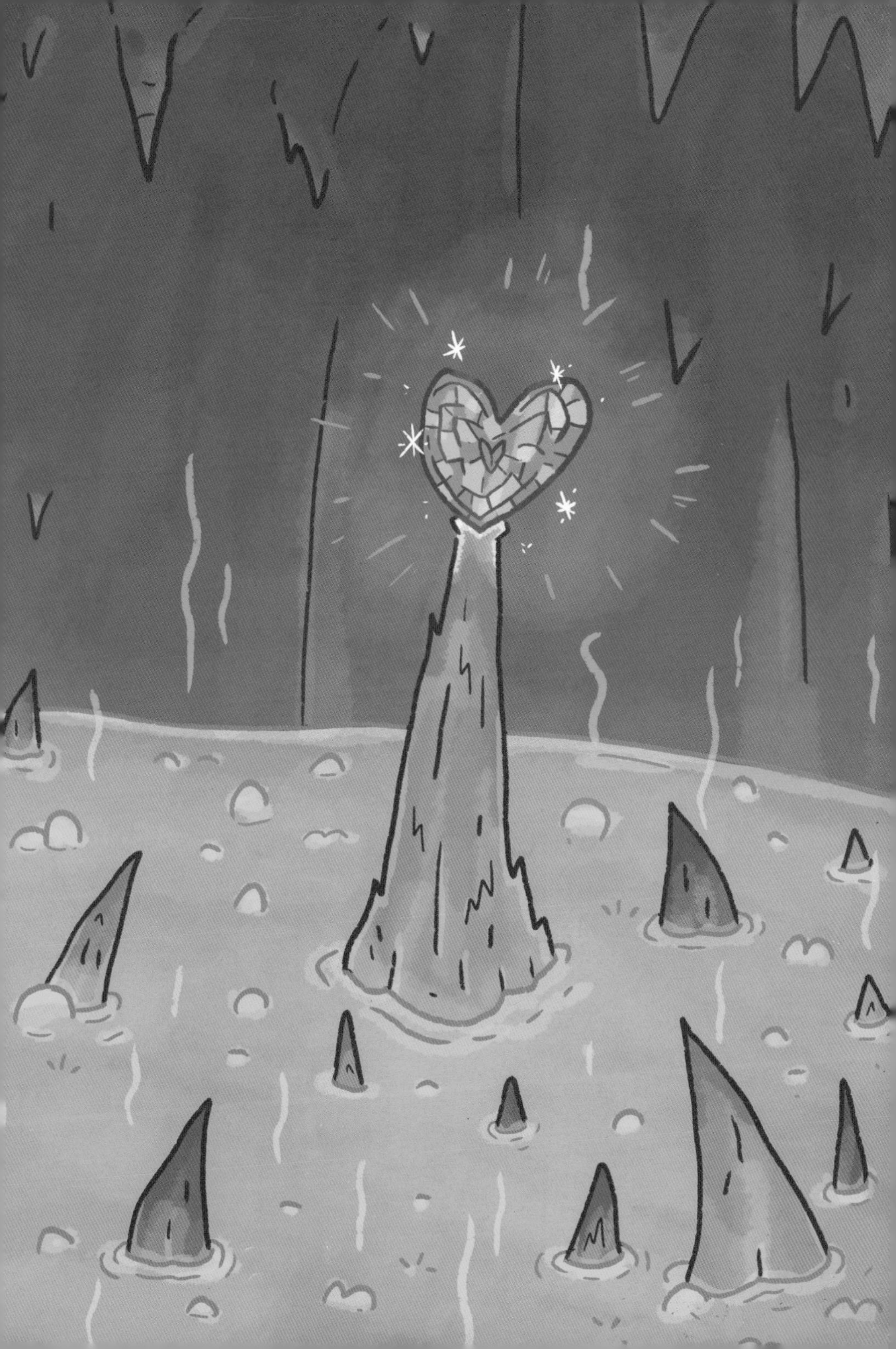

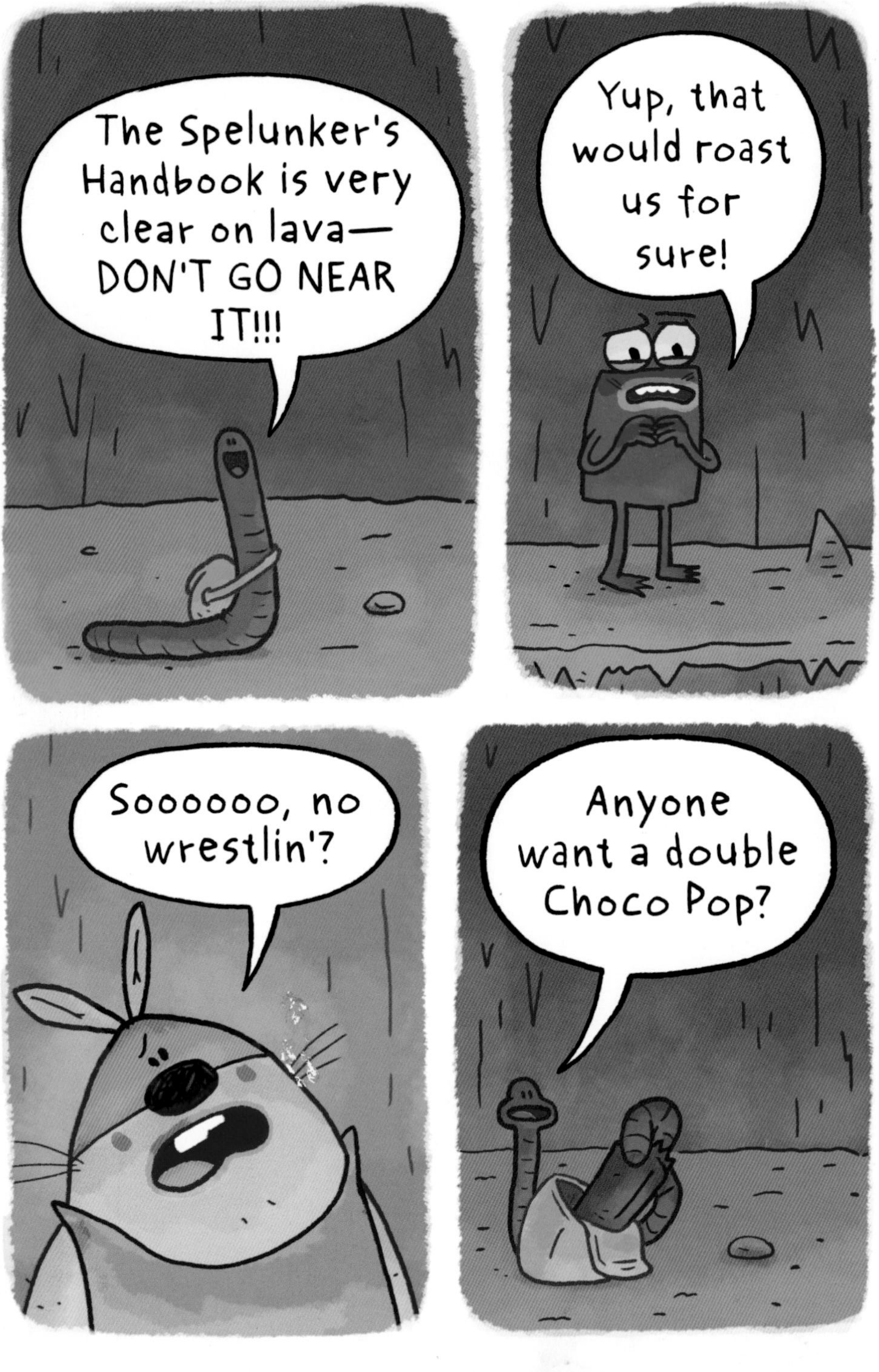
The Spelunker's Handbook is very clear on lava—DON'T GO NEAR IT!!!
Yup, that would roast us for sure!
Soooooo, no wrestlin'?
Anyone want a double Choco Pop?

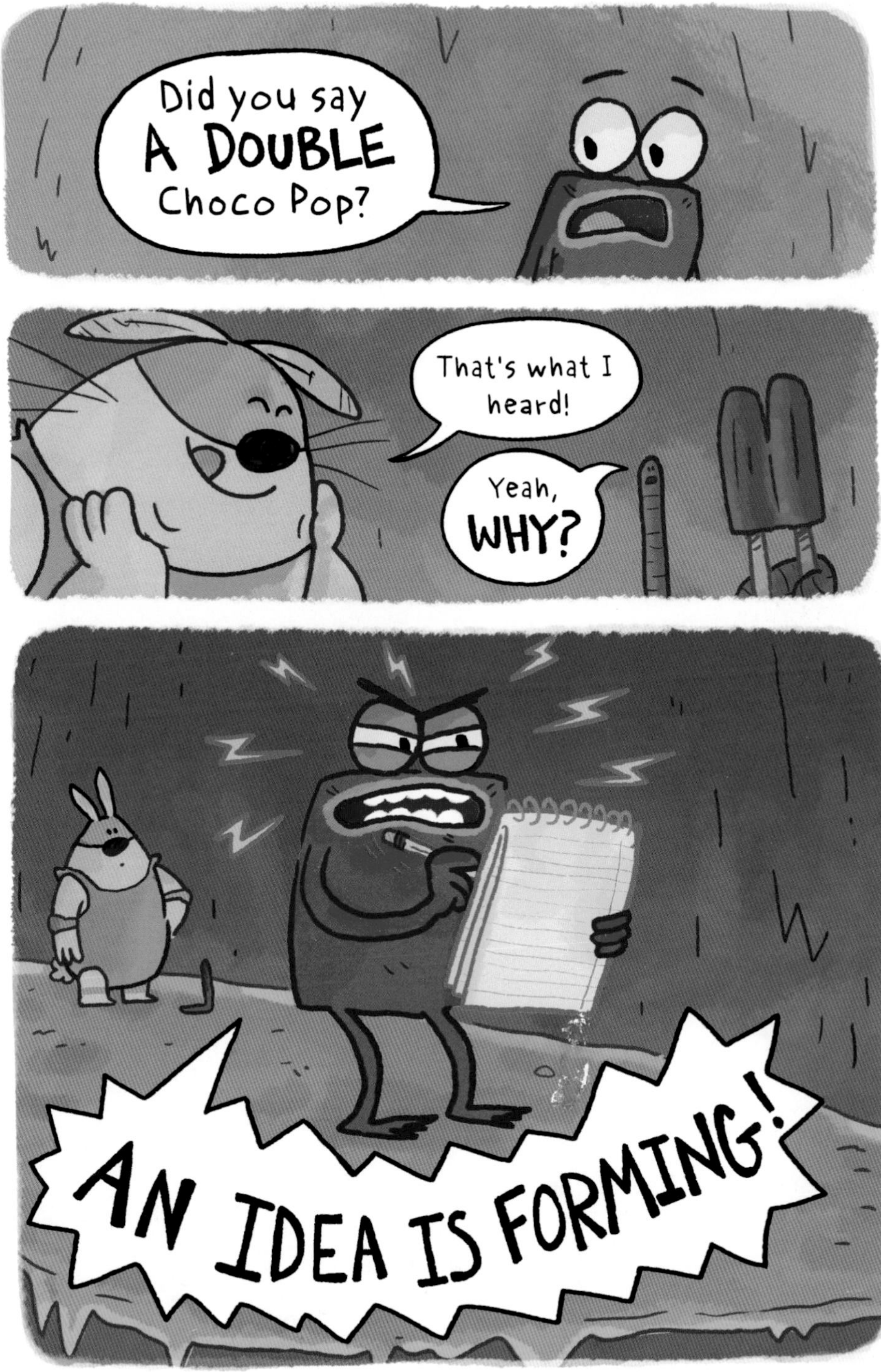
Did you say A DOUBLE Choco Pop?
That's what I heard!
Yeah, WHY?
AN IDEA IS FORMING!

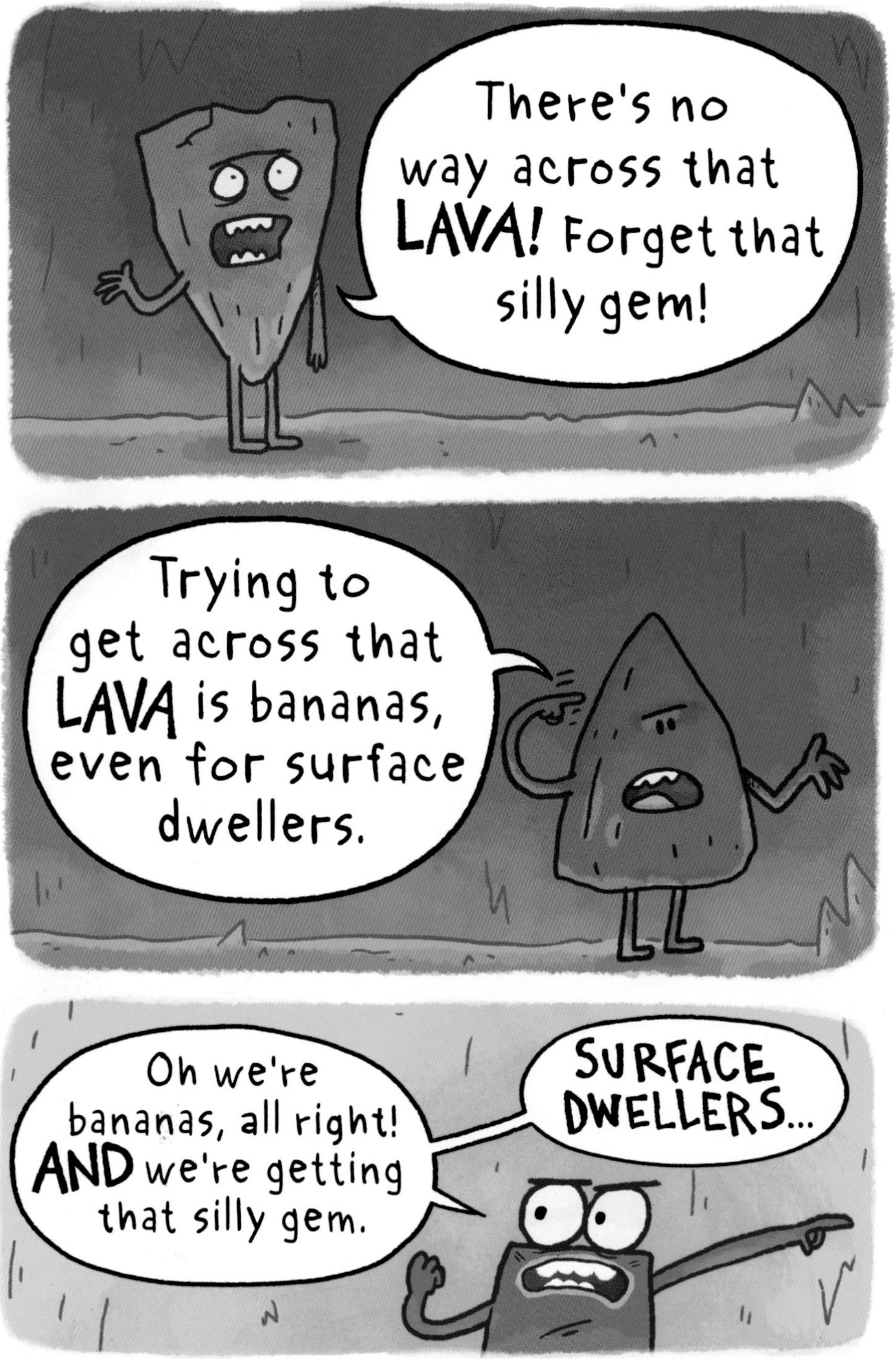
There's no way across that LAVA! Forget that silly gem!
Trying to get across that LAVA is bananas, even for surface dwellers.
Oh we're bananas, all right! AND we're getting that silly gem.
SURFACE DWELLERS...

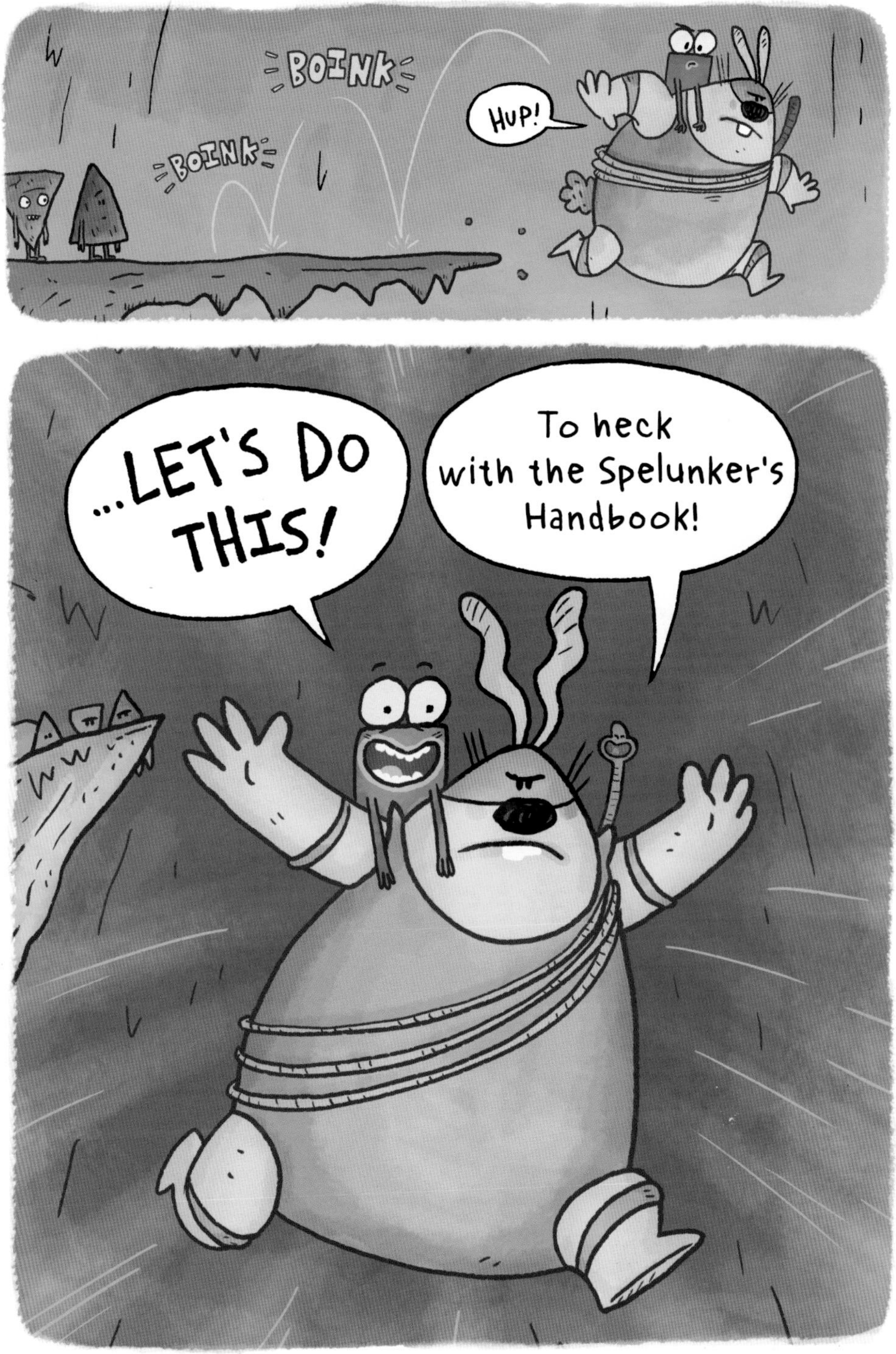
BOINK
BOINK
HUP!
...LET'S DO THIS!
To heck with the Spelunker's Handbook!

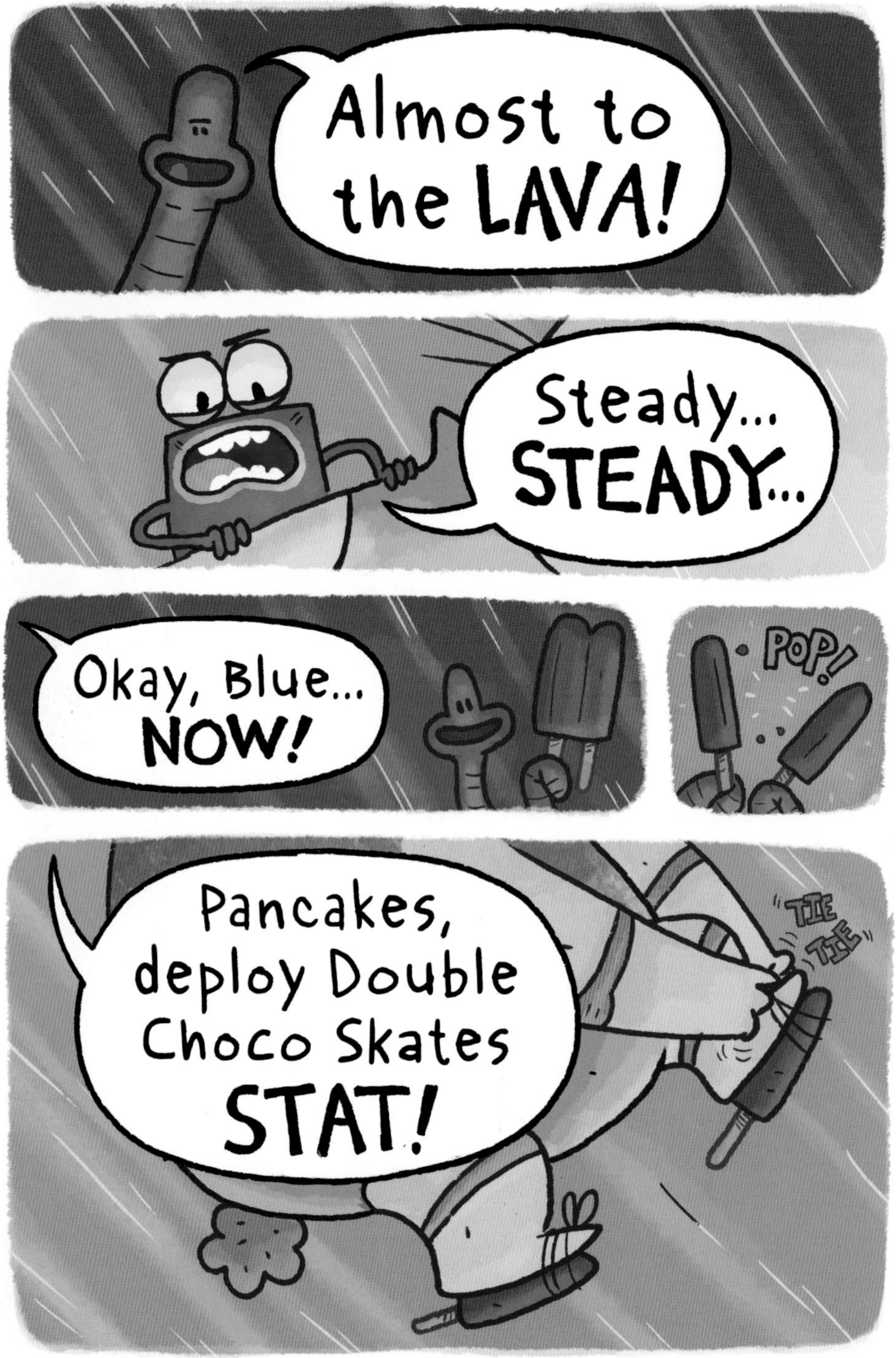
Almost to the LAVA!
Steady... STEADY...
Okay, Blue... NOW!
POP!
Pancakes, deploy Double Choco Skates STAT!
TIE
TIE

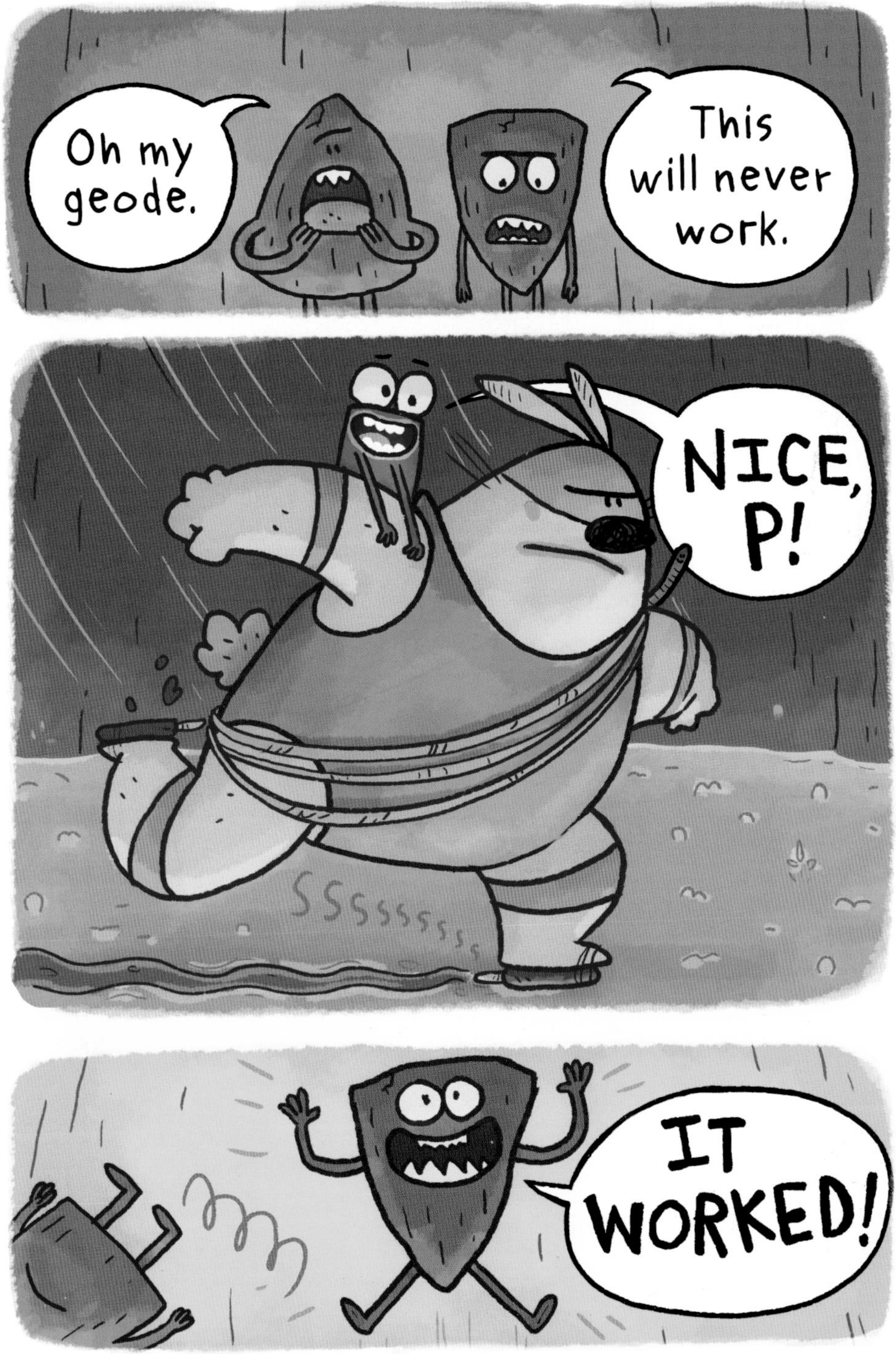
Oh my geode.
This will never work.
NICE, P!
SSsssssss
IT WORKED!

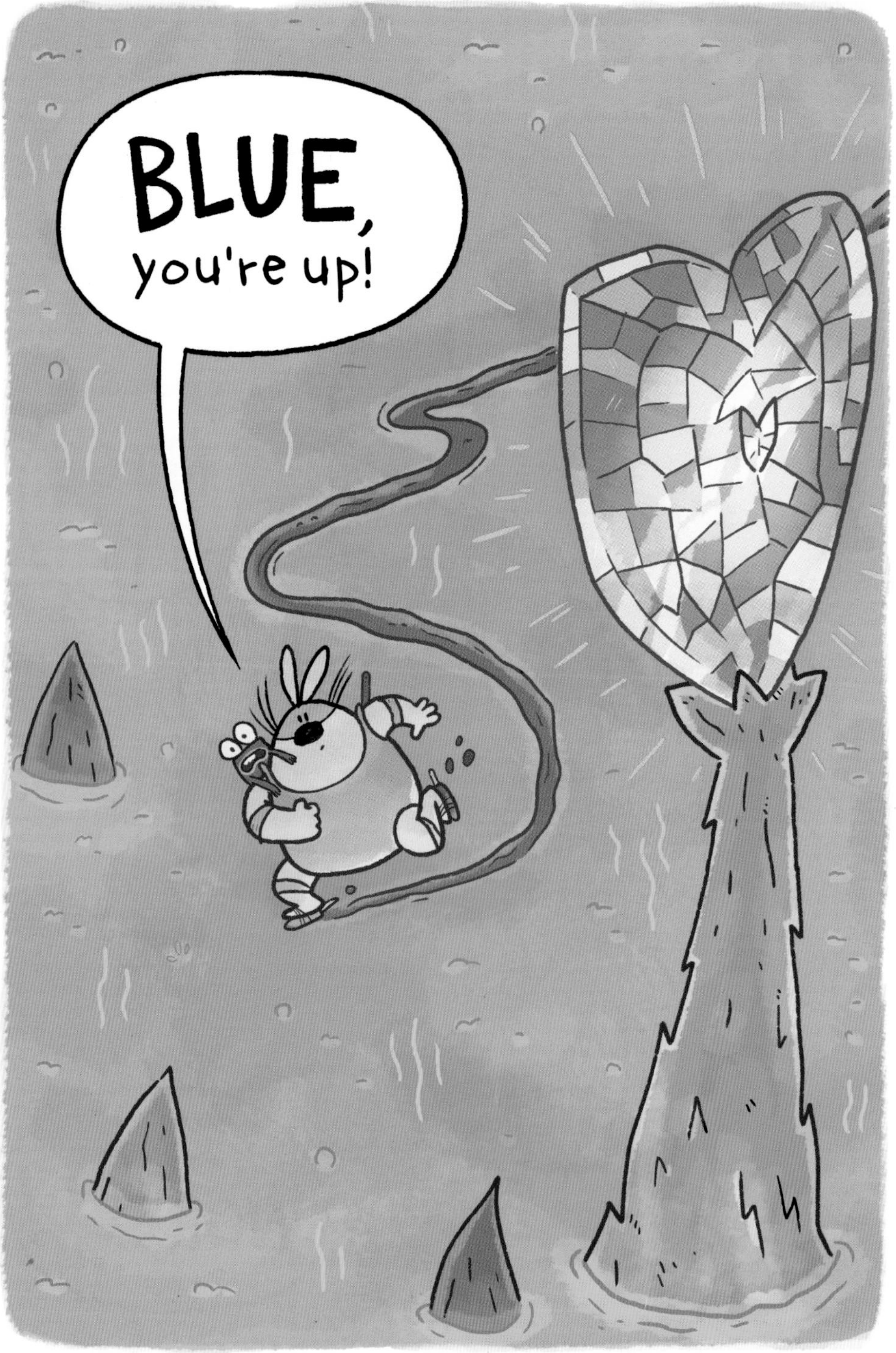
BLUE, you're up!

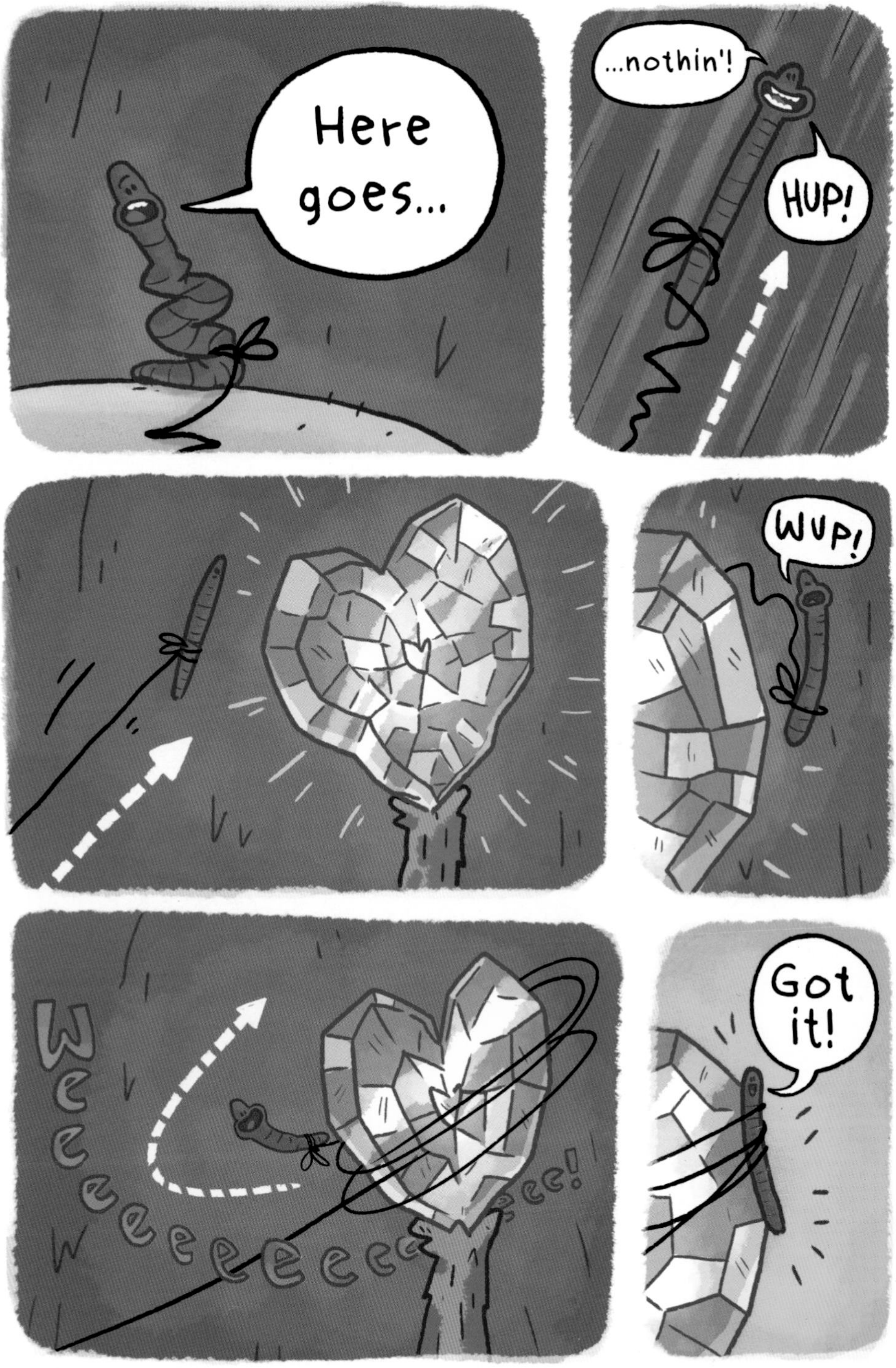
Here goes...
...nothin'!
HUP!
WUP!
Weeeeeeeeeeeeee!
Got it!

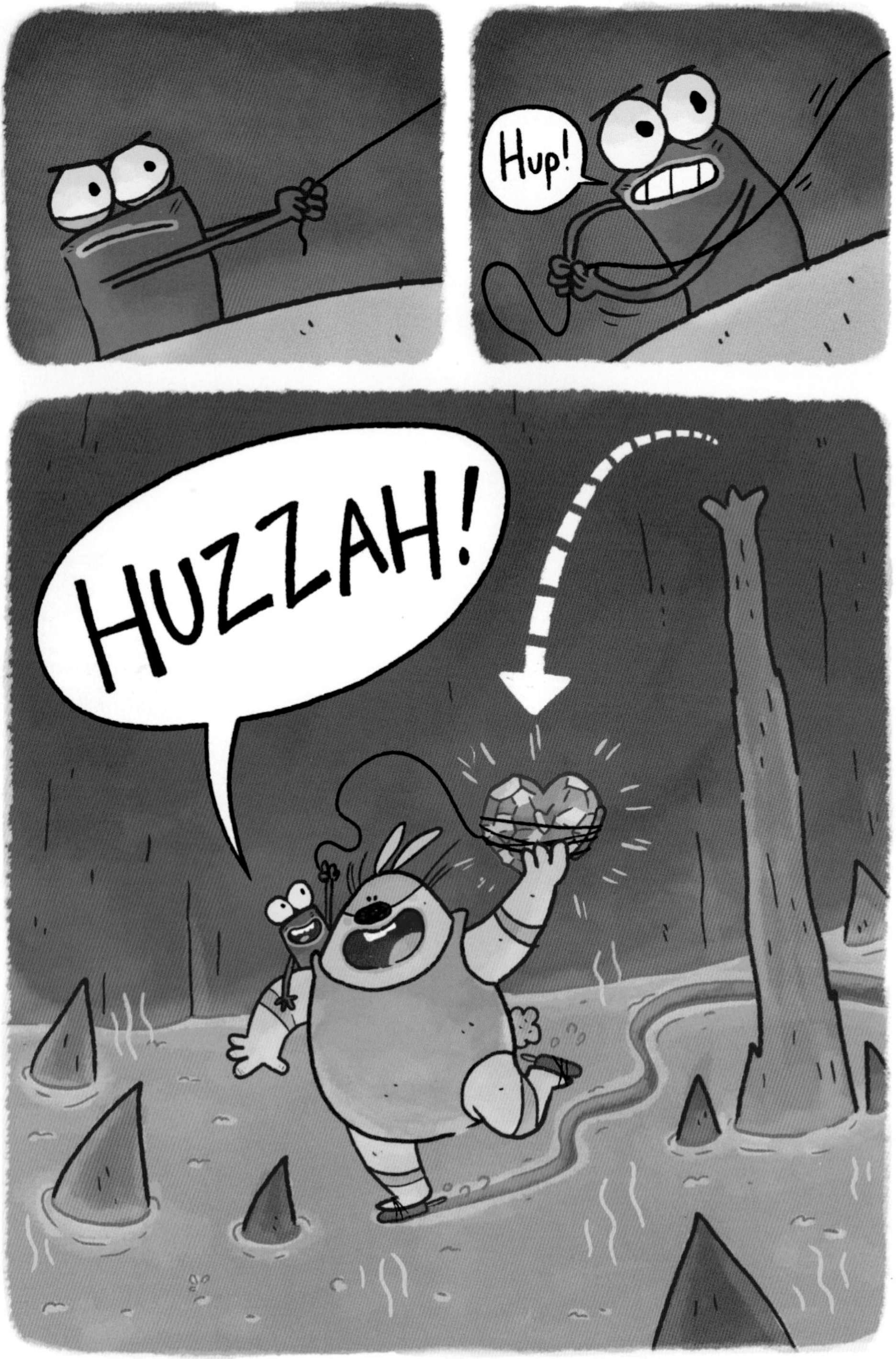
Hup!
HUZZAH!

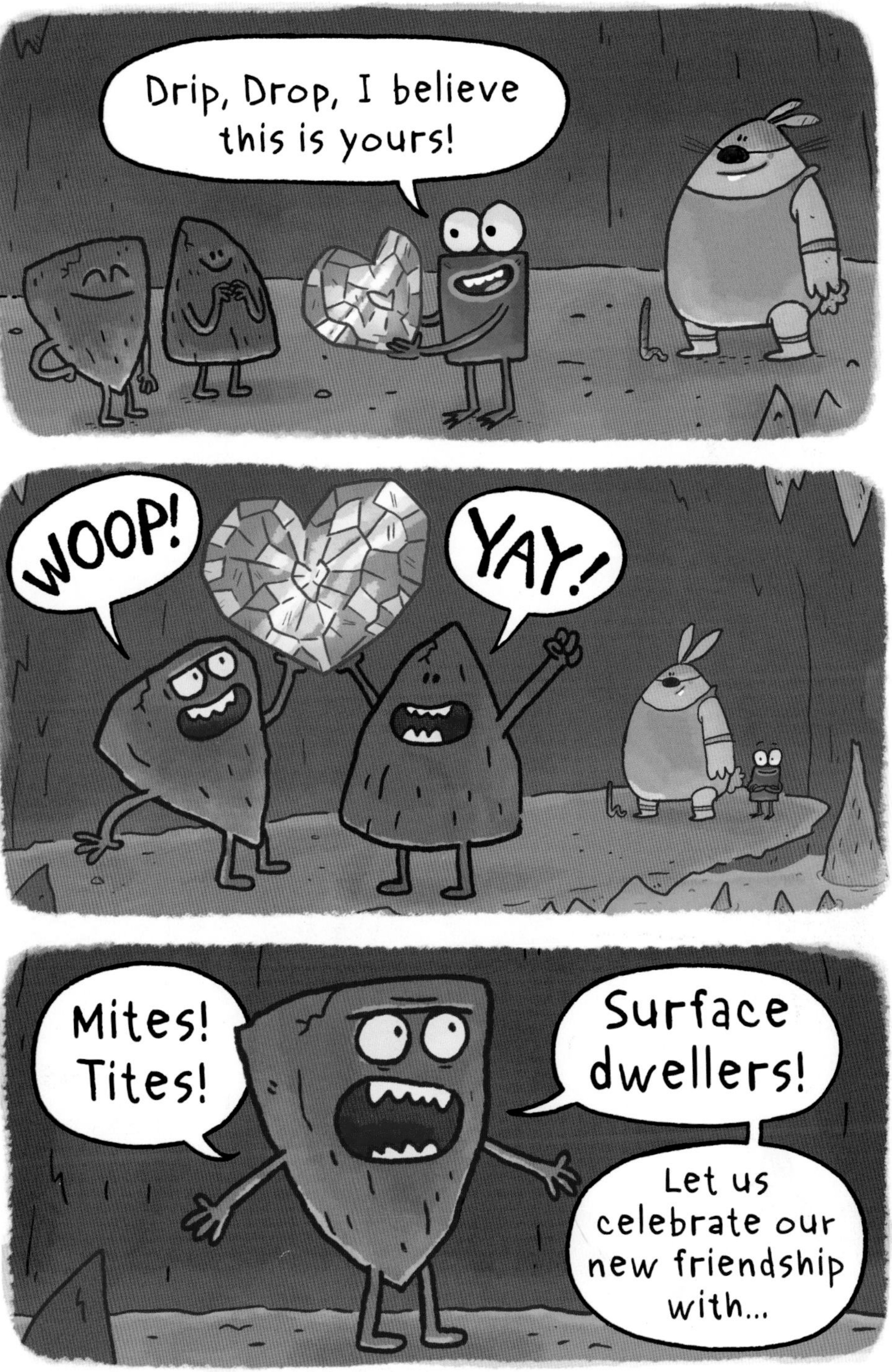
Drip, Drop, I believe this is yours!
WOOP!
YAY!
Mites! Tites!
Surface dwellers!
Let us celebrate our new friendship with...

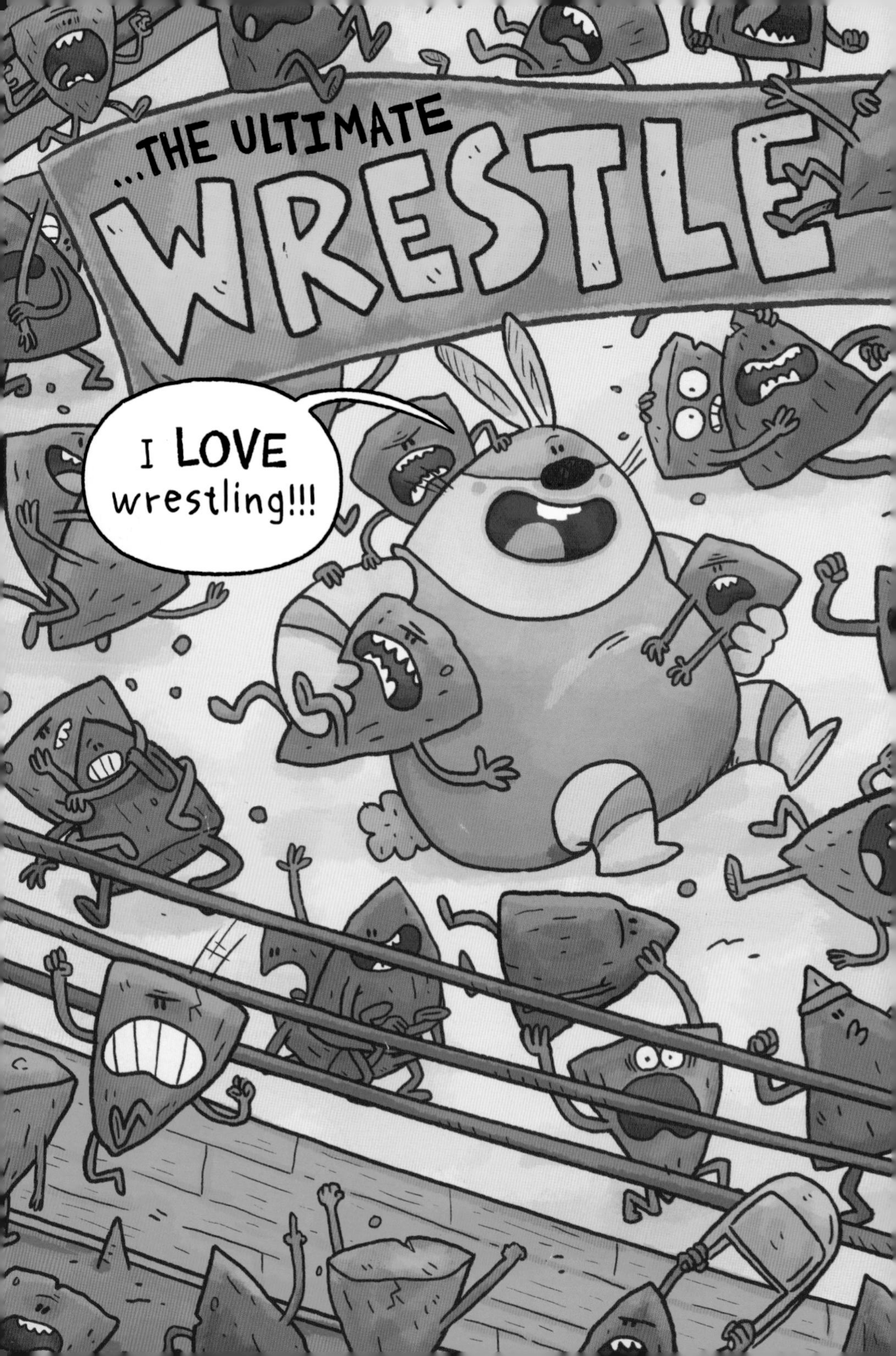
...THE ULTIMATE
WRESTLE
I LOVE wrestling!!!

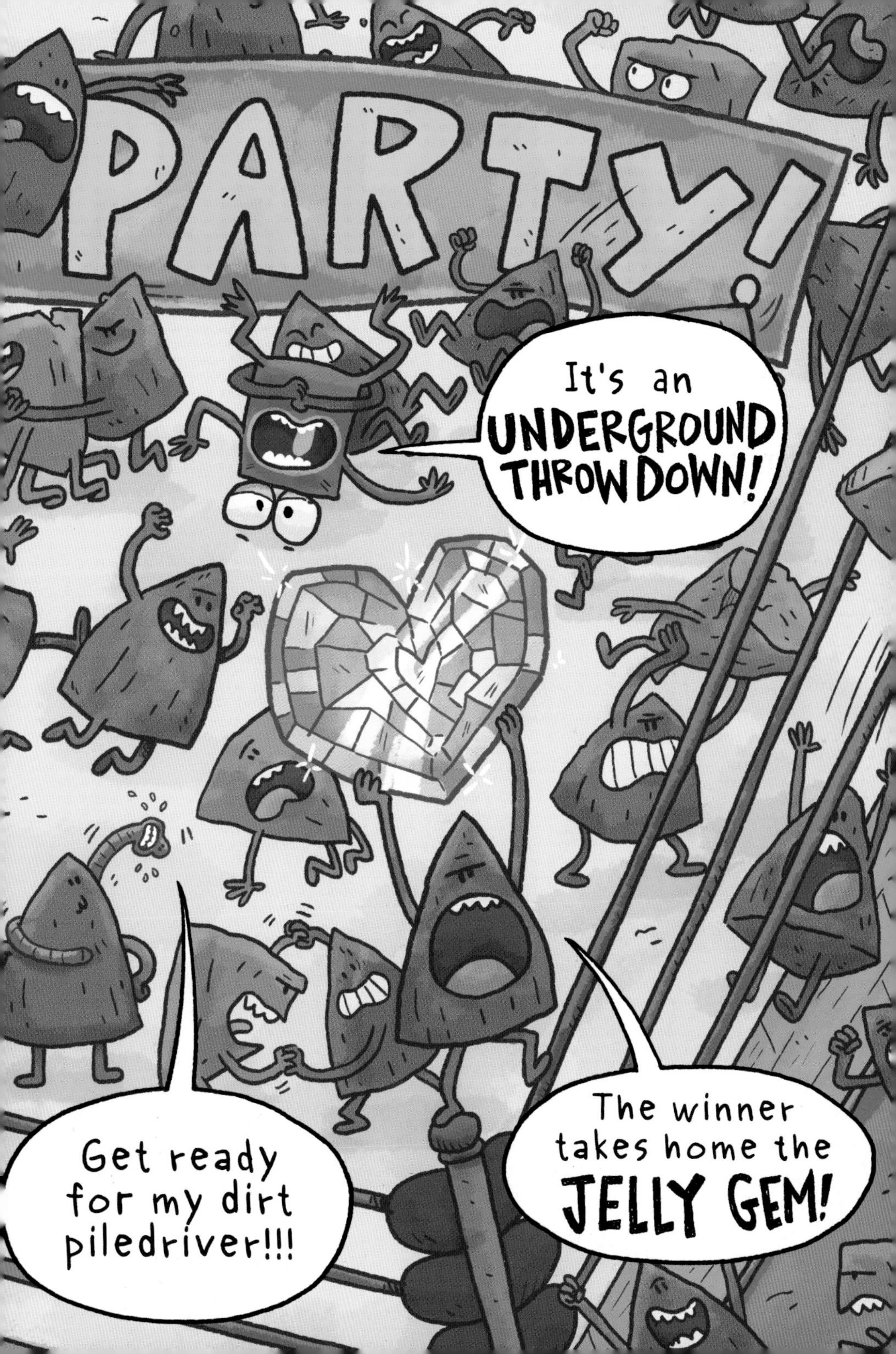
PARTY!
It's an UNDERGROUND THROWDOWN!
The winner takes home the JELLY GEM!
Get ready for my dirt piledriver!!!

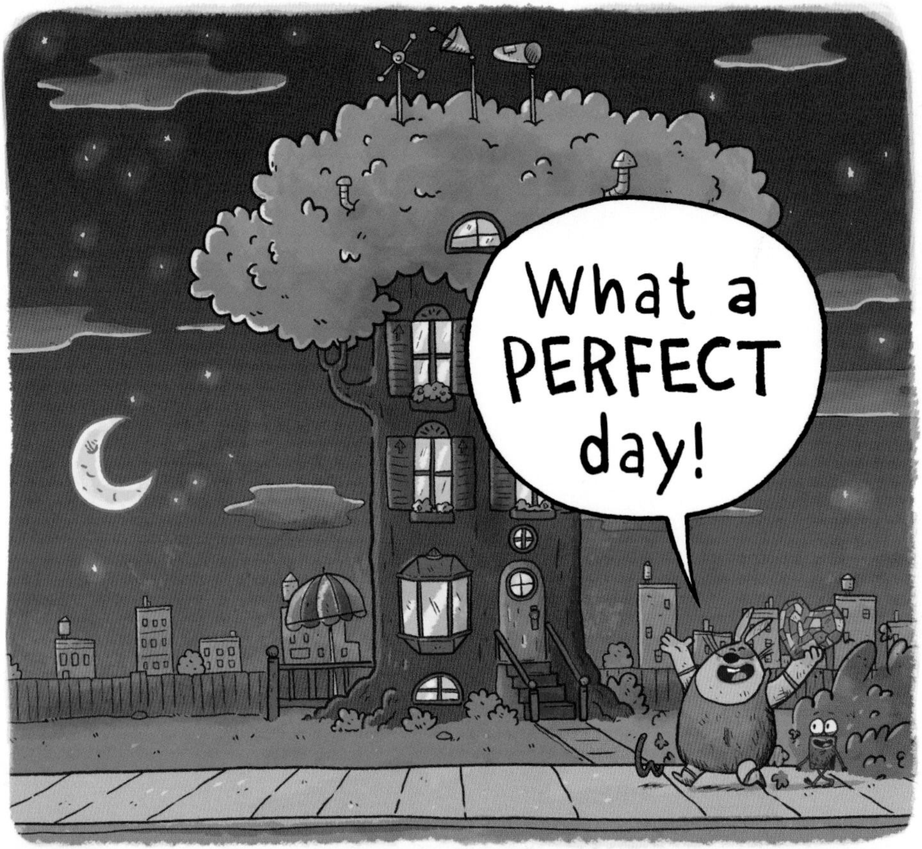
What a PERFECT day!

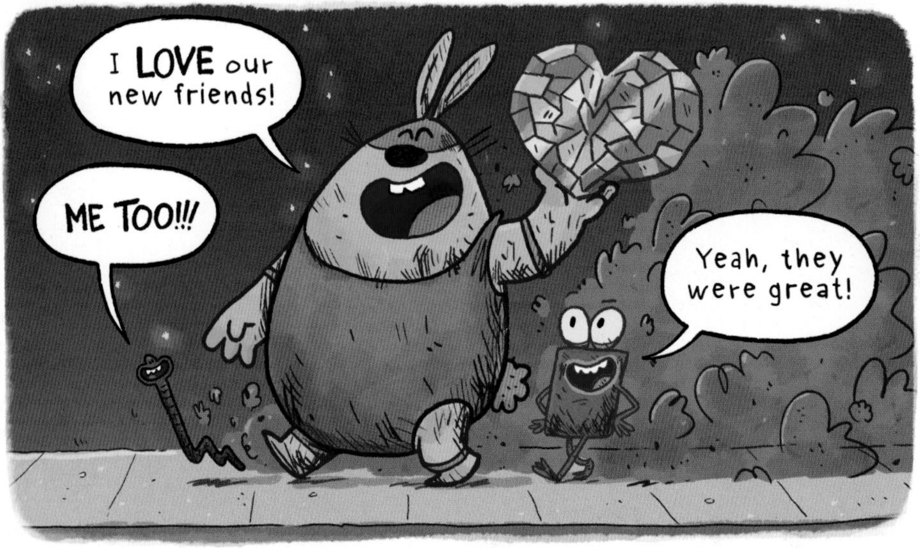
I LOVE our new friends!
ME TOO!!!
Yeah, they were great!

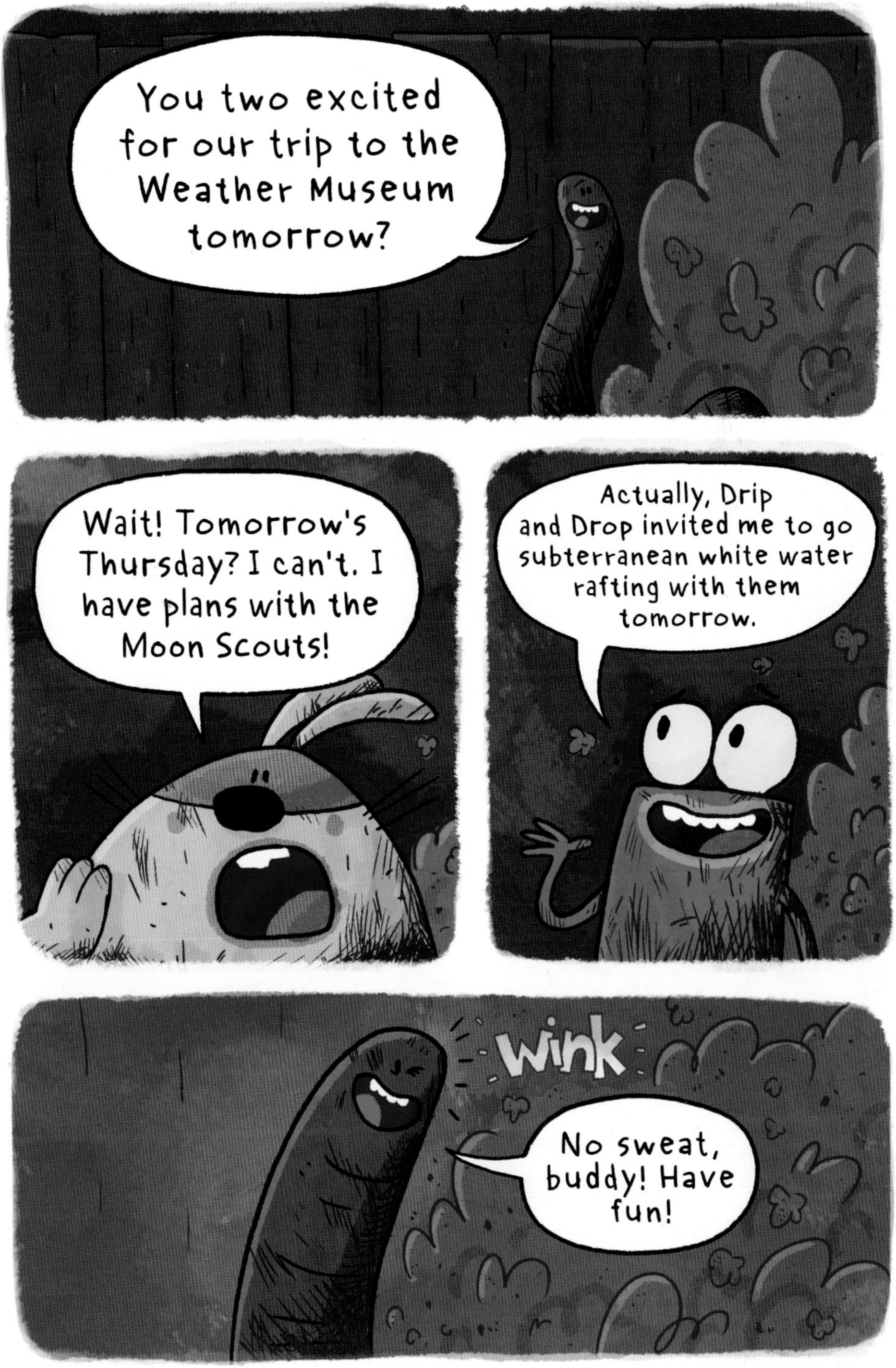
You two excited for our trip to the Weather Museum tomorrow?
Wait! Tomorrow's Thursday? I can't. I have plans with the Moon Scouts!
Actually, Drip and Drop invited me to go subterranean white water rafting with them tomorrow.
WINK
No sweat, buddy! Have fun!

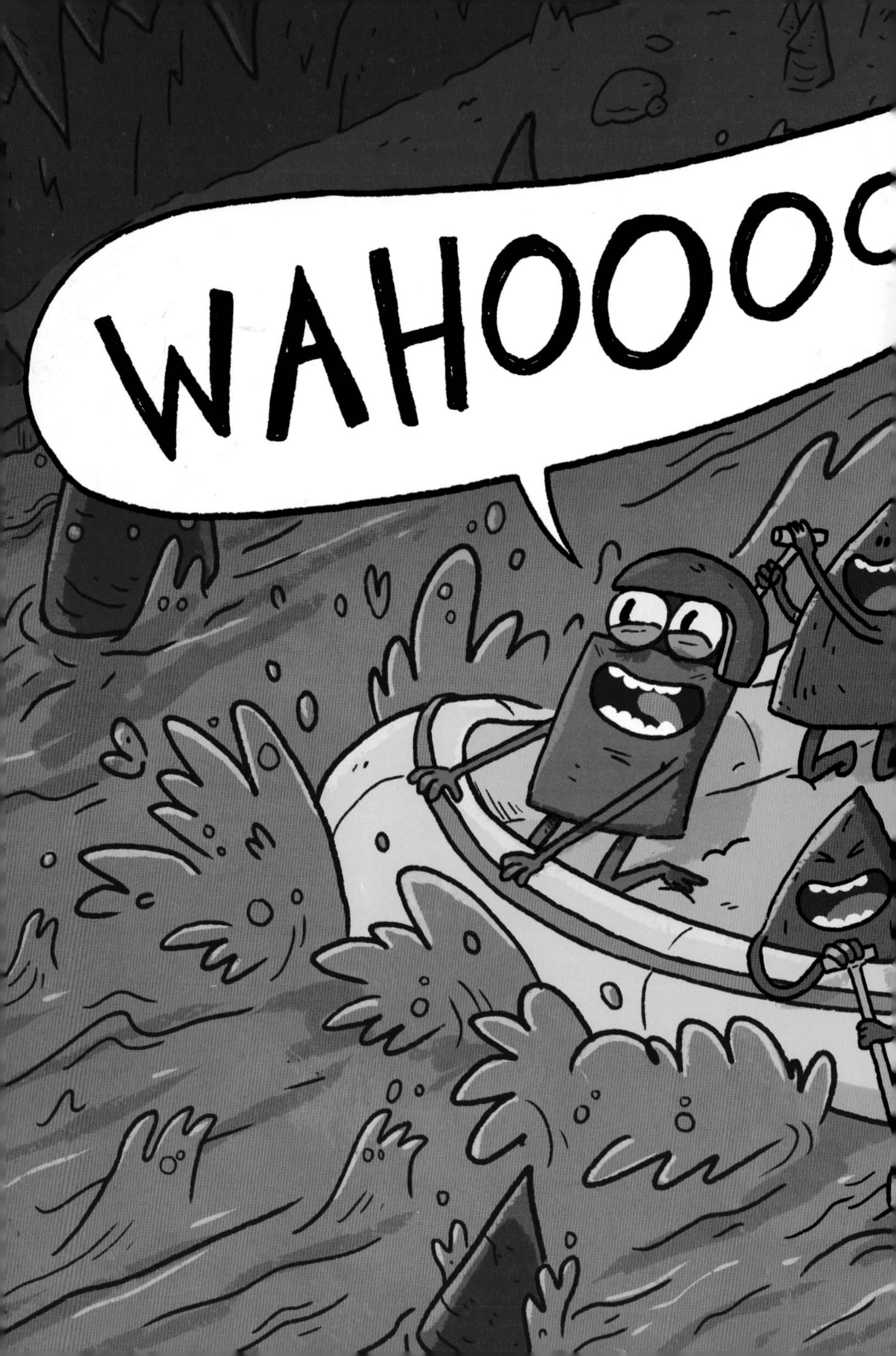
WAHOOO

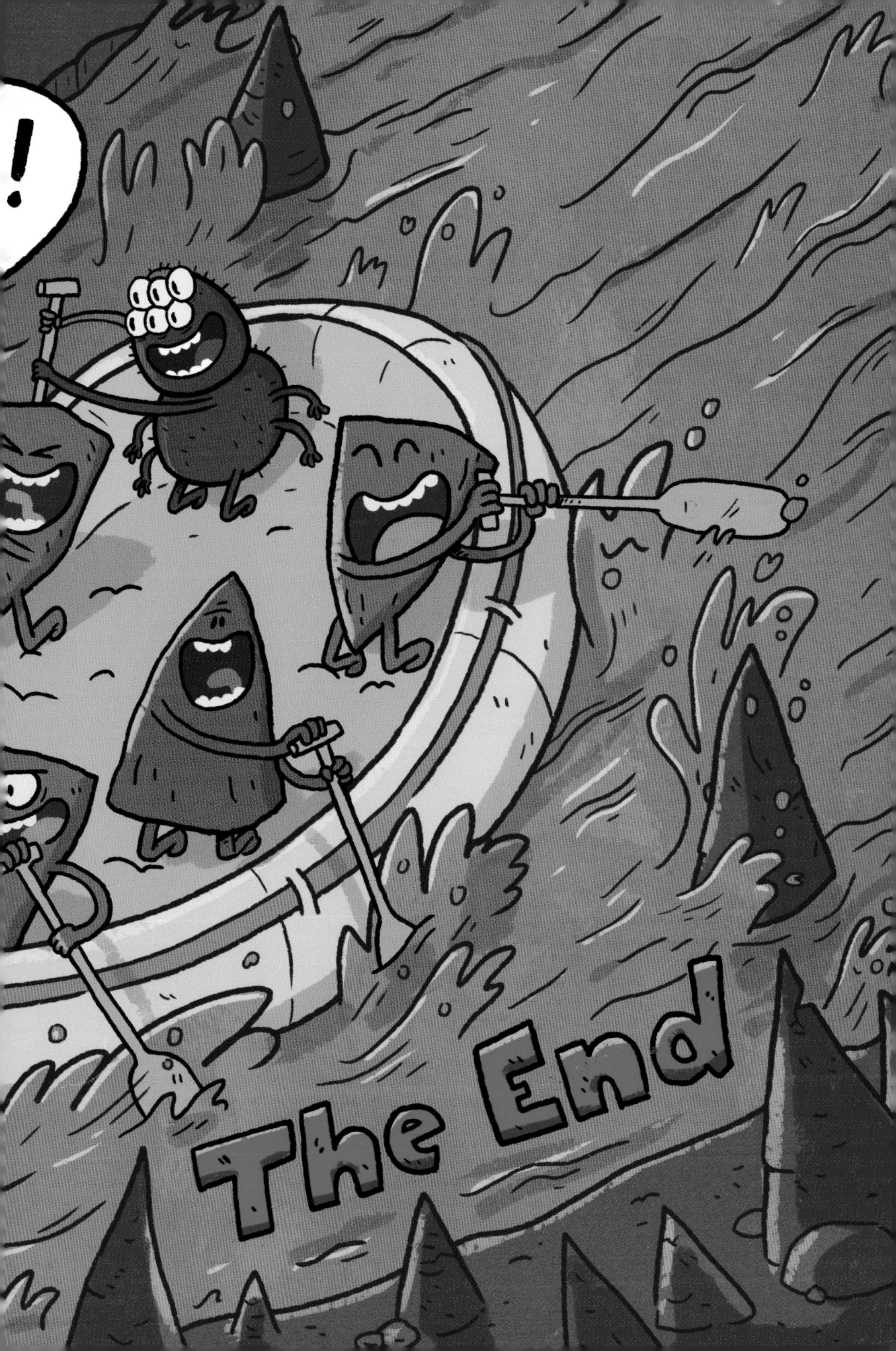
!
The End

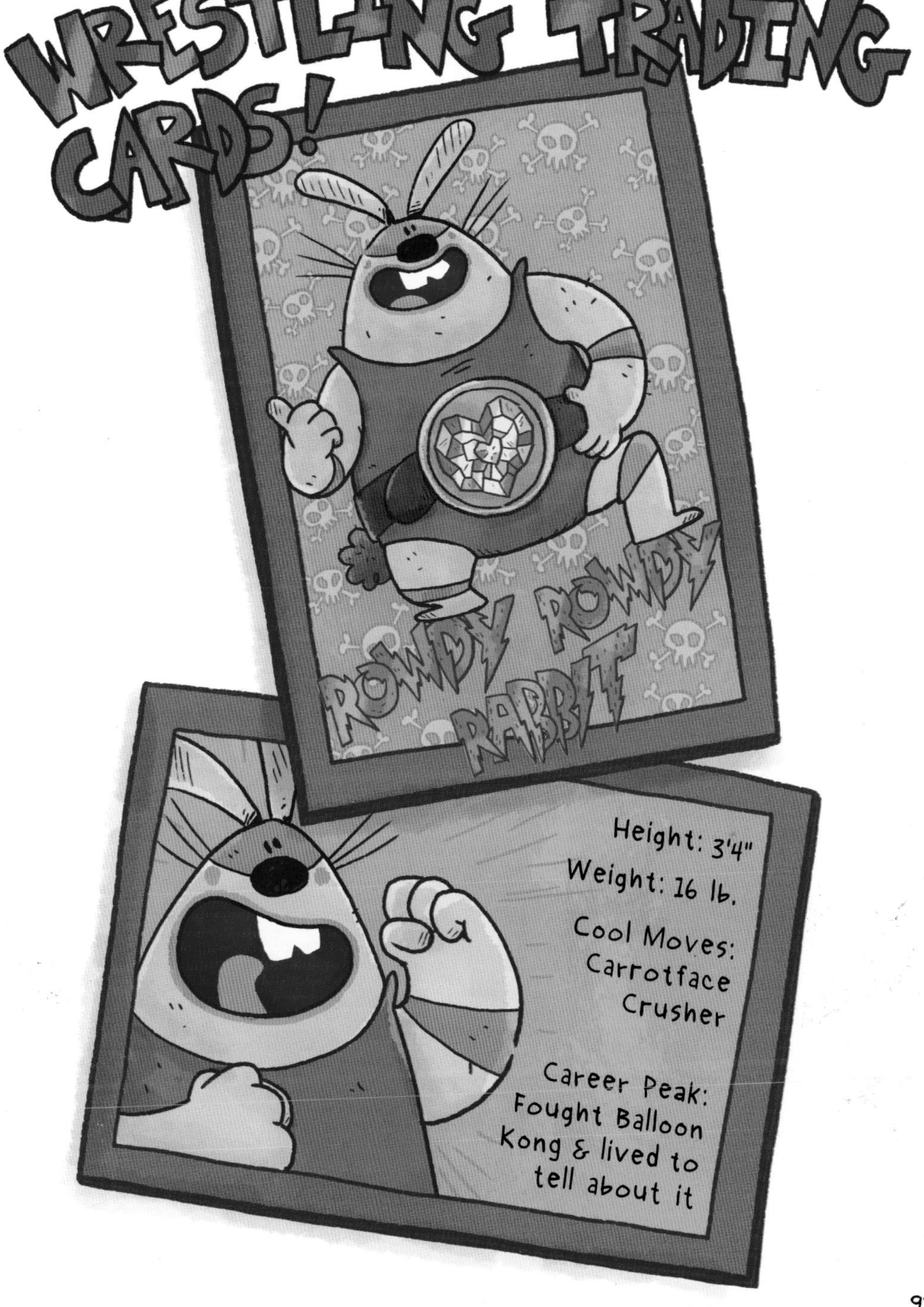
WRESTLING TRADING CARDS!
ROWDY ROWDY RABBIT
Height: 3'4"
Weight: 16 lb.
Cool Moves: Carrotface Crusher
Career Peak: Fought Balloon Kong & lived to tell about it

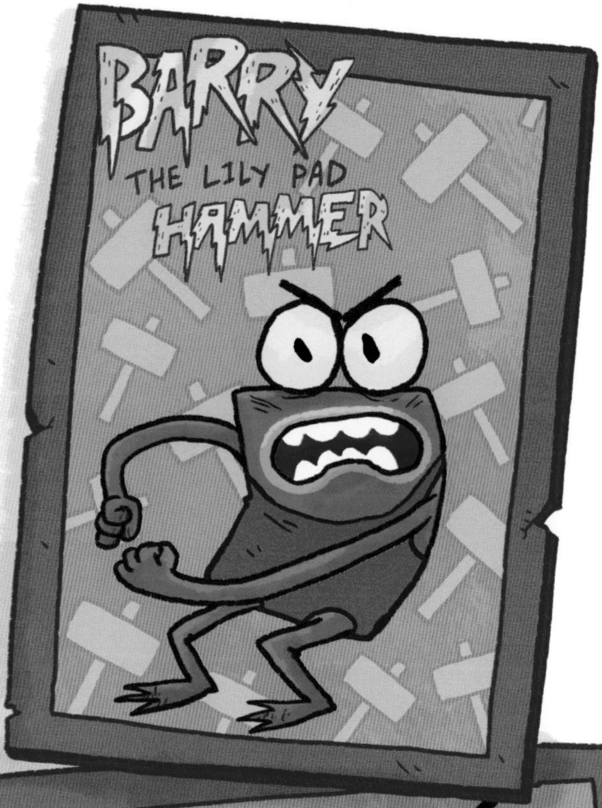
BARRY
THE LILY PAD
HAMMER

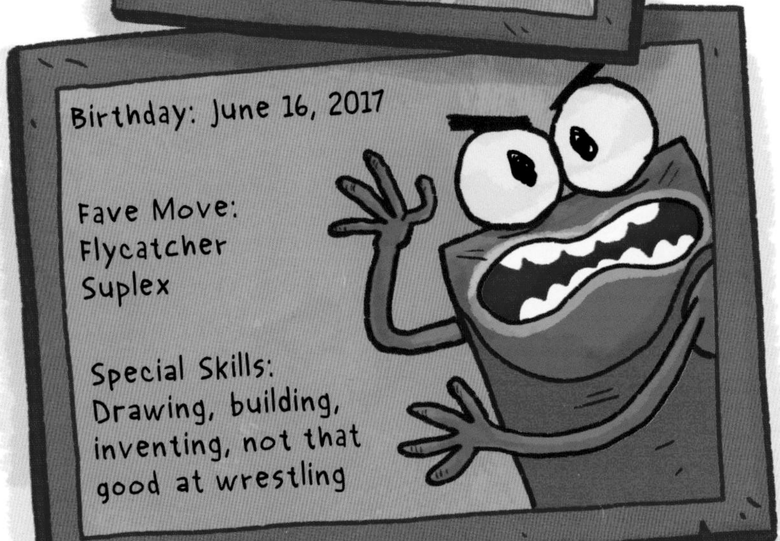
Birthday: June 16, 2017
Fave Move:
Flycatcher
Suplex
Special Skills:
Drawing, building,
inventing, not that
good at wrestling

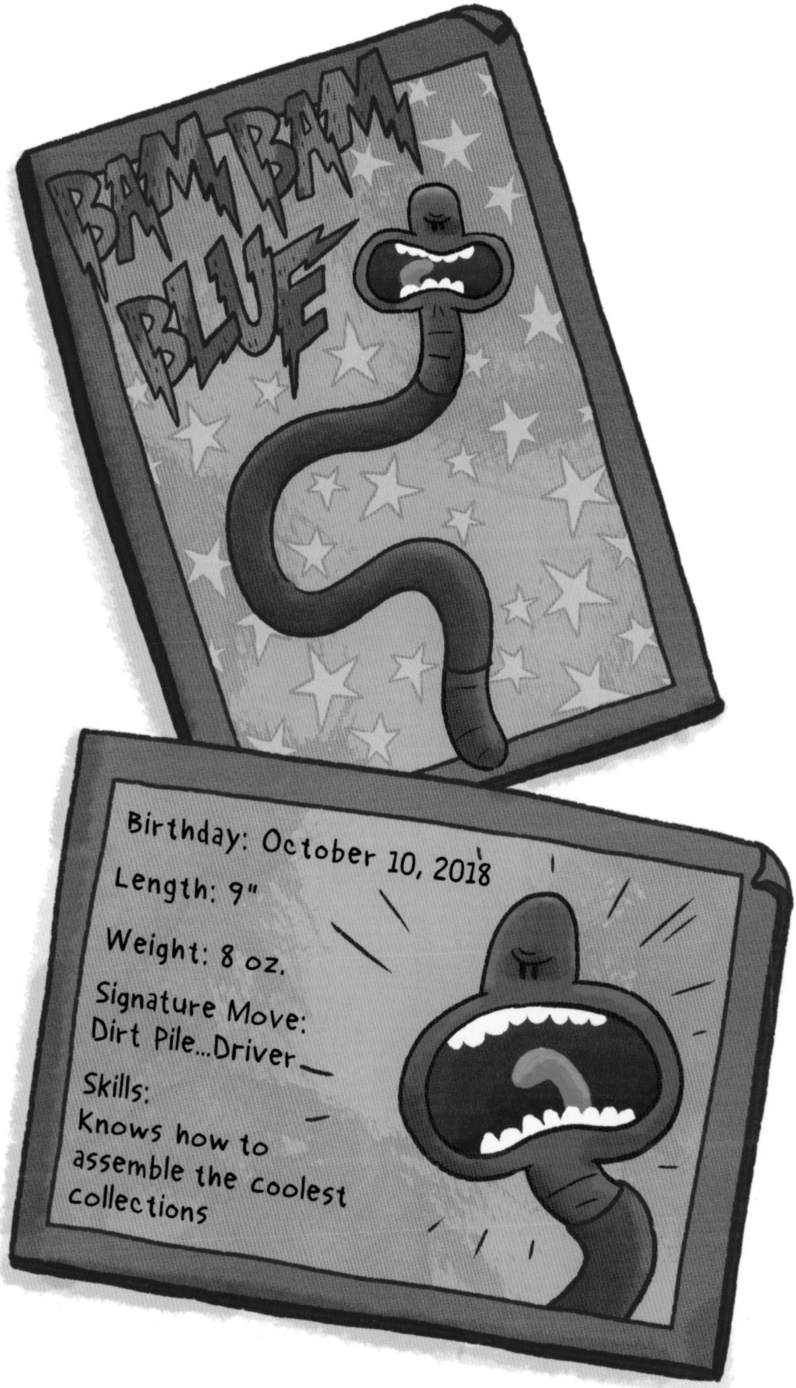
BAM BAM BLUE
Birthday: October 10, 2018
Length: 9"
Weight: 8 oz.
Signature Move:
Dirt Pile...Driver
Skills:
Knows how to assemble the coolest collections

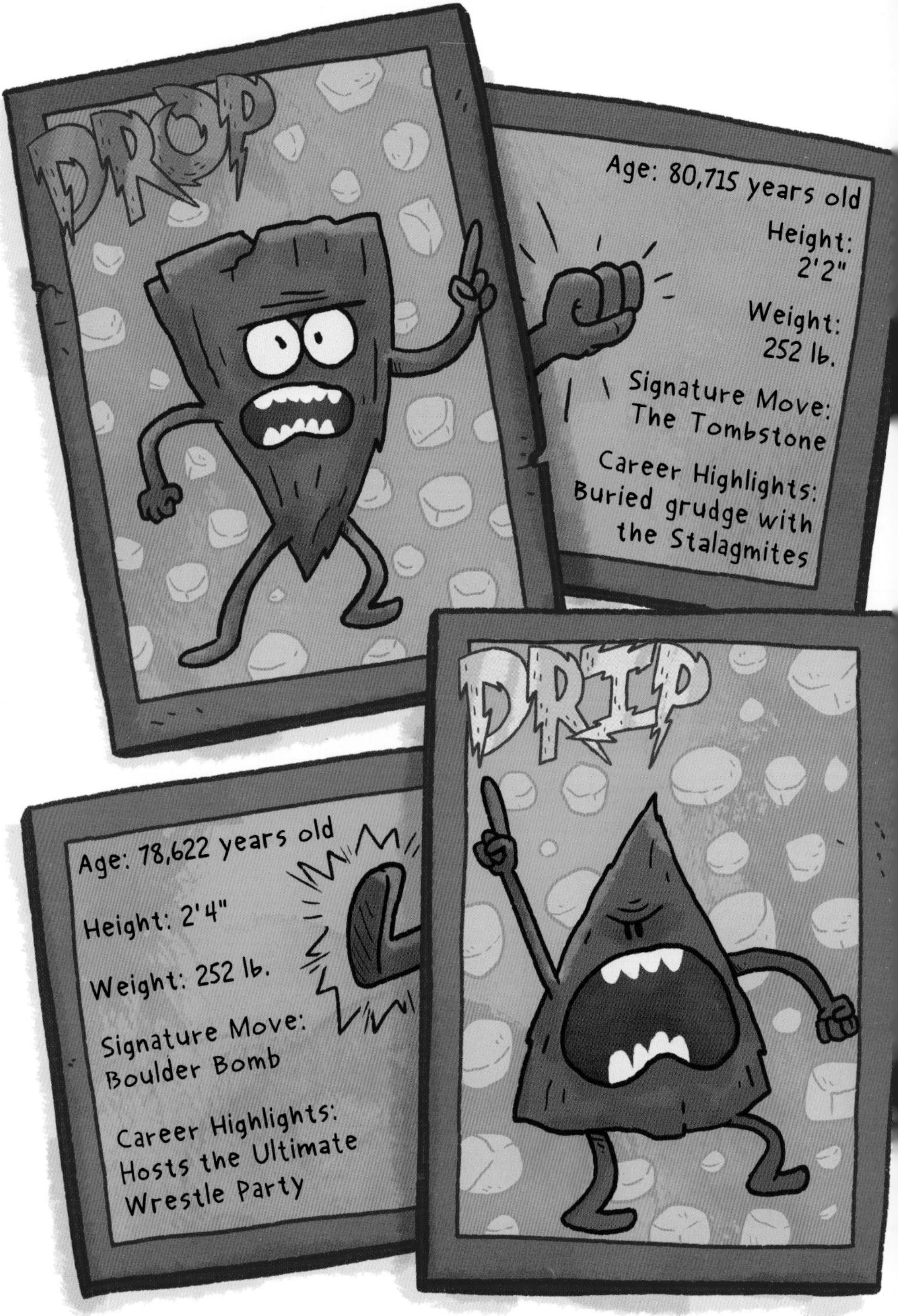
DROP
Age: 80,715 years old
Height: 2'2"
Weight: 252 lb.
Signature Move: The Tombstone
Career Highlights: Buried grudge with the Stalagmites
Age: 78,622 years old
Height: 2'4"
Weight: 252 lb.
Signature Move: Boulder Bomb
Career Highlights: Hosts the Ultimate Wrestle Party
DRIP

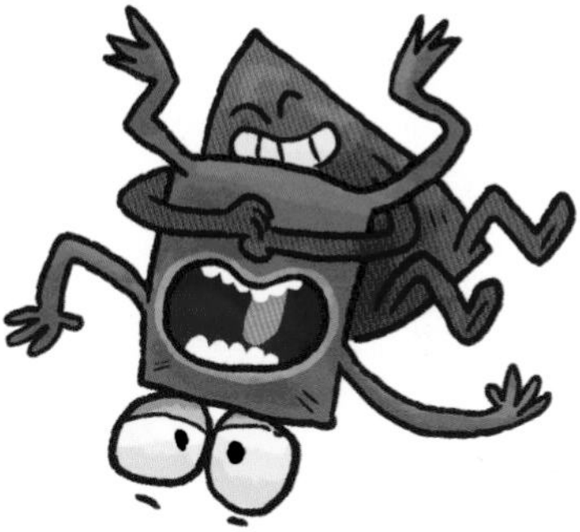

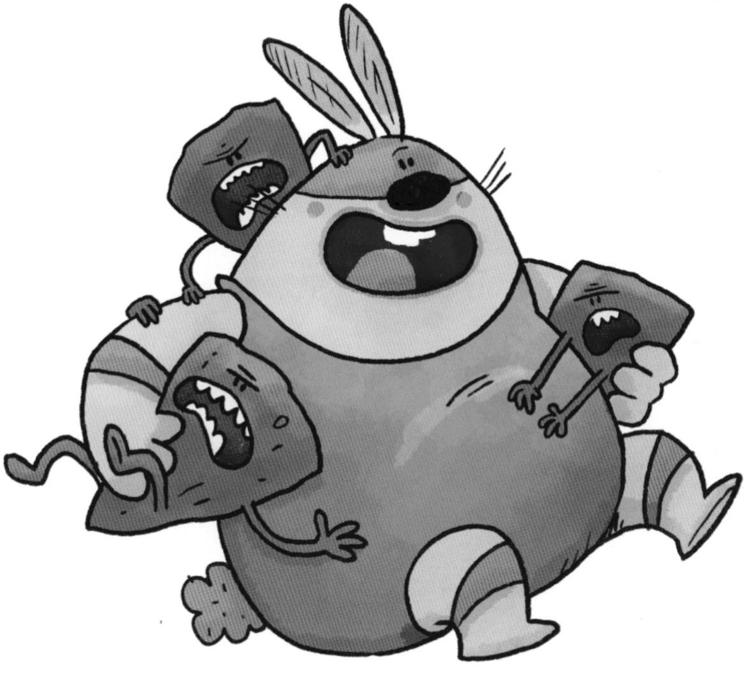

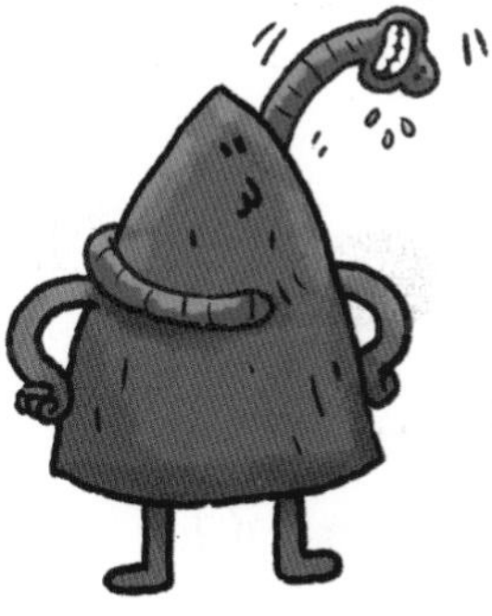

FREESTYLE WRESTLING BASICS

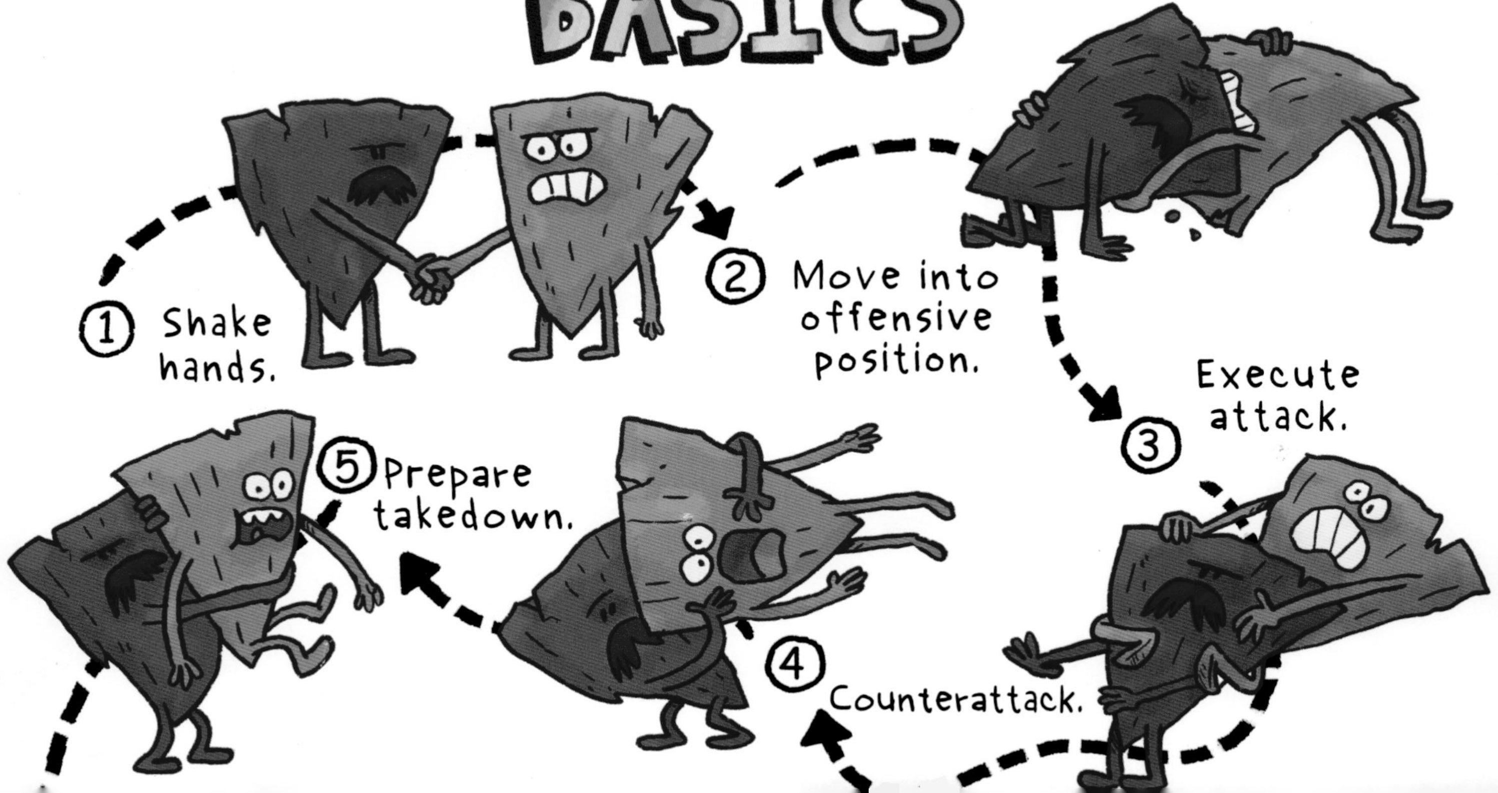

1 Shake hands.
2 Move into offensive position.
3 Execute attack.
4 Counterattack.
5 Prepare takedown.

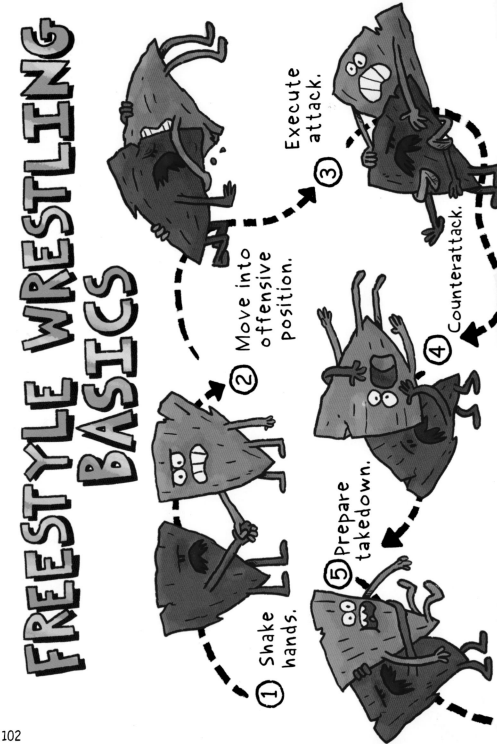

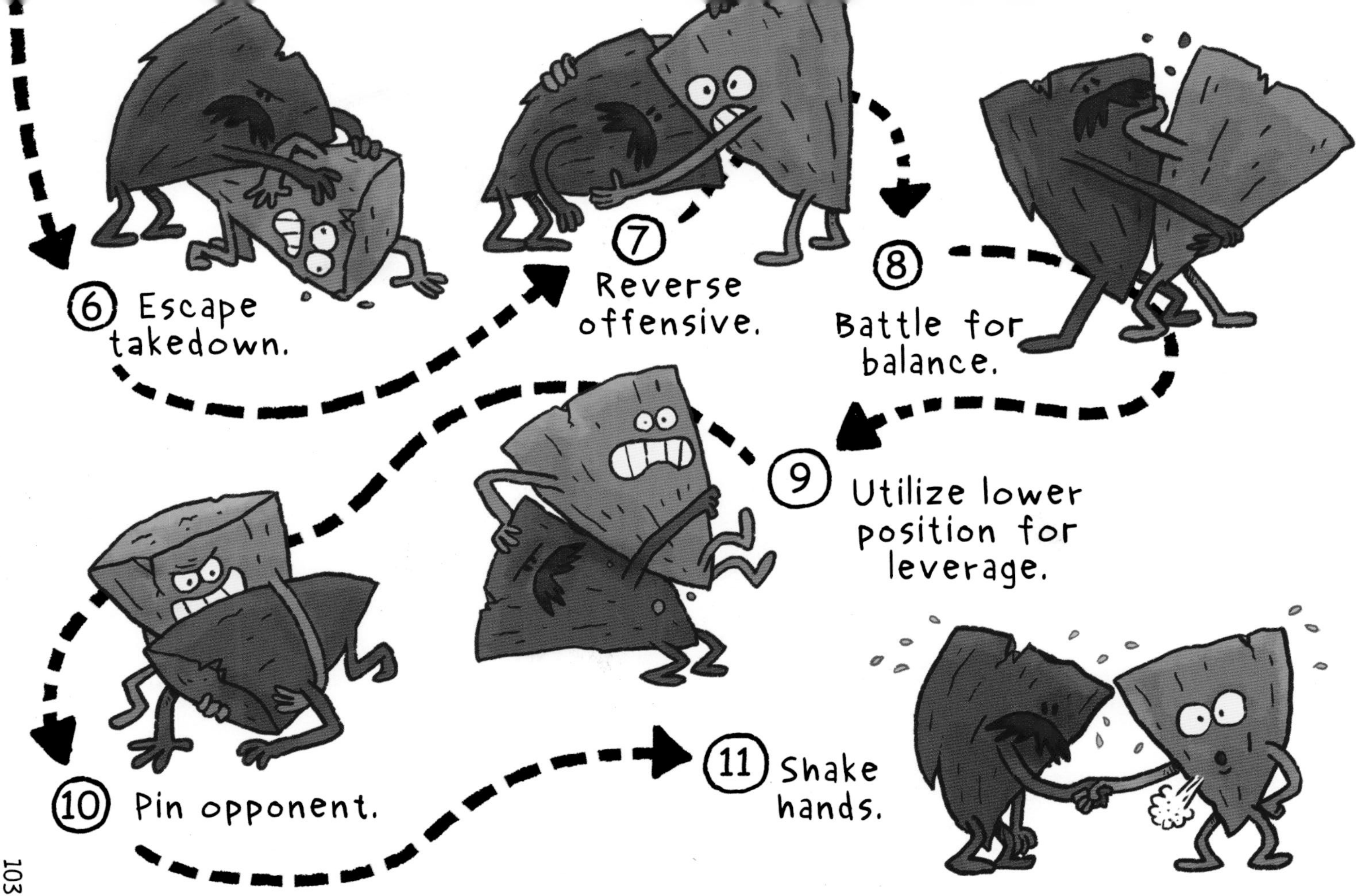

6 Escape takedown.
7 Reverse offensive.
8 Battle for balance.
9 Utilize lower position for leverage.
10 Pin opponent.
11 Shake hands.

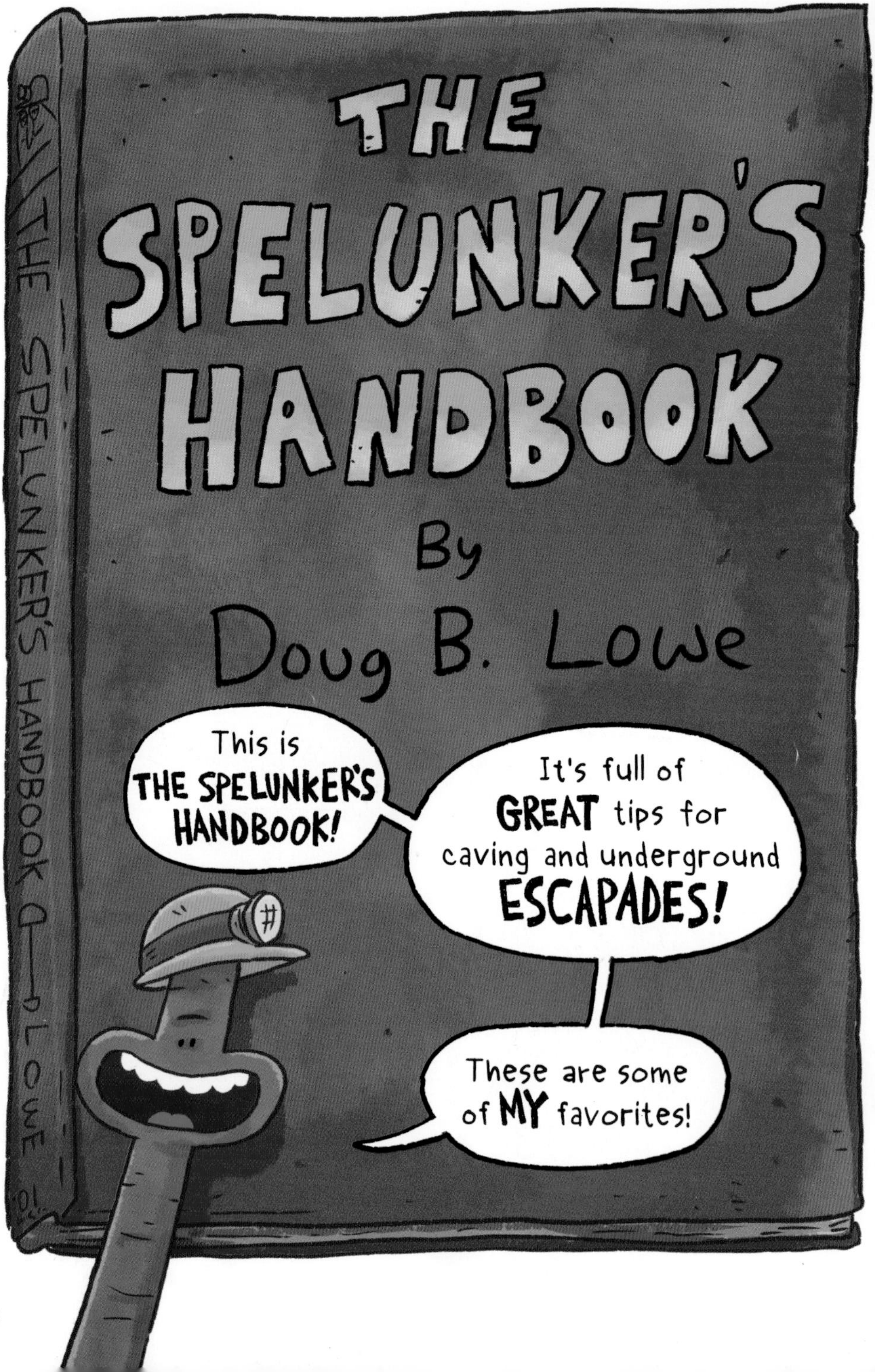
THE SPELUNKER'S HANDBOOK
By Doug B. Lowe
THE SPELUNKER'S HANDBOOK
This is THE SPELUNKER'S HANDBOOK!
It's full of GREAT tips for caving and underground ESCAPADES!
These are some of MY favorites!

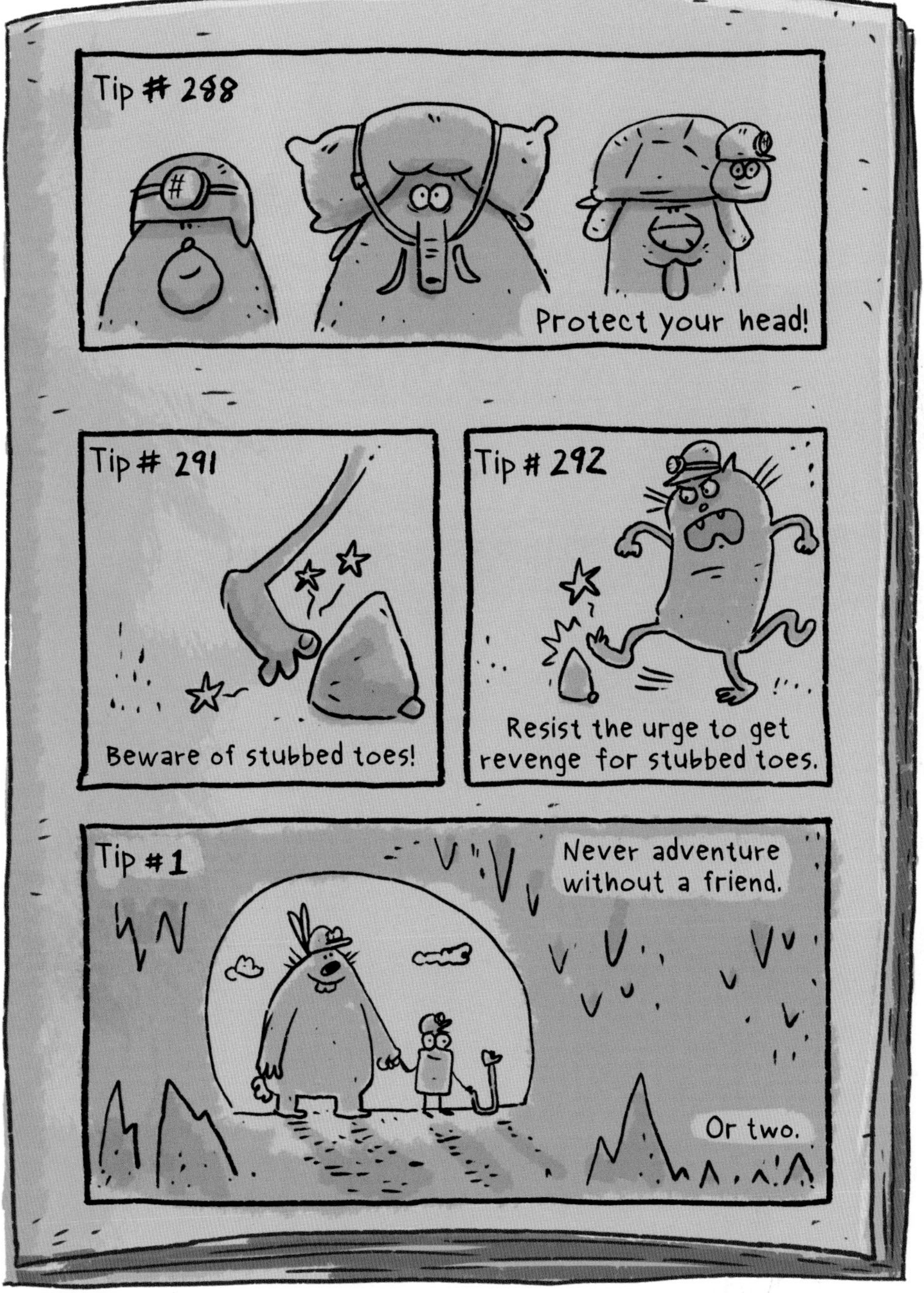

Tip # 288
Protect your head!
Tip # 291
Beware of stubbed toes!
Tip # 292
Resist the urge to get revenge for stubbed toes.
Tip # 1
Never adventure without a friend.
Or two.

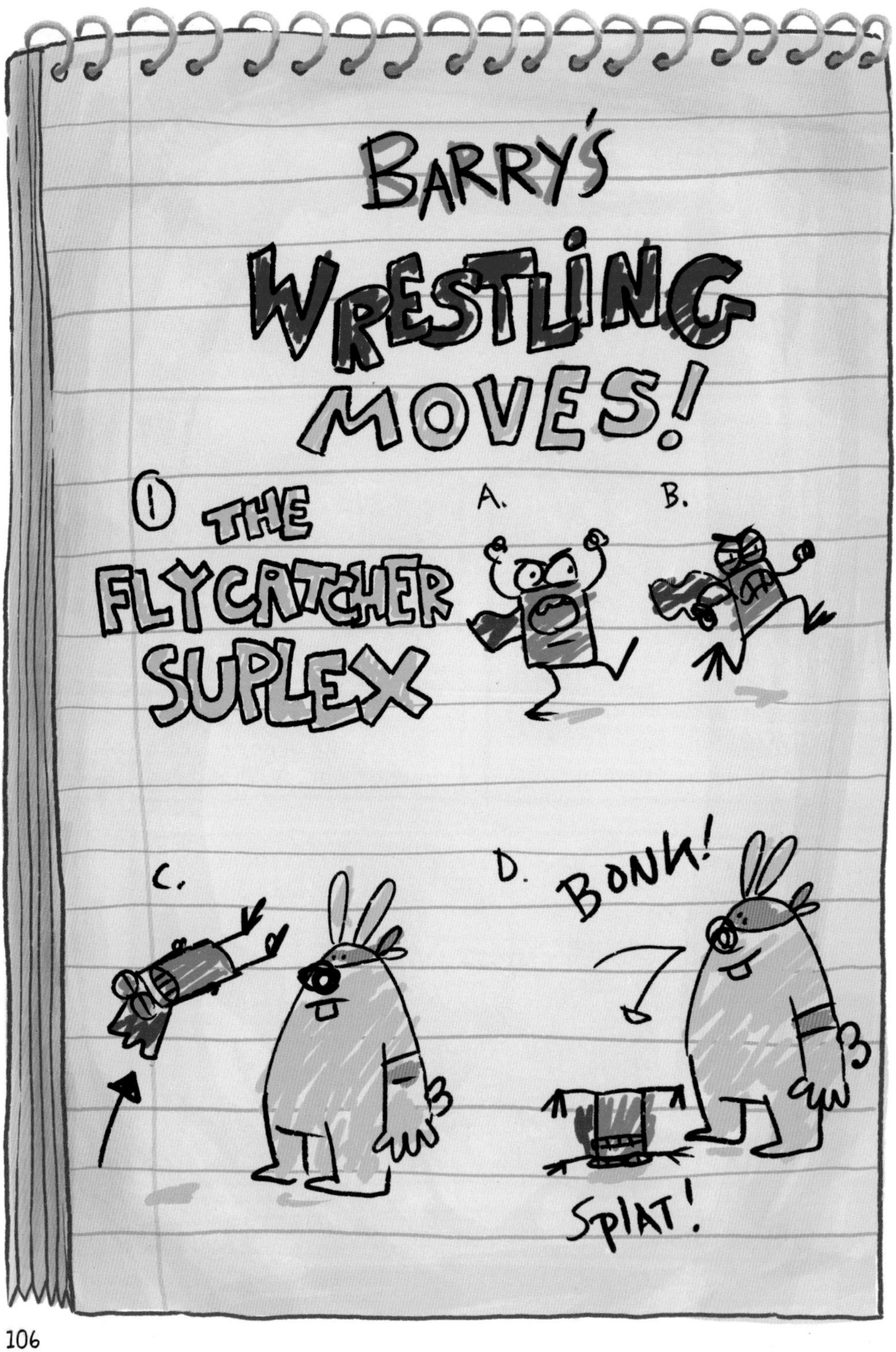
BARRY'S
WRESTLING
MOVES!
① THE
FLYCATCHER
SUPLEX
A.
B.
C.
D.
BONK!
SPLAT!

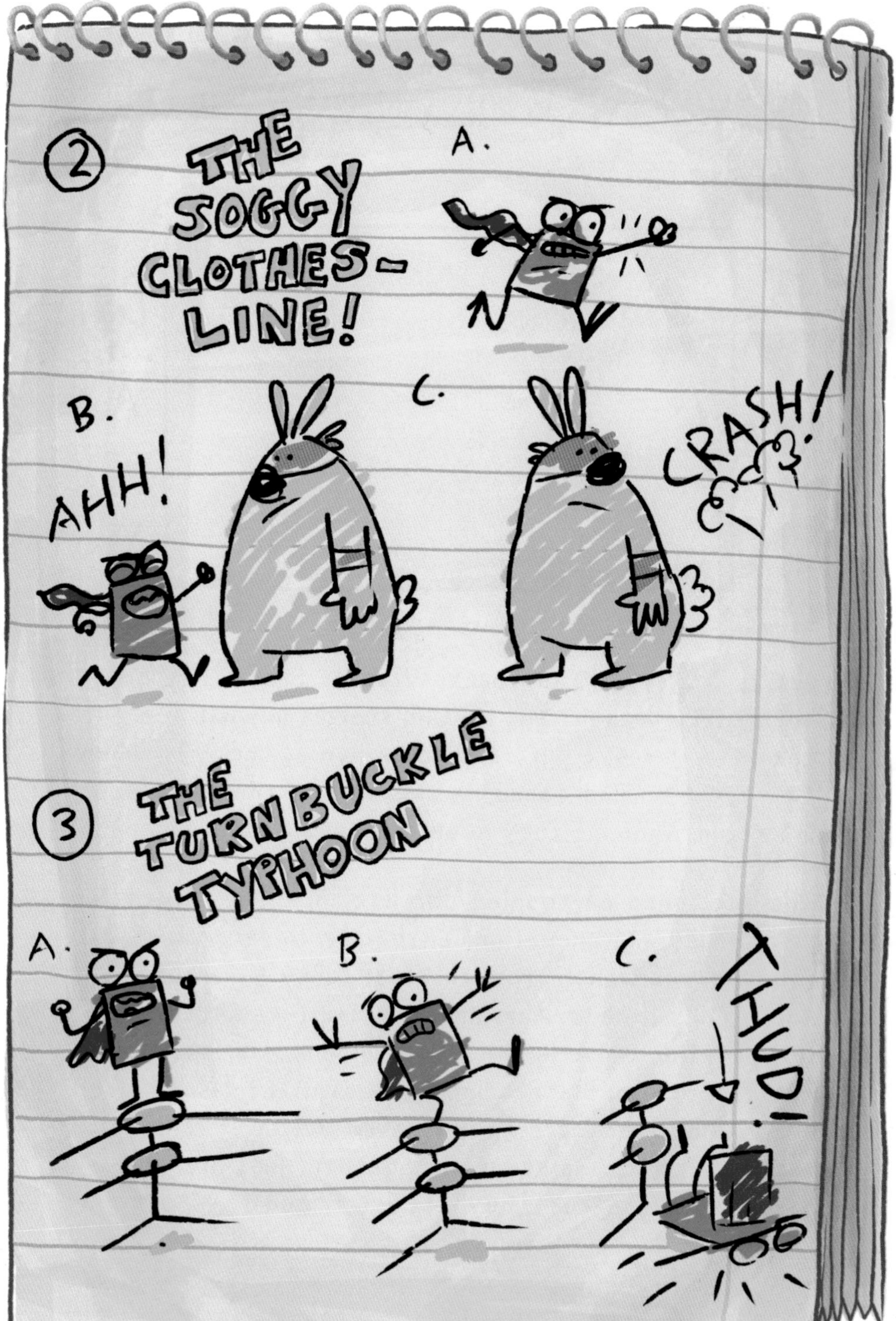

2
THE SOGGY CLOTHES-LINE!
A.
B.
AHH!
C.
CRASH!
3
THE TURNBUCKLE TYPHOON
A.
B.
C.
THUD!

About the Authors

Jason
TNT
Patterson →

← Dan-ger
Zone
Abdo

Dan & Jason go back. Waaaaay back. They got their start drawing and writing stories in what feels like the early Jurassic period, also known as the '90s, when they were making comics in the back of their high school art room. Annnnnd they never stopped!

The acclaimed cartooning duo live, breathe, and eat comics and animation. *Enter the Underground Throwdown* is their fourth Blue, Barry & Pancakes book. They love writing and drawing these stories more than anything else in the whole wide world, and they really hope you like reading them. Dan and Jason make everything together! They think it, write it, draw it, mix it, bake it, and serve it together. Just like Blue, Barry, and Pancakes, they're best friends!